PEKING
A MOSES WINE DETECTIVE NOVEL
DUCK

by ROGER L. SIMON

SIMON AND SCHUSTER / NEW YORK

Published by Simon and Schuster
A Division of Gulf & Western Corporation
Simon & Schuster Building
Rockefeller Center
1230 Avenue of the Americas
New York, New York 10020

Designed by Irving Perkins

Manufactured in the United States of America

1 2 3 4 5 6 7 8 9 10

Library of Congress Cataloging in Publication Data

Simon, Roger Lichtenberg.
    Peking duck: a Moses Wine detective novel.

    I. Title.
PZ4.S5984Pe [PS3569.I485]   813'.5'4   78-27839
ISBN 0-671-22880-3

FOR RICHARD HUNTER

"*Men fight and lose the battle, and the thing they fought for comes about in spite of their defeat, and when it comes out not to be what they meant, other men have to fight for what they meant under another name.*"

—William Morris

Delegates, Friendship Study Tour Number Five:

RUBY CRYSTAL, 32, movie actress, Malibu, California
MAX FREED, 31, publisher, San Francisco, California
STAUGHTON GREY, 66, "Movement" leader, Walnut Creek, California
REED HADLEY, 65, real estate & investments, Palm Desert, California
NANCY LEMON, 39, social worker, Newport Beach, California
NATALIE LEVINE, 52, politician, Oakland, California
LI YU-YING, 49, college professor, Logan, Utah
SONYA LIEBERMAN, 64, "Responsible Person," Los Angeles, California
FRED LISLE, 46, college professor, Redlands, California
MIKE SANCHEZ, 44, culinary worker, Portland, Oregon
NICHOLAS SPITZLER, 43, radical attorney, Los Angeles, California
ANA TZU, 38, housewife, Downey, California
HARVEY WALSH, 34, Gestalt therapist, Santa Barbara, California
MOSES WINE, 33, detective, Los Angeles, California

Their Guides

YEN SHIH, 42, male
LIU JO-YUN, 29, female
HU JUNG-CHEN, 26, male

I I RECEIVED the invitation the same day I bought the Porsche.

A '73, mind you, but still a Porsche: silver, air-conditioned, FM stereo cassette—a 911T.

I clipped on my beep alarm, slipped a .38 in my shoulder holster, and tooled around the Hollywood Hills for a morning pretending I was James Bond.

Tacky.

That afternoon I picked up the kids at Suzanne's and took them for a spin.

"Now, whatever you do, don't tell Aunt Sonya," I told them as they clambered into the jump seat. "I'll never hear the end of it."

They giggled and we took off, veering down an access road along the Los Angeles River.

"It's terrific," said Jacob as I kicked it into fifth.

"Wowee!" said Simon. "Faster!"

We were climbing from sixty to ninety-five in what seemed like nothing flat and I was scared of losing control.

"How much did it cost?" asked Jacob.

"What?"

"How much did it cost?"

"None of your business."

"Come on, Dad. You can tell me."

"What difference does it make? And besides, I told you, it's none of your business."

"More than a hundred dollars," chimed in Simon.

"Right," I said, anxious to get off the subject. I caught a glimpse of a highway patrolman in my side-view mirror and downshifted in a hurry.

"I bet it cost over ten thousand," said Jacob.

"No, it didn't. It's a used car."

"Nine thousand?"

"Eight." There. I told him.

"Oh." He sounded disappointed. There was a momentary lull in the conversation as we headed up Fountain toward my house. Then: "When I'm a teenager, I think I want an MGB."

"Wonderful," I said, turning to Simon. "What do you want?"

"Corvette."

"Jesus Christ, when I was a—" But I stopped myself. My heart wasn't in it. After all, I had bought the Porsche.

Actually, I considered the car compensation for the Leonard case. It was something I don't do under normal circumstances—personal injury work. Splitting fees with an attorney is illegal for a detective in the first place and going to interview witnesses to a three-car collision in San Luis Obispo is not my idea of high-class entertainment. But it paid well, really well. Al Rothstein let me have fifteen per cent of his fee on the settlement and Al Rothstein's fees are legendary in every lawyers' bar from Nob Hill to Century City. So, through a series of rationalizations common to most middle-class American males on the way to middle age, I figured if I was going to eat the forbidden fruit, I at least ought to take a good bite. Hence the Porsche.

I was mulling this over for the umpteenth time while the kids watched the Betamax at my place when the call came from Aunt Sonya.

"So I hear you got a new car...."

She got right down to it with a directness that comes from

sixty-four years of abhorring small talk. Who told you, I was going to ask, but one look at the grin on Jacob's face made it scarcely worth the effort.

"You're disgusting," she continued.

"You're right. Disgusting."

"Fascist!"

"Absolutely. Fascist."

"Now you won't go for sure."

"Won't go?"

"No, you won't go."

"Go where?"

"Go where? What're you asking me?"

"I'm asking you what you're talking about."

"It doesn't make any difference. You won't go anyway."

"How the hell do you know?"

"Because you just bought a Porsche!"

"So goddamn what?"

"Who ever heard of someone with a Porsche going to China?!"

"To China?"

"That's right, shmendrik. The People's Republic of China. Remember them? Or did you burn your SDS card when you bought your automobile registration?"

"This is August 1977, Sonya. I haven't been in SDS for eleven years."

"That's what I thought." She muttered incoherently into the speaker. "Well, are you going . . . or did you blow your whole wad on the Gestapomobile?"

"Are you serious?"

"Sure, I'm serious. U.S.–China Friendship Study Tour Number Five."

Friendship Study Tour Number Five. I eased myself down onto the sofa to digest this. For the last few years Sonya had been an officer of an organization called the China Friendship Society, which arranged guided tours of China for those lucky enough to be chosen by a mysterious travel committee. She had even been on one of the first tours herself. Figuring this gave me an in, I filled out several long forms, sent in the requisite passport pictures, and paid my dues annually—but nothing ever happened.

"This doesn't have anything to do with my application of four years ago, by any chance?"

"What application?"

"Never mind."

"I don't know what you're waiting for. Are you going or are you not?"

"Am I going . . . am I going . . . I, uh . . ." I glanced over at Simon and Jacob. They had slipped a cassette of *Fantasia* into the video tape deck and were watching the dinosaur sequence, "The Rite of Spring," blaring just a few decibels above comfort level.

"When does it leave?"

"Thursday."

"Three days from now?"

"What's the matter? Some rich client have a motel room you absolutely have to—"

"Sonya!"

"Moses, if you knew the trouble I went through to get you on this tour—a private detective. Do you think they've heard of a private detective over there? Or a private anything? When they want justice, the people decide. They—"

"I know. I know." I could see going to China with Aunt Sonya would present its difficulties. Like going on a tour of the Vatican with Saint Bernadette.

I stalled a moment. But any delay was a charade, of course. There was nothing I wanted more at that particular point in my life than to get away. The farther the better. Alpha Centauri would have been perfect, but China wasn't bad. And Thursday was fine, too. Five minutes from then wouldn't have been too soon for me.

The Porsche was compensation for more than I cared to admit. The truth of the matter was I had had it. If one more creep at a cocktail party asked me what I did and then said, "You're putting me on!" when I told him, I would have punched him through the floor. If another hostess said, "Come over here. I want you to meet Moses Wine. He's a real private detective. He makes his *living* at it!," I would have set fire to her house and turned the fire extinguisher on her guests.

It was as if life had turned into the eighty-third rerun of *What's My Line?* The classic symptoms of incipient middle age were creeping up on me. I was bored and alienated. I had fantasies: Sometimes it was opening a bookstore in Berkeley. Sometimes it was joining the working class on the GM assembly line. Sometimes it was even going back and finishing law school. I didn't know what I wanted. All I knew was I wanted out.

"Moses . . . you still there?"

"Yup."

"I'm waiting for an answer."

"What do you think? I'm crazy? Of course I'll go."

"Well," she said, "at least there's *some* hope for you."

"Sonya, you're a godsend."

"Please, no mythology."

"Sure, sure." I started jumping around the room, glad she couldn't see my excitement through the telephone. "How'd you do it? How'd you get me on a trip to China with only three days' notice?"

Suddenly there was an uncontrollable fit of coughing on the other end.

"What's the matter? You okay?"

"Shhh!" said Jacob. I was interrupting the movie.

"Sonya?" The coughing subsided as quickly as it came.

"I asked you a question."

"What?"

"How'd you get me on the trip?"

"One of the delegates from the Bay Area dropped out at the last minute. A death in the family . . . besides, it was easy. I'm Responsible Person this time."

"Responsible Person?"

"Your tour leader, shmendrik. I'm going with you."

II "Wʜᴀᴛ'ʀᴇ ʏᴏᴜ going to bring me?"

The inquisition had been going on for most of the day, first Jacob, then Simon, accusing, demanding, testing. How dare I, their father, disappear across the globe for three weeks, dissolve into an alien culture, see the Great Wall, smell lotus blossoms, eat Chinese food, without them?

I didn't have any answers. I just mumbled something about once-in-a-lifetime chances—it should happen to them someday (I'm sure it would: they would probably even go to the moon, to Mars—who knew?) and continued organizing my imminent departure, passing a few cases to a friend at an agency, and arranging for my new car to be garaged at the mechanic's in Hollywood.

But the kids didn't relent. The questions became more and more specific. Simon wanted to know if they had swords in China, could I bring him a sword? Jacob was worried they wouldn't have anything to sell since it was a Communist country and everybody had the same. Didn't they? I tried to explain they had special stores for foreigners where, I heard, they kept fancy silk embroidery from the seventeenth century for rich tourists to admire and buy. Jacob didn't think that was fair. I tried to defend it, but the whole thing seemed ridiculous.

16

It was almost a relief when I went to pick up Sonya that night at the Fairfax Senior Citizens Center.

"So this is the Messerschmitt," she said, depositing a warm tray of tamale pie in my hands. "When do we strafe Warsaw?"

"Come on, Sonya. It's only a machine."

"Some machine!" She held on to the top with her frail fingers and stepped into it as if it were a poison ivy bush.

"Now, where's the party?" I said, climbing in next to her.

"Malibu. The Colony."

"The movie colony?"

"Something wrong with that?"

"Movie stars aren't exactly proletarian."

"It's Ruby Crystal. She's going to be on the tour and I asked her to have a party so we could all meet each other."

"Who else is coming on this tour?" I asked, suddenly interested.

"First get going," she said, motioning the car forward. "I want to see how the Luftwaffe flies."

I gave Sonya a look and shot out onto Fairfax, heading toward the freeway.

"This isn't one of those radical chic tours, is it?"

"Chic . . . and not so chic."

"What's that supposed to mean?"

"What it says . . . of course, to the Chinese it wouldn't make a difference anyway."

"Of course."

"Though they are making a special effort to give this group one of the most thorough exposures to their society."

I glanced at Sonya as I turned up the freeway ramp. "According to whom?"

"My correspondent."

"Your correspondent?"

She nodded opaquely, but I knew exactly what she meant. Sonya had reminded me on numerous occasions that she was one of the few foreigners who still kept in contact with her guide from her first trip to China. It was the closest she came to bragging.

17

"Come on, Sonya. Out with it. Who's on the tour?"

"You'll see," she said.

I gritted my teeth and continued along the freeway. Obviously she was enjoying what little suspense she could generate. Earlier that evening Suzanne had been the same way. I had delayed telling her as long as possible because it was my month to handle child care while she prepared for her summer law school final.

"Suppose I flunk?" she told me.

"You won't flunk. I'll pay for a babysitter. Besides, you got A's your first semester."

"Don't you think I've got a right to get A's the second time too?"

"You'll always get A's with me."

"Oh, get fucked!"

"The trip is important to me, Suzanne. I'm thirty-three years old. I've got to get out of town to figure out what to do with my life."

"China's pretty far out. Maybe you should try Palm Springs for the weekend."

"You were the one who always said I was wasting my life."

"I merely said someone who wrote a critique of More's *Utopia* like you did at Berkeley shouldn't spend his life serving processes on runaway housewives."

"That's not all I do!"

"Oh, yeah, one or two little heroic cases to get your picture in *Rolling Stone*. All you are is a sucker for publicity, not to mention the image of a dime-store Bogart with a hashish pipe. You love that."

And so it went. Until she disappeared into the bathroom to get ready for a date with her tax law professor.

She never did say I could go, although she never said no either. I left her house with that wonderful unresolved feeling that makes divorce so special.

"*This* is the Malibu Colony?" said Sonya as we turned left off the Coast Highway, jogging behind a gas station and a taco stand to a nondescript stucco gate. There wasn't much in

18

the way of landscaping. Most of the houses were not very prepossessing either—simple clapboard affairs, imitation Cape Codders or fifties modern, shoehorned onto thirty feet of beachfront land that just happened to be worth six hundred and twenty-five thousand dollars.

We gave our names to the gatekeeper and continued on to Ruby Crystal's house, number 37, an A-frame near the end of the Colony. On Sonya's insistence, we were the first ones there, and Ruby was standing in the doorway to greet us. She was in an antique lace blouse and jeans, with no makeup, and looked younger than she did in the movies. I could hear the voice of Linda Ronstadt singing *Love Is a Rose* coming from the room behind her. Considering where I was, I wondered if it was live or recorded. It was probably Memorex.

"Ruby, this is Moses Wine—a late addition to our tour."

I smiled.

"Make yourself at home," she said. "I'm just finishing the tabouli."

Sonya followed her into the kitchen with the tamale pie she had brought, while I wandered around Ruby's place. It was unostentatiously but expensively furnished in the Design Research fashion, with unfinished pine shelves housing a large collection of antiquities. The walls were decorated with original lithographs—Lichtenstein and Johns—and a sprinkling of political posters, including some I had never seen before from Tanzania and Chile. A brightly colored gouache of Chinese peasants in a cotton field, titled *Criticizing Lin Piao and Confucius Promotes Production*, hung over her mantelpiece. Ruby may have come later to politics than Fonda or MacLaine, but she was trying hard to catch up.

Her South American housekeeper was offering me sangria when the others started to arrive. I moved to the window to watch their cars pull up. The first was an old Peugeot 304 which looked well cared for, with a new paint job and fresh faculty parking sticker on the rear window. A tall man in his forties, with a pepper-and-salt beard and wearing a cable-knit sweater, got out just as a purple Seville drove up behind him.

A thin, intense woman with a flattened-out chin emerged in a cracked-leather jacket and Cacharel scarf, and followed the bearded man into the house. I was about to turn away from the window when another car pulled up—a beat-up VW of middle-sixties vintage, with Oregon plates and a frayed bumper sticker reading DON'T LIE DOWN FOR THE BOSSES—SUPPORT THE WILDCAT CULINARY WORKERS OF SOUTH PORTLAND! I watched as the door swung open and a Chicano in his forties got out carrying a brown grocery bag. He stopped and looked at the house, smirking slightly before he started in.

I was still staring out the window when the man with the beard slipped around me and extended his hand.

"Fred Lisle," he said. "Asian Studies at California Lutheran. Specialist in the Taiping uprisings of the 1850's."

We shook as I digested his pedigree. "Moses Wine."

"Moses Wine . . . Moses Wine . . . I don't remember your name."

"Latecomer," I said.

"Oh, an alternate."

Lisle surveyed me carefully. From closer up he had the distinct air of someone trying to look younger than he was—styled hair, tight-fitting pants, an expensive silver pendant of the type sold in boutiques at the Marina.

"You missed your orientation reading," he said. "I hope you're up on the Gang of Four."

"Only what I read in the papers."

"That's the key right now—the Gang of Four. . . . What do you do, Moses?"

"Detective."

Lisle burst into a loud laugh. "Oh, don't tell me!" He turned to the woman from the Seville, who was standing nearby. "Someone's hired a detective for this tour."

"No one hired me," I said, restraining myself. "I'm just along for the ride, same as you."

"But suppose someone steals something, like a piece of the Great Wall? Or suppose there's a murder?" Lisle seemed pleased by the prospect.

20

The woman beside him smiled and introduced herself as Nancy Lemon, a social worker from Newport Beach. But judging by her car and her clothes, she wasn't living on a social worker's salary.

"Where should I put these?" said the Chicano, joining us with a couple of half-gallon bottles of Italian Swiss Colony. The slight edge in his voice told me he knew two-dollar jug wine wasn't usually the drink of choice at Ruby Crystal's house. We didn't have a chance to answer before the housekeeper whisked them away, hiding them at the back of the buffet table behind a magnum of 1970 Schramsberg Blanc des Blancs.

The Chicano introduced himself as Mike Sanchez.

"Don't tell me. Let me guess," I said. "The culinary workers of South Portland."

"You saw my bumper sticker."

I nodded. "What's going on up there?"

"You could say we got our own Gang of Four. The *cabrones* tried to take over the union and use it for their own purposes."

"Someone's going to have to explain this Gang of Four business to me," said Nancy Lemon.

Another couple of cars pulled up just as Sonya and Ruby emerged from the kitchen with the tamale pie and tabouli. I helped myself and sat down on the couch. Nancy sat down next, letting her thighs rub lightly against mine. It wasn't exactly what I had in mind.

"Did you see the exhibit?" she said.

"What exhibit?"

"The Chinese archaeological exhibit." She indicated an art book on the coffee table in front of us. "It was in the county museum in May. Ruby must have gone, too. . . . It's incredible stuff. I can't wait to see them again."

"You like Chinese antiquities?"

"They're gorgeous." She touched my sleeve. "Take a look at the one on page thirty-four."

I picked up the book—*Treasures Unearthed During the*

Chinese Cultural Revolution—and opened it, flipping forward to page thirty-four, when my attention was diverted by a group at the door. Two more members of our tour had arrived—a Chinese-American woman of about forty, and a distinguished white-haired gentleman at least twenty years older. His face looked familiar but I couldn't place it.

"Who is he?" I asked Nancy.

"Staughton Grey," said Mike Sanchez.

Staughton Grey. I hadn't thought of him since I was fifteen years old and he was the leader of what was called the Peace Movement in the late fifties. I still remembered pictures of him sprawled across the desert sands of Yucca Flat, Nevada, in the first protests against nuclear testing. He was a hero to me then. Sonya introduced the woman as Ana Tzu, a housewife from Downey. I was already staring at her. She wasn't particularly attractive, but Chinese women have always held a tremendous fascination for me. Call it sexism, racism, or just plain inaccessibility, I could never take my eyes off them. It got to be a joke among my friends when I went to Berkeley and we would go into San Francisco Chinatown for dinner— poor old Moses, smitten like a Shakespearean swain by Oriental women. But I had never had the opportunity to act on my attraction.

"You went to the exhibit, too," Ana Tzu said, wandering over to us. I realized I was still holding the book of archaeological treasures. "It's a pity they didn't have that duck."

"Vy a duck? Vy a no chicken?" I cracked, but it was obvious from their reaction that no one else had seen the Marx Brothers in *The Cocoanuts*.

"Western Han Dynasty," Ana Tzu continued, regarding me strangely. "The Chinese government wouldn't let it out of the country. It was their most important find."

"Page thirty-four," said Nancy Lemon.

Ana Tzu nodded her concurrence.

I turned easily to the page, which had been marked with a receipt from the museum bookstore. It showed a duck, all right, intricately carved in silver and jade; but in a black-and-

22

white reproduction it was difficult to see what all the shouting was about.

"I hope we get a chance to see it when we're there," said Nancy.

"So you'd rather see some feudal relic than the glories of the New China."

There was something very familiar about the sarcasm in that voice and I looked up to see an equally familiar body standing there.

"Nick Spitzler!"

"Only the best people go to Peking."

I got up and shook his hand. I hadn't seen the lawyer in several years, since I was doing a follow-up on the California Four trial, but he looked fine, as if his righteous political lifestyle had unlocked the secret of eternal youth. Actually I would have assumed Spitzler had already been to China. He had been to Hanoi, after all, arranging the prisoner exchange after the war. And someone once told me he was the first American in Albania.

"There's someone else you know on this tour," he said. "Max Freed."

I didn't know whether that was good news or bad. The young publisher of *Modern Times* was a self-centered bastard, and his formerly counterculture magazine had gone establishment in the worst way.

"He's not coming tonight, needless to say."

"Needless to say," I repeated.

"Mr. Spitzler," said Nancy Lemon, "do you think we're going to see the real China? I mean, more than Nixon?"

"That's the idea of being 'friends' of China, isn't it?"

"Well, I hope you'll be able to interpret some of the more complex questions of ideology for me." She batted her eyelashes at him.

"Who can tell?" said Nick. "Maybe you'll get a chance to see the Great World."

"I've heard of the Great Wall, but not the Great World, Mr. Spitzler."

"Oh, it's at least as interesting."

I seized the opportunity to slip off for a refill of tamale pie.

"What'd you think of Staughton Grey?" asked Sonya, dishing it out.

"What am I supposed to think? I just met him . . . I'm impressed."

"What for? He's only a human being." She seemed annoyed.

"It's the people who make history."

"He's only two years older than I am!" She walked off to introduce three more members of our group.

The first of these I recognized immediately from the media as Natalie Levine of Oakland—once the most outspoken woman in Congress. She had just made an unsuccessful pass at the California Senatorial nomination and I imagined she was glad to get away to forget about her huge campaign deficit, which had made headlines in Sunday's paper.

The second was another Chinese-American, Li Yu-ying—a language professor from Utah State. He was a shy man with an academic stammer, who had been born into a bourgeois family in Shanghai but had left China in the thirties, when he was only nine years old, to wander the world. After living in France, Switzerland and South America, through one of those odd twists of twentieth-century history, he ended up teaching Italian in Utah. Now he was going home.

I wanted to know more of his story, but before I could ask him, the third man—a heavy Rotarian in a blue Banlon shirt and matching pants—started glad-handing his way through the room. He shook mine a little too firmly, depositing his card in the breast pocket of my jacket: REED "CALL-ME-RED" HADLEY/REAL ESTATE & INVESTMENT/13 TAMARISK DRIVE/PALM DESERT, CALIFORNIA.

"It's printed in Chinese on the back," he said. I turned it over and saw that it was. "I'm also an appraiser."

"An appraiser?"

"Of artifacts." He looked past me at the room, as if sizing

24

up Ruby Crystal's collection. "What's this?" He suddenly moved to the sofa, where Mike Sanchez was perusing the catalog of the archaeological exhibit. "Where'd you get this?"

Before Mike could say anything, Hadley grabbed the catalog from his hand and started riffling through it. His fingers stopped at page thirty-four.

"I don't suppose you think you'll have a chance at that!"

"A chance at that?" said Mike. "What're you talking about?"

"You know what I'm talking about. The Han Duck. I'm sure half this tour wants to buy it!"

He looked at Sanchez with the hypocritical smile of a real estate developer. Around Palm Desert, Hadley's type was as common as jackrabbits.

"This is the opportunity of a lifetime!" he continued.

"You think we're on a shopping spree?" Natalie Levine broke in.

"It's no accident that catalog was on the table!"

"I'm here to learn about the People's Republic," said Mike.

"So am I," said Nancy Lemon, coming over.

"Uhuh. Well, as far as I can tell, there isn't a single red-blooded American who could resist an object like that if they could get it at a price. And I'm holding to my first statement —half the people in this room have their eye on it."

"How're you going to prove that?" said Fred Lisle.

"I don't have to. It's a fact."

"Oh, come on!" said Natalie Levine. "It's too absurd."

"How'd he get on this tour?" whispered Nick Spitzler.

"This is the China Friendship Society," said Mike Sanchez.

"Oh, yeah?" said Hadley. "Then how come I found this in the driveway not more than twenty feet from the front door of the house?"

He held up a bent postcard. There was no writing on the back, but even at thirty feet I could see the object on the front. It was the duck, and this time it was in living color.

Ruby tapped on a wineglass. "Your attention, please! I'd

25

like to introduce the last member of our tour to join us tonight—Harvey Walsh of the Personal Growth Gestalt Institute of Santa Barbara." She indicated a man in a boat-neck sweater and droopy mustache, standing behind a large cardboard carton. "Harvey's been good enough to prepare an icebreaker for us."

"Hi, everybody." He smiled at us. "When a small group like this goes on a long trip there can be a lot of tensions. You know, hostilities build up, making it unpleasant for everyone. That's why I brought these tonight—so we could get it *all* out in advance."

He reached into the box and took out an armful of clublike objects.

"Don't worry," he said, starting to distribute them to us. "They don't hurt. They're called 'batacas' and they're made of foam. . . . Well, start hitting each other."

Nobody moved.

III "How come Aunt Sonya never got married?" Simon asked. It was fifteen minutes to the flight and we were sitting in the coffee shop of the international departures building of L.A. International. "How come?" he repeated, his elbow moving precariously close to his chocolate milk shake. I glanced over at Sonya, whose eyes were glued to a recent issue of the *Peking Review*.

"I didn't get married because marriage is a bourgeois institution of questionable value." She didn't bother to look up, but she wasn't about to get an argument from Suzanne, who was feeling about as friendly that morning as a tankful of piranhas. She had just informed me that she had to drop legal theory that summer because of my trip and was going to graduate late.

"Did you even have a boyfriend?" Simon was being obnoxious.

"You're being obnoxious," his older brother informed him.

"Yes, I had a boyfriend," Sonya answered, turning the page to an article entitled "Vice-Chairman Yeh Relentlessly Criticizes the Gang of Four."

"In the thirties. Back at the Bronx Co-ops," I said. "She slept with every Bolshevik on the block!"

"I did not!" She looked at me in annoyance. "Sexist!"

I waited for the echo from Suzanne.

"You know that I was essentially a monogamous person. There was only one man in my life. That's more than I can say for some perverted tastes at this table." She eyed me pointedly.

Simon leaned forward, sending the milk shake bouncing off the saltshaker onto the empty chair next to him. I hurried up to the counter for a refill before he complained and I became the recipient of some last pre-flight licks from Suzanne.

I was waiting in the food line, trying to pick out the rest of our group at the various tables, when a man stepped out from behind a display of San Francisco sourdough and accosted me. He was somewhere in his forties and elegantly dressed in the kind of cashmere jacket you don't find marked down at J. C. Penney's.

"Excuse me," he whispered. "Mr. Wine?"

"Yes."

"My name is Arthur Lemon. I'm a manufacturer." He presented me with his card, glancing nervously behind him. "You're going on the trip to China, aren't you?"

I nodded.

"And, uh, I gather you're a private detective."

"Uhuh." I didn't sound my most enthusiastic.

"Well, um, I'm not going myself but . . . see that woman over there?" He nodded to a table in the corner, where Nancy Lemon was sipping coffee. "She's my wife. You may have met her at the party last night. She's going and, uh . . . I was wondering if you'd, uh, keep an eye on her?"

"Keep an eye on her?"

"Yes, you know, when, uh, she goes on vacation she . . . well, even when she doesn't go on vacation she . . . Look, Mr. Wine, how much do you want?"

"Oh, for crissakes!"

"Please, Mr. Wine. It's very important to me. You must—"

"Look, Mr. Lemon, I don't want to offend you. But I'm

28

going on a study tour of the People's Republic of China, not a working vacation. I don't intend to watch your wife or anybody else for that matter. And if she feels like kicking up her heels, shacking up with the pilot, or even shtupping the corpse of Chou En-lai—that's her affair."

"If it's a question of money—"

"Sorry, Mr. Lemon." And I started off, just as an announcement came over the loudspeaker for the flight to Hong Kong, our port of entry to China.

The kids were already up when I got back, watching some press flacks photograph Ruby Crystal's departure.

"Is *she* going with you?" Jacob said.

"What do you want? An autograph or a lock of her hair?"

A couple of other photographers had surrounded Natalie Levine and the recently arrived Max Freed, who was giving some last-minute dictation to a secretary in aviator glasses.

"Congratulations, Sonya," I said as we started for the gate.

"For what?"

"All those famous people. They better like China or you'll end up doing winter guard duty on the Russian border."

"Don't get fresh. Besides, that's your department."

"Oh, I'm a commissar, eh? I have to watch out for them."

"Something like that."

The name Hong Kong was repeated on the loudspeaker and for the first time a shiver went straight up my spine. This was actually it. I grabbed the boys by the hand and moved faster for the gate. Sonya walked right along beside us, clutching my sleeve in excitement, Suzanne following a few steps behind. I could feel my pulse beating with the rhythm of a thousand Chinese fans. We reached the gate and Sonya and I gave our boarding passes to the steward. The boys seemed to be taking it pretty well, but at the last moment tears started to appear in little Simon's eyes. I bent over and kissed him.

"I'll bring you a panda," I said.

Then I hugged them both.

"Have a good time," said Suzanne, and I think she mostly meant it.

"Give my regards to Chairman Hua."

Sonya started onto the plane. I lingered there a moment, looking at my children, then followed her through the gate.

I was feeling a little guilty, but the inside of the fuselage was another world and I forgot them almost completely as soon as the plane started to taxi down the runway. A kind of giddy determination was coming over me. It was that curious euphoria of traveling, amplified by something hard to define yet even more powerful. No matter how lightly I took it, whatever wisecracks I made, going to China for me was not like taking a trip to New York or London, or even to Tokyo or Bombay. It was a search for self, a search for values that were waning so fast I wondered if I ever had them. After fifteen years of flirting around radical movements, playing footsy with commitment, I wanted to find out if it was worth resolving the ambivalence in my life, an ambivalence which had reduced whatever idealism I had left to copping attitudes at cocktail parties and making donations at liberal fund-raisers. And if there was a resolution, I thought it would be in China, the one place where the egalitarian ideal did not seem to have been completely vitiated by self-serving bureaucrats and distinctly nonsocialist expansionism. At least not yet.

So, in the few quiet moments of the last couple of days, I had begun to see this trip as a new beginning, a spiritual journey of sorts. Sonya wasn't the only one making her pilgrimage to Mecca. I was, too—the skeptical son, the doubter who encompasses within his doubt the kernel of a yet stronger belief.

It made me resent even more that I would be categorized as a detective—"Moses Wine, 33, detective, Los Angeles," it said on the list of "delegates" to Friendship Study Tour Number Five—a career I fell into by accident, that inherently distanced me from the world, turning me into a kind of photographer who perceived everything at one remove. I looked over at Fred Lisle, seated in the nearest aisle seat of our 747, and was irritated with him for being so eager to put me in that position. Sonya, seated beside him, was already dozing, a copy of the *Barefoot Doctor's Manual* in her lap. In the next row, Ana Tzu was showing Harvey Walsh some photographs of her children, while Nancy Lemon, a whiskey sour in her hand, introduced herself to Max Freed. I heard some mention of how pleased she was to meet him, how she had read every issue of *Modern Times* since the one on the murder at the Rolling Stones concert in 1969.

In the row behind them, Nick Spitzler and Mike Sanchez were going over lists of people they knew in the union movement. Reed Hadley, who had cornered Ruby Crystal by the emergency exit, was bemoaning the escalating prices of Chinese bronzes. Some of those he had seen at the archaeological exhibit had quadrupled in value in the last five years.

I had started to drift off when Li Yu-ying leaned over to me. "I thought you'd want to read this," he said. "I sent it to the other members of the group several weeks ago." He handed me a mimeographed sheet on Utah State stationery.

WHAT IS THE "GANG OF FOUR"?

Reports from China these days are filled with news of the attack against the so-called "Gang of Four"—Chiang Ching (Mao's widow), Wang Hung-wen, Chang Chun-chiao and Yao Wen-yuan. On the surface, this is an ideological struggle, with the "Gang" and their supporters upholding the idealistic gains of the Cultural Revolution against a collection of Soviet-style bureaucrats, essentially a battle of those who favor pure communism now against those who uphold a gradual process of socialist consolidation leading to communist utopia and withering away of the state somewhere in the indefinite future. The Chinese say, however, that this is not true, that the "Gang's" objectives were not idealistic but actually an opportunistic attempt to seize state power by exploiting a naive revolutionary fervor and creating a debilitating anarchy throughout the productive sector of the entire society. They also accuse the "Gang" of stifling free expression in the arts (Chiang Ching's province) and of attempting to suppress the legitimate contribution of older revolutionaries like Chou En-lai.

31

The "Gang" was arrested as a direct result of events precipitated by the death of Mao. They are all now supposedly under preventive detention in Chang An Hai on the edge of the Forbidden City, the historic home of the Chinese Emperors.

We arrived in Hong Kong about eleven P.M. local time, seven o'clock in the morning in Los Angeles, after fourteen hours on the plane. Most of us seemed pretty wasted, except for Fred Lisle, who had that magic ability to fall asleep an hour after takeoff and wake up as the captain was announcing the descent.

Through the window we could see our first glimpse of the Orient, a hillside city resembling San Francisco, with skyscrapers growing like wild grass along the oceanfront. The flight path, the shortest I had ever experienced, took us directly over those buildings and down with the suddenness of a helicopter.

And then we were on the ground, walking with equal abruptness from the plane to the baggage claim area, a scant fifty yards away. It was raining, and chic Hong Kong Chinese in tight skirts and newly purchased California denim suits hurried ahead of us. But before we had a chance to become confused, a short, round-faced man in a white sport shirt and blue pants came forward to greet us. He was wearing what seemed like a chauffeur's hat and a simple red star on his left breast. How he knew who we were, among the many Westerners traveling on that plane, I still do not know; but it was only the first of many confusing events that occurred in the next few days.

He introduced himself as Mr. Kau. With him were two other men similarly dressed and six other men wearing blue work shirts and blue shorts, also with red stars on their breasts. They smiled at us as if we all shared some wonderful secret, produced umbrellas, and escorted us into the terminal. These men were much earthier, far more peasantlike, than the Chinese on the plane. The Hong Kongers did not look at them and they did not look at the Hong Kongers—as if there were some *entente cordiale* between the two Chinas not to embarrass each other with stares of recognition. Maybe it was my lack of sleep, but these mainlanders had a primitive, almost holy quality about them, like disciples of an early Christian saint come to labor among the heathens. And they were much shorter. Or maybe that was because they wore sandals instead of high heels and platform shoes with gold lamé side straps.

Mr. Kau squired us into a modern air-conditioned bus while our bags were lashed onto a rickety old truck by the men in blue shorts. I found myself sitting in an aisle seat next to Fred Lisle as our bus lurched to a start.

"That's Victoria Harbour." He pointed out at the passing parade of freighters and ferries.

"You've been here before?"

"Oh, yes. Several times," he said, as if it were the most obvious thing in the world.

The bus turned down the Nathan Road and we were assaulted with a barrage of neon signs longer and more intense than Times Square: watches, pens, stereos, calculators, cameras—all the products of the Japanese industrial colossus, presented through the genius of Chinese retailing. Mr. Kau nodded apologetically, as if sorry he had to expose us to such crass commercialism. Then we turned again onto a side street, arriving at the elaborate *porte cochère* of our hotel, the New Kowloon, where two immense jeweled ceramic tigers guarded an electronically operated sliding door. Above that, a row of glittering pink-and-orange flower boards advertised all-night dancing in the hotel's rooftop restaurant—a Ching Dynasty version of the Ramada Inn.

Fred and I got up behind Max Freed and Ruby Crystal, following them out of the bus.

"I bet they don't show," he whispered darkly.

"What?"

"The celebrities. I bet they don't show up at the orientation tomorrow morning."

Twenty minutes later I was watching *Cinderella Liberty*

with Chinese subtitles. It was the late show on Hong Kong television and I was sprawled out on the bed, too exhausted to change the channel although I had already seen the movie. It was vaguely reassuring anyway, a kind of cultural bridge. My body might be in Asia, but my soul was still doing fifty-five in a thirty zone on Sepulveda Boulevard.

Harvey Walsh, my roommate for the first night of the trip, slouched in an easy chair, going over a list of restaurants given him by an *est* trainer from Palo Alto who used to be in import-export. I looked from him to the television screen. The little black kid in the movie was making some wiseass reference to Mao Tse-tung and I smiled.

That's the last thing I remember that night until there was a sharp rapping on our door. Walsh and I both sat up in our beds.

"Yes?" I said.

"Ana Tzu?"

Walsh and I looked at each other. For the moment, I had no idea who Ana Tzu was.

"Ana Tzu?" the voice repeated. It was definitely Chinese. Then I remembered. Ana Tzu was the Chinese-American woman on our tour. I had scarcely spoken to her on the way over.

"Ana Tzu?!" More knocking.

I got out of the bed a few steps ahead of Walsh and went to the door. The digital clock in our room registered two-thirty-five A.M.

I opened the door a crack, carefully leaving it on the latch. Outside in the corridor three well-dressed middle-aged Chinese people—a man and two women—stared anxiously at me.

"Ana Tzu?" said the man again, but this time his voice lacked conviction. If Ana Tzu were in *this* room, something was clearly awry.

"She's not here," I said. "Wrong room."

He muttered something in Chinese and started backing away. The two women stared at me a second longer.

"What is it?" I asked. But they didn't answer. They fol-

34

lowed the man around the corner, where I heard him knocking again, at the next room.

"Ana Tzu?" The voice remained insistent.

I shut the door. Walsh and I looked at each other, then went back to our beds.

I didn't sleep much the rest of the night. The intrusion disturbed me, and my inner clock was already scrambled from the time change. At six A.M. I decided to give up and went downstairs for some exercise and a look at the city. Outside, it was drizzling. A typhoon was passing, the early morning doorman told me. I jogged a few blocks up the Nathan Road, past some massage parlors, a place called the Lee Kee Go-Go Club and a McDonald's stand.

IV A NERVOUS expectation pervaded our orientation session, held at ten that morning in the "Aberdeen Room" on the second floor. We sat around a large circular table with several pots of tea steeping in front of us and stared at each other. Americans had been moving in and out of China for several years now, since before the Nixon visit, but the number of places remained limited and each of us knew it. We were the chosen, the elect.

And despite Fred Lisle's warning, everyone was there, including the celebrities: Natalie Levine, her crushed-velvet hat tipped rakishly to one side; Max Freed, wearing what must have been the most expensive safari suit from Abercrombie & Fitch. Staughton Grey sat at the far end in what seemed like the same crew-neck sweater he had worn when he accompanied Bertrand Russell on the Aldermaston marches of the late fifties. It was probably threadbare even then.

At the mythical head of our round table was our "Responsible Person," my Aunt Sonya. It was hard to think of her in that position. To me she had always been a vaguely comic figure—warm and affectionate, yes, a surrogate parent since my mother died; but still comic, a female Don Quixote tilting at social windmills. I remembered when I was seven and she tried to teach me the words to "The Internationale" in Russian. My mother threw a fit, but it didn't matter. I never learned them, in English or Russian.

"Sometimes it's difficult for Americans to act as a group," said Sonya, passing out mimeographed sheets on which we were to indicate our principal areas of interest. "But in China that's the best way to get results. So when you fill these out don't be disappointed if your individual requests go unanswered. But if five or six of you can get together on something, you will find the Chinese bending over backward to accommodate you."

Sonya had put on her glasses and was looking straight at me. I knew she thought of me as a lone-wolf individualist, but I resented being singled out. "Now there are certain places you won't be allowed to go," she continued, with an authority I had never heard before. "The Chinese have an itinerary for us. They've made hotel reservations. So if you want to go to Tibet, forget it. Also, mental hospitals have been placed off limits, as have prisons and courts. I know this may be a disappointment to some of you." She eyed Spitzler and Harvey Walsh. "You'll just have to live with it. Now, about sex . . ." Suddenly my sixty-four-year-old aunt had riveted everybody's attention; everybody, that is, except Ana Tzu, who had been dozing in an armchair ever since the meeting began. "I guess you all heard the Chinese have a different attitude toward it. Maybe it's prudish, maybe it's just common sense, but Peking is not Hollywood Boulevard. You won't find any drag queens or hookers in short skirts. Everything they do, they do in private. So don't be an idiot— no touching, no feeling, no holding hands between men and women. And if someone on this tour strikes your fancy and you feel you just have to do it, at least wait until you're back in Hong Kong. And for crissakes don't get palsy-walsy with one of our guides. It'll only make trouble for both of you."

"What kind of trouble?" grinned Reed Hadley, playing the court jester.

"Well, to begin with, there's the story of the newspaper

reporter who told his elevator operator in the Peking Hotel she had nice legs. He was out of the country in twelve hours. But if you've got a bigger imagination than that, let me remind you that adultery in China is a crime called 'Sabotage of the Family,' punishable by thirty years in prison."

Max Freed whistled, considering, no doubt, the many years he could have spent in the Shanghai jail.

"One other thing," said Sonya, "while we're on the subject of Western decadence. Most of us like to collect souvenirs of our travels—stationery, matchbooks, ashtrays, maybe an occasional towel from the Rome Hilton. The Chinese do not take kindly to this. Put everything back unless you pay for it. It all belongs to the people."

We then started to complete our preference forms. I saw Reed Hadley writing the words "Han Duck" on his sheet. Three seats away, Nancy Lemon was asking about the Great World. "No, no," Li Yu-ying was saying. "You won't be able to see that. It's off limits now." But she was going to put it down anyway. I didn't know what to write, so I scribbled something about cooperating with the group. It seemed to be in the proper spirit and I figured it would please Sonya.

"All right, who's going to be the baggage chief?" she said, collecting the forms. "We need someone to be responsible for our bags as we go from city to city."

Nobody responded.

"Well, that's terrific. That's the spirit," she said.

Finally Mike Sanchez raised his hand.

"Uhuh. Now that's interesting."

Sonya looked at us archly as we all registered the awkwardness of the sole working-class person on our tour—and a minority member, to boot—having been the only one to volunteer.

"I'll do it, too," said Staughton Grey, raising his hand.

"It's too late," said Sonya. "We only need one. You should have spoken up earlier." And we were dismissed for lunch.

I had wanted to go with Harvey Walsh, who had the name of a restaurant specializing in shark's-fin soup in a district called Mongkok, but was buttonholed immediately by Max Freed, who insisted I come with him.

"What're you doing on this trip?" he demanded the moment we got outside the door of the hotel. They were building a subway beneath the sidewalks of the Nathan Road and the din of jackhammers was inescapable.

"The same thing you are, I imagine—taking a peek at Utopia."

"Oh." He studied me carefully.

"You had a different idea?"

"Not particularly." We walked a few more feet. Some tourists passed by in a red rickshaw with a green canopy. "Do you think there's an agent on the tour?"

"An agent?"

"You know—CIA, FBI, whatever."

"I don't think we're that interesting . . . anyway, I'm surprised to see you on the tour, too—associating with radicals. I heard your magazine's gone uptown. Truman Capote and Richard Avedon."

"Who're you to talk? Somebody told me *you're* chasing ambulances."

"Better than gossiping over cocktails with Princess Radziwill!"

"I never should have used you on the cover." He looked at me with that boyish sneer of his. "Hip detectives, it didn't sell."

"Next time stick to punk rock groups."

Our relationship was picking up where it left off. The last time we met we'd traded insults for an hour at an actors' bar on Santa Monica Boulevard. But this time he laughed.

"Bring any dope?" he asked.

I smiled and shook my head.

"Oh, come on, Wine. You used to be a big doper. I remember when you sucked nitrous for three hours straight in Gunther Thomas's room at the Château Marmont."

"Salad days," I said. "I'm thirty-three going on thirty-four."

"Well, I don't know about you, but I brought *my* overnight bag—a half a gram of coke, two ounces of Maui zowie, and six tabs of MDA. Who's going to take it with me if you don't?"

"The Fourth Plenary Session of the Eleventh Party Congress."

He shook his head. "I knew this was going to be a dull trip," he said.

It was then that Nancy Lemon came running up to us.

"Ana Tzu's sick," she said. "They're taking her to the hospital!"

V THE DAY before I left, I found the old copy of *Quotations from Chairman Mao Tse-tung* I had bought my second year of law school. It wasn't the familiar Chinese publication with the red plastic jacket, but a fraying Bantam Book published in 1967 with an introduction by Stuart Schram to "clarify" what the back cover trumpets as " 'THE LITTLE RED BOOK' THAT HAS SHAKEN THE WORLD!!!" I remember being mocked for paying a dollar for it when the Peking original cost fifty cents.

Actually I had bought the book at the behest of two friends —David and Jane Petrakis—who even then thought China the acme of civilization. They were film students at USC who gave up potential movie careers to become assembly-line workers, and had the irritating ability to give me a guilty conscience at a moment's notice. My answer to their sinophilia was an ostrichlike "we-know-so-little-about-it," but in reality I didn't want China to be so special. I had a vested, ethnocentric interest in its failure and also, I suppose, a vested interest in the Petrakis's being wrong. Later they gave me copies of *Important Documents of the Great Proletarian Cultural Revolution* (never read) and *Five Articles by Chairman Mao Tse-tung* (two read).

41

I opened the book, bypassing the epigraph from Chairman Mao's now mysteriously deceased great comrade in arms Vice Chairman Lin Piao, and flipped through the pages for the quotations the Moses Wine of ten years ago had starred and underlined. The first one came right to the point:

Whoever sides with the revolutionary people is a revolutionary. Whoever sides with imperialism, feudalism and bureaucrat-capitalism, is a counter-revolutionary. Whoever sides with the revolutionary people *in words only* but acts otherwise is a *revolutionary in speech.* Whoever sides with the revolutionary people in deed as well as in word is a revolutionary in the full sense.

It was underlined twice and had three stars.

Another quotation that was heavily underlined came from the essay "On Contradiction," written in August 1937, in which Mao contended that revolutionary struggles never cease—that there will always be "contradictions." As the essay put it, one always splits into two. Therefore, there is no final *end* to revolution, no perfected society.

I liked that then, in sixty-seven, and I still liked it. I could see why: it gave me an excuse for my ironic, pleasantly alienated view of life. Mao himself had let me slide out of commitment. After all, what was the use in participating in a dialectic that would not resolve itself?

And as for the Red Book itself, why bother? It was now in disrepute anyway—a document of the Cultural Revolution and its adherents, the infamous Gang of Four. Now, in the new, new China, Volume V of Mao's works is stressed, its "Ten Major Relationships" pushing ever onward for modernization, increased production, and technology.

But I, the parlor Maoist from the Hollywood Hills, had a soft spot for the unruly idealism of the Cultural Revolution, that revolution which, Li Yu-ying told us at our afternoon orientation, he thinks actually began in 1927, at the time of the Autumn Harvest Uprising, and not, as those of us who have made only a cursory study of China would assume, with the so-called excesses of the Red Guard in 1966 and '67. It was then, in 1927, that the struggle between the mass line and the bureaucratic line first appeared in the Chinese Communist Party.

My major struggle at the moment, however, was to stay awake. It was already one in the morning back home, as Li Yu continued his survey of Chinese revolutionary history, a crash course in more ways than one. Actually, I liked him and under more normal circumstances he wouldn't have been boring. But right now I couldn't tell the Gang of Four from the front line of the Chicago Bears or the Shanghai Commune from the latest boutique in Beverly Hills.

We were all pleased when Sonya seized the initiative as Responsible Person and let us go for the evening—all, that is, except Ana Tzu, who was long gone anyway.

When Max and I arrived back at the hotel from our aborted lunch, they were already putting her on a stretcher, Sonya standing beside her, tapping her toe impatiently with a gesture I remembered from when she was housebound for six months with arthritis.

"What happened?" I asked her.

"Something in the stomach—I don't know. She says she was vomiting."

I looked down at Ana Tzu, who was clenching a white sheet to her shoulder and staring at the ceiling. Her complexion gave no clue to her condition.

"How are you?" I asked.

"Okay," she said. "Don't worry."

Two orderlies picked her up and carried her through a side door.

I turned to Sonya. "Someone woke us up last night, looking for her."

"You and everybody else."

"Who was it?"

"I have no idea."

"What're you going to do?"

"What're you—a nudge?"

"Well, you're going to do something about it, aren't you?"

"I told Mr. Kau . . . they're going to watch over her stay here and try to arrange for her to meet us inside, if she feels better."

"Suppose she doesn't?"

"Then she doesn't. What can I do?"

I didn't have an answer. Through the window, Ana Tzu was visible being lifted onto an ambulance and driven away.

"It's really a shame," said Sonya. "She was born in Canton and wanted to see her old house."

That evening, after Li Yu's history lesson, I decided to go out alone. It was my last chance to see Hong Kong and, I thought, my last opportunity to be by myself, away from the group, before we entered China.

I took a shower and went down into the lobby to write a postcard to my kids. At the magazine kiosk I selected a photograph of two little boys on a sampan and started to write. Out of the corner of my eye, I could see Nancy Lemon sitting by the elevator watching me. She smiled and I had the distinct impression she wanted me to come over. But I chose to ignore it, smiled back politely, and finished my card.

Outside, it was still raining, the night lights of Hong Kong glistening on the pavement. I headed south for the Star Ferry. Crowds of local people pushed past me in both directions on their way home from work. They were smartly dressed and the women were attractive, very attractive. It was the chic area of town. A pair of Bentleys were parked in the driveway of the Peninsula Hotel.

I was hurrying past them to the ferry gate across the street when I noticed Staughton Grey getting out of one of the cars. Staughton Grey in a Bentley? I stopped and looked at him. For a moment it seemed as if he were going straight into the hotel, the oldest and richest in Hong Kong. But he caught my reflection in the glass of the revolving door, stopped, and turned back to me.

"I borrowed it from an old friend in the British Dip-

44

lomatic Corps," he said, before I could ask. "I wanted to see the view from the top of Victoria Peak."

"How was it?"

"Terrible. All fogged in . . . I have to return these to him." He waved the keys at me. "He has drinks at the Peninsula Bar every night at seven."

"Bombay gin and tonic?"

"Pimm's Cup number two."

We smiled uneasily at each other for a second.

"You won't tell anybody I was driving a Bentley, will you? It'd play havoc with my image."

"That's okay. I drive a Porsche."

He grinned. "See you tomorrow," he said and started inside, but stopped himself. "How's your aunt?"

"She's fine," I said. "She's napping."

He nodded and continued inside. I stared at the Bentley, its hood still smoking in the rain, while a liveried doorman watched me from the top of the stairs.

I walked off and rode the Star Ferry back and forth a few times. It was amusing, but a thick fog obscured the legendary view. You couldn't see the lights of the Hong Kong skyline until you had practically bumped into it and the top of Victoria Peak was completely enshrouded in clouds. So I gave up and got off again on the Kowloon side. It was getting late anyway and we had an early start the next morning.

On the way back to the hotel, I passed a bar called the Club Barcelona. A tall Chinese woman in a blue slit dress and long black hair with a gardenia pinned to it smiled at me through the doorway. She was gorgeous and I stopped and smiled back at her. In the background I could make out a silver beaded curtain in a shaft of green-tinged light, the silhouette of a chaise longue covered in brocade. She nodded for me to enter, but I didn't move. Somehow it didn't seem right. At seven A.M. I was crossing into the People's Republic of China. I should go pure.

VI ENTERING PEOPLE'S China is like entering the waiting room for an Early-Renaissance version of the afterlife, only the heraldic choir plays "The Volunteer Army Marching Song" and the angels of mercy wear pigtails and rope sandals and distribute copies of the *Peking Review*. Everything is clean, simple and green—pale green, like Piero della Francesca—not bold proletarian red. The baggage inspection station on the Chinese side has two large murals showing people of all nationalities joyously arriving in the People's Republic, multicolored ribbons swirling about their heads, but even these are painted in subdued pastels. You almost expect someone to tap you on the shoulder and lead you off to sit forever on soft, overstuffed armchairs covered with lace antimacassars.

We got there by taking a crowded train across the New Territories. It was a slow eighteen-mile ride passing through ramshackle suburbs of Hong Kong and then along the Tide Cove of Mirs Bay. By the time we reached Tai Po the landscape had widened to verdant farmlands, rice paddies and water buffaloes, a picture unfolding like pictures of China in children's books I had read as a boy.

I sat next to Mike Sanchez. Across from us, Natalie Levine

dictated into a miniature Sony. I heard the words "Dear Constituents, It is hard to believe that I am now . . ." Outside, a cloudburst dumped water on a group of peasants standing by a truck. They ran for cover under a banyan tree. Sanchez looked worried.

"How much did you pay for this?" he asked.

"The trip? Same as everybody. Twenty-four hundred."

"I took a loan from my credit union. Now I'm in the hole for everything. My television, a washing machine, two cars and a trip to China."

"Join the club," I offered.

He didn't smile.

We stopped for a moment at the market town of Fanling. A Coca-Cola vendor jumped off the rear car, a last vestige of capitalism. We were drawing closer to the border. The train started up again, half of us standing in the aisles now, snapping photographs through the water-stained windows or straining for a first view of the Sham Chun River, which separates the New Territories from the province of Kwangtung.

I felt a hand on my shoulder. It was Harvey Walsh.

"You turned in early last night," he said.

"I was bushed."

"You should have seen *them*." He nodded to Nancy Lemon and Fred Lisle, who were sitting next to each other in the front seats. "Doing the hustle at the Lee-Kee Go-Go Club until a quarter to three."

I was staring at the deep rings around Nancy's eyes when the train slowed again, hugging the edge of a cliff planted with jasmine. "I can't wait," Harvey continued. "The last time I led a group at Esalen there were twelve divorces."

We pulled up hard at the station at Lo Wu, a few low-slung white-stucco buildings running along the wall of the railroad bridge. A solitary red flag waved over a block house on the other side. It took me a second to realize where we were: This was it. Mr. Kau stood at the back of the car, signaling for us to follow.

Soon we were pushing our way through the Hong Kong border control building, jammed up with more than a hundred overseas Chinese on their way to visit relatives. A young inspector stamped my passport and returned it to me. I looked up to see Kau beckoning to me from under a doorway. A sign over his head read, improbably, TO CHINA.

I headed through the door with the others. We waited for Kau, but he waved to us to keep going. We were walking across the border on foot, over the railroad bridge, Kau standing on the Hong Kong side, waving goodbye. A girl of about eighteen, a pair of pigtails hanging over her shoulders, cheeks glowing like the peaches in some brush painting, waited at the other side, smiling beatifically. I glanced over at Li Yu, walking beside me. Tears were welling up in his eyes. My heart pounded. This was the Bamboo Curtain.

We were ushered to an outdoor desk where our papers were examined, a scene that resembled registration day at Berkeley. Then a strange segregation process occurred. The overseas Chinese were led around the back while we, the foreign guests, were taken along a corridor to a large, inviting waiting room with a distinctly nineteenth-century cast—doilies on the tables, a blue rug with a panda design on the floor. My first reaction was to wonder, Why us? We don't deserve this special treatment. But the young girl smiled at me and I melted onto a sofa, a cup of tea in my hand and copies of the *Peking Review* spread out in front of me in five languages.

Our permanent guides were then introduced to us. There were three of them: Mr. Hu, a young man, in his mid-twenties, with a flattop haircut; Mrs. Liu, a woman in her late twenties, with closely cropped hair and a skirt down to the middle of her calf; and Mr. Yen, a tall man in his forties, with aquiline features and dark, rather charismatic eyes. They would be augmented in each of the cities with local guides, but they still would have the primary responsibility for overseeing our trip and, I imagined, be our most significant connection with the people of China.

Yen was the first to speak, in warm, ingratiating tones that mirrored our excitement at being there.

"Good morning. We are very pleased to greet our American friends of U.S.–China People's Friendship Study Tour Number Five and warmly welcome them to the People's Republic of China." Our applause was matched with applause from our guides in the Chinese fashion. "We see there are many special friends of China on this tour and we would like to make extra welcome to our old friends: Mrs. Sonya Lieberman, Responsible Person; Mr. Li Yu-ying, returning to the nation of his birth after forty years; and to Mr. Fred Lisle, also returning to the country where he spent his childhood." Fred Lisle in China—that was a surprise. "Another old friend, Mrs. Ana Tzu, is, I understand, missing, and will join us later in our visit. I hope you will enjoy your stay in the People's Republic of China and that you will return with a better understanding of how we build socialist revolution and construction."

Mrs. Liu was next to speak. "Welcome, American friends! You have come to China at a great time. All the people are rejoicing at the overthrow of the ultra-Rightist Gang of Four and at the new direction of our wise leader Chairman Hua. Taking class struggle as the key link and agriculture as the leading factor, we continue to learn from Tachai in agriculture and from Taching in industry, to guard against the danger of capitalist restoration and to march eagerly along the socialist road."

"And now for some . . . launch," said Mr. Hu.

"Lunch," said Mr. Yen.

"Yes. Lunch," said Mr. Hu, reddening.

We followed our guides down another corridor past some empty offices and another lounge. Sonya was in the front with Mrs. Liu, whispering to her conspiratorially as if they were long-lost friends at a reunion. I watched them as we continued on to the other side of the railroad station, where two round tables were laid out for us beneath a brown needle-point portrait of Chairman Mao at his desk.

Yen nodded for us to sit and I took a place between Ruby Crystal and Mr. Hu. Mrs. Liu, Harvey Walsh and Reed Hadley sat opposite me. We began what proved to be an eleven-course meal with boiled pork in hot-pepper sauce, steamed oxtail, prawns in clear sauce and abalone in oyster sauce. A waitress filled up glasses of beer, orange soda and mao tai, the Chinese version of White Lightning.

"What's that?" I asked Mr. Hu, pointing to a mixture of chicken and some other ingredients which were unknown to me. He looked over helplessly at Mrs. Liu.

"Achilles tendon of pork with chicken and ham," she said. "Made with scallions, ginger and a little bit of rice wine . . . you do not eat?"

She was looking directly at Ruby Crystal, who indeed was sitting behind an empty plate.

"My fast day. I fast two days a week."

Mrs. Liu stared at Ruby, totally baffled. Then she burst into laughter. "Ah, Americans, you are always on a diet." She patted her own stomach, which was as flat as Ruby's. "Here in China, we work."

Ruby looked down at her plate uncomfortably. A dish of spareribs with fermented beans was brought to the table, followed by deep-fried bean curd in sesame sauce. Mr. Yen stood, holding aloft a glass of mao tai. We all rose with him.

"To the friendship of the Chinese and American peoples!"

"To friendship!"

The mao tai went down my throat and into my feet in less than a second. Harvey Walsh leaned over to me. "She's gorgeous, isn't she?"

"Just like in the movies."

"Not Ruby," he said. "Mrs. Liu."

After lunch, we descended a couple of flights and emerged in the courtyard of the railroad station. "The East is Red" was playing over loudspeakers. I stopped and listened to it, staring out across the railroad tracks to a rice paddy where peasants were busy planting. Nearer in, a crew of women in hard hats worked on a power line.

Maybe it was the mao tai, but I immediately felt an intense identification with planters and with the women on the line. In fact, with everyone around me. The music was having a powerful effect on me, too, the way it did in the sixties, when I would get tears in my eyes singing "We Shall Overcome" at peace marches and demonstrations. It was that rare feeling of belonging, yet here it was belonging to something so alien as to be almost incomprehensible.

But I let myself flow with these emotions as I crossed the courtyard, passing an immense waiting room where hundreds of Overseas Chinese were cued up at ticket windows, to the Canton train. We were directed onto an air-conditioned coach with more Victorian doilies and propaganda literature. I chose a seat by the window. Another pigtailed waitress came by with tea in white ceramic cups and protective lids. But she did not feel like my servant. She felt like my equal. I smiled at her as I took the tea. It tasted like ambrosia. Everything I had hoped about this country was coming true.

Mr. Yen must have read my emotions, because he got up from his seat next to Mr. Hu and sat down beside me.

"Well, how do you feel about being in China, Mr. Wine?" he asked.

"Incredible," I said. "I can hardly believe it!"

"We are pleased to have you," he said. The train pulled out, chugging past the rice paddy where the peasants were working, their bent bodies like figures in a brush painting.

"I understand you are a 'private detective'!" said Yen.

I nodded.

"That sounds interesting. What do you do?"

"I investigate things the police can't . . . or don't want to."

Yen looked puzzled.

"You know, a businessman wants to find out about his competition . . . or someone's looking for a missing child, or someone else wants to prove another man's running around with his wife."

"You do that?"

A head popped up from behind the next seat before I could answer. "Sure he does. He's terrible—a complete sellout!" It was Sonya.

"Sellout?" Yen didn't understand.

"He does everything for the money and rides around in a Porsche!"

"Is that true?"

"Basically," I said, not feeling like advertising the two or three times I might have used my skills to do something worthwhile.

But Yen didn't look disturbed. "That is nothing to be ashamed of," he said. "We are all a product of our historical conditions. You are the product of the conditions of your society as much as we are the product of ours."

"That doesn't mean he shouldn't know better," Sonya muttered.

But it didn't bother me. I had Yen on my side. And I was in China.

The train was fully up to speed now. I sat back as other members of our group peppered Yen with questions. Yes, he said, hard as it was to visualize, the area we were passing through had been barren before Liberation. But extensive programs of reforestation and water conservancy had changed the face of the land. Poor peasants once lucky to bring in one scanty rice crop were now members of communes harvesting two or three bumper crops a year. Hills had been terraced and irrigation systems established everywhere. And, despite the interference of the Gang of Four, the people were pushing onward to turn the whole province into a garden spot.

As we drew closer to Kwangchow the land became more populous, isolated factories dotting up among the rice fields. We crossed the Pearl River, wide and yellow-brown, with peasants wheeling bicycles across the trestle bridge. A jaunty camaraderie was developing among the group. Max Freed tried to teach Mr. Hu the latest American slang, while Mike Sanchez and Harvey Walsh competed for photographs off the rear of the car. Spitzler, who must have been feeling some of the same emotions I was, paced up and down the aisle humming Movement songs. As we approached the Kwangchow railroad station, Mrs. Liu began to sing us a Chinese peasant song from the Great Leap Forward. Later, she translated the words:

> There is no Jade Emperor in heaven.
> There is no Dragon King on earth.
> I am the Jade Emperor.
> I am the Dragon King.
> Make way for me
> You hills and mountains
> I'm coming.

VII It was later that afternoon that Reed Hadley—our investment counselor—told me Canton was a center for jade. We were standing under the pavilion of the memorial park dedicated to the martyrs of the 1927 uprising. One of our guides was explaining how Chiang Kai-shek's troops crushed the Canton Commune and slaughtered five thousand people, when Reed asked me to keep my eye out—in case I saw any bargains. I told him I didn't know anything about jade.

Back on the bus, Hadley buttonholed Mr. Hu and asked him if Canton was a good place for antiques. We only had two and a half days in the city and he wanted time off to do some shopping.

Mr. Hu looked a little nonplussed and fumbled around a moment, saying he would see what could be done. We were driving along the bund by the Pearl River. This was downtown Canton, traffic and people swarming everywhere. Across a bridge lay Shamien Island, the old French and British concession, its fading pastel villas reflecting in the water. In past days, we were told, no Chinese were allowed there without permission and the bridges were shut at ten P.M.

We pulled up in front of a monument in memory of the demonstrators who were killed on that spot in 1925 by bullets fired by European soldiers on the island. The Chinese were protesting the "unequal treaties" which resulted in a general strike which paralyzed the harbors of Canton and Hong Kong.

Now those same Chinese were staring at us, their faces pressed in curiosity against the windows of our bus.

"Could we walk around?" Spitzler asked Yen, expressing a desire we all felt, to get out and mingle with the Chinese people. We had been swept up by local guides on our arrival in Canton and taken from monument to monument without so much as a stop at our hotel to deposit our bags. There was so little time to see Canton, they said, and we agreed.

Yen looked at his watch. "All right," he said, "but we must be back at the hotel in time for dinner."

We got up quickly and filed off the bus, the Chinese dispersing politely to observe us from the nearest sidewalk. I was feeling a little uneasy, maybe guilty about the actions of some European soldiers who died years before my birth, when an open truck roared by, a half-dozen men with red handkerchiefs tied around their foreheads standing on the back, shouting and banging giant kettledrums and cymbals. Long red streamers trailed from the door handles and bumpers.

"Is this a holiday?" I asked Mrs. Liu.

"Workers from Canton Number Three Steel Plant celebrate the second conference on learning from Taching in industry."

"It looks like Chinese New Year back home."

"Many old traditions exist in the New China, Mr. Wine."

Mrs. Liu looked amused. I could see that Harvey Walsh was right. She was beautiful. But not like the apple-cheeked girls we had seen at the border, the kind that adorned the covers of Chinese magazines. She was at once more familiar and more remote—like the disputatious, attractive women I knew in graduate school, but totally different.

The truck doubled back again, banging louder as it passed our bus.

"It is for socialist emulation," she explained. "Workers

study the achievements of other workers so they may learn to serve the people better."

We watched the bus disappear around the corner and she turned away, answering a question from Ruby Crystal.

I joined Nick Spitzler and Natalie Levine for a walk through Shamien Island. The old imperialist bastion had clearly been taken over by the people, laundry strung from window to window between the former mansions. What must have been the "Club" stood along the water's edge, a row of red flags decorating the promenade where once their excellencies took the air.

Nick, Natalie and I decided to leave the main street, turning down a narrow alley where some older women were playing a checkerslike game. They looked up at us, astonished, and Natalie waved to them with the practiced hand of a politician.

Spitzler and I hadn't seen each other in a while and we joked about the time, a few years ago, when I had come to him for help in locating an underground figure he once represented. For a year after that he suspected I was an FBI agent.

"What do you think *that* is?" he said, pointing to a formidable building at the end of the block, surrounded by a high brick wall. Jagged pieces of broken glass were embedded in cement around the windows and at the top of the wall, with the apparent intention of discouraging visitors.

"The Sun Yat-sen Memorial Home for Political Dissidents," I cracked, but my heart wasn't in it.

"Let's have a look," he said, making for the front gate, a large iron affair that looked like it would require a battering ram to push open. He started to put his shoulder to it.

"Nick, for crissakes!" said Natalie, moving to stop him.

"Oh, come on," he said. "What're they going to do? Besides, aren't you interested? We're supporters of the people!"

"We've been in China for four hours!"

"If they've got something to hide, then we should know about it!"

He turned to the door again. I grabbed his arm, restraining him. "Nick!"

"Nick what?!" He stared at me, his muscles tightening. I knew Spitzler could be excitable. He had been cited for contempt more times than any lawyer west of Omaha.

"Don't," I said.

"Don't what?!" He wrenched himself free and pushed on the door with his foot. He nearly fell in when it swung open with almost no resistance.

"Holy shit!" He grinned. "Will you look at that?"

We took a step forward and stared past him. Inside were about a hundred nursery school children sitting on their knees, engaged in a rehearsal of choral singing. When they saw us, they stopped and started applauding. Their attractive young teacher waved and gave us a broad smile. I felt embarrassed I had been so protective.

Our little adventure made an amusing story on the bus to the hotel. Even the guides had a laugh. It seems, one of the Canton group explained, we had stumbled on the child-care center for the local silk factory. True, it had once been a prison, but that had changed even before Liberation, during Kuomintang rule, over fifty years ago.

We were still smiling when we assembled in the lobby of our hotel, the East Wind, a rather dismal, barnlike affair that reminded me of Atlantic City before they decided to institute gambling. Mike counted our bags while Sonya distributed the room assignments for our first night inside.

"I can't believe our rooms don't have keys!" said Nancy Lemon.

"Isn't it terrific?" said Ruby. She had already bought a Mao suit and wore a little red star on her lapel.

"Sure puts him out of business," said Sonya, nodding toward me.

"God," said Nancy, "there must not be any crime at all."

"Is that true?" asked Max Freed, turning to our guides, who were standing nearby, making sure everything went smoothly.

"There are still some crimes," said Mrs. Liu. "We are in a period of transition, when there remain class enemies under socialism, contradictions among the people. It may be that way for many years."

"But you will have nothing to worry about," Yen added reassuringly.

Nancy shook her head in an amazement that held for all of us. Then Sonya assigned her and Natalie Levine to a room. They started for the elevator. "Knock on the way to dinner," I heard Nancy tell Fred Lisle before it slid shut.

My Canton roommate was Staughton Grey. I wanted to tell him his speech at the Cooper Union in 1958 was the reason I joined the Student Peace Union at the age of fifteen. But, exhausted from jet lag, he fell asleep immediately after dinner.

I walked out on the balcony of our hotel room instead and stared out over Canton. In one direction I could make out the Pearl River winding its way back to Hong Kong, in the other a row of factories ending in the delicate pagoda of the Temple of the Six Banyans. Old and New China.

I shook my head like Nancy Lemon and took a deep breath. Here I was, standing on the balcony of a hotel room eight thousand miles from home, surrounded by one-quarter of the human race. I knew no one except the people on my tour and some guides I had met a few hours before. I did not speak a word of the language. I would be totally lost twenty yards from the hotel and there were no locks on my door—but I felt absolutely no fear. I could still hear "The East Is Red" ringing in my ears.

VIII THE NEXT day I learned a lot about the Gang of Four—at least I thought I did. We were at the New China Commune, about an hour out of Canton, sloshing around in the mud from the still-lingering storm. We had had our first taste of what the Chinese call a "Brief Introduction," followed by visits to the commune peanut fields and repair shop.

We were returning for lunch in the building where we had the introduction when I stopped to admire a blackboard with elaborately drawn calligraphy in pastel chalk. I was about to continue on when I noticed Mrs. Liu standing beside me. She had come up silently on the soft earth.

"Production Team Number Three—news of the day," she said, alluding to the blackboard.

"Local, national or international?"

"All kinds."

She clearly disapproved of the irony in my voice, not realizing it didn't mean anything. It was just my style.

While pretending to examine the board, I took a look at her out of the corner of my eye. She wasn't wearing proletarian blue this morning, but a short-sleeve blouse with the kind of prissy little flower pattern you'd see on college girls in the early sixties, before everyone got hip. But on her it didn't seem prissy at all.

"What does that say?" I asked, pointing to some writing in the lower right corner.

"Production Team Seven—first in hog production May 1977."

"And that?"

"Our brothers and sisters on Taiwan joyously await liberation."

"And that?" I pointed to the most prominent of the calligraphy, large Day-Glo-pink ideographs bordered by meticulously drawn water lilies.

"Continue the life-and-death struggle between the proletariat and the bourgeoisie to the end. Thoroughly smash the Wang–Chang–Chiang–Yao Gang of Four!"

I smiled.

"You think that is funny?"

"Not what it says. Just the rhetoric."

"What does that mean?"

"You know, the language. It's a little overblown."

"You do not understand. Our whole Party, the dictatorship of the proletariat, was in jeopardy."

"From whom?"

"The Gang of Four." She sounded impatient. "I do not understand why you consider this a frivolous matter."

"I don't consider it frivolous."

"Do you realize the Gang of Four set production back ten years?"

"How'd they do that?"

"By preaching revolution but practicing revisionism."

"I don't understand."

"They were left in form but right in essence. Have you heard of the concept 'Red and expert'?"

I shook my head.

"During the Cultural Revolution, it was determined it was not enough to be good at something, to be an expert. One must also have good politics, be at one with the masses . . . Red *and* expert." She waited a moment for this to sink in. Beyond her, the courtyard was empty. Everyone else had

60

gone in for lunch. "The Gang of Four made—how do you say?—a mockery of that idea. They said being Red was all-important and being expert nothing. Production slowed down. The factories were thrown into disorder. Anyone who was a good technician, who wanted to do his work well, was accused of the fallacy of productive forces. Made into a ridiculous."

"Made ridiculous."

"Yes. I do not speak very well."

"You speak marvelously."

A smile flickered across her face and vanished.

"Where'd you learn English?" I asked.

"The Foreign Language Institute in Peking. Now do you understand this?"

"Some of it."

We heard a door opening and turned around. Mr. Yen was standing at the entrance to the meeting hall.

"You are late for lunch," she said quickly. "If you have more questions about the Gang of Four, you will have an opportunity to ask them later."

We ate in a downstairs dining room with portraits of Marx and Engels on the wall and an expansive view of the countryside. The chairman of the revolutionary committee, a gregarious type with a stocky peasant build, stood and served us himself with foods that were, he proudly stated, grown exclusively on their commune. Later he told us how he lost his job during the Cultural Revolution because the peasants felt he was becoming a high-and-mighty bureaucrat. Even now, to show his proletarian spirit, he spent only half his day at official functions and the other half working in the fields.

He showed us his callused hands, but I was not paying great attention. I had spent my lunch mulling over the conversation in the courtyard, wondering whether Mrs. Liu had realized we were the only ones there—and why she had picked me to converse with in the first place. China was obviously a country of small signs, of vast shifts in ideology masking subtle human changes.

I drank some tea, knowing this course of speculation was not a smart one. Even to ruminate on a relationship with a Chinese woman was foolish, not to say absurd, given the warnings Sonya had been so careful to lay out at our first meeting. Yet here I was, on my second day, a veritable Jimmy Carter practicing adultery in my mind. Romanticism, I thought, bourgeois romanticism and nothing more. I downed the tea and tried to forget it.

We spent the afternoon tromping around the pigpens and the animal husbandry area of the commune. The rain was still misting gently, once again giving the hills the feeling of a Chinese brush painting. I stopped to photograph a water buffalo and a bullock for my children. I also photographed a young man carrying a butterfly fishing net for them. They would like that.

We followed the chairman of the revolutionary committee uphill along a stream leading to the commune reservoir. The hill climbed sharply and we continued up to where there was a view of the entire valley. Seemingly by accident, I found myself locking steps with Mrs. Liu. She didn't say anything and I didn't either. We walked on for a while, silently, until she was stopped by a couple of members of our group who had specific requests. Mike Sanchez wanted to know if there was time to visit the machine shop and Harvey Walsh asked if it would be possible for us to sit in on a session of criticism and self-criticism. She handled these and seemed to be starting up again, when she turned to me instead.

"I am surprised you have nothing more to ask about the Gang of Four." There was a twinkle in her eye.

Quickly, I came up with a few questions. "Uh, to begin with, if this Gang was so bad, how did they get into such high positions in the first place?"

"This is a complex question to do with the Communist Party and class struggle under socialism."

"Do you think I'm advanced enough to understand?"

"I don't know . . . do you understand the concept of 'Red and expert' yet?"

"I imagine it means putting your expertise at the service of the people."

"And?"

"And what?"

"Is that all?"

"I suppose."

"Don't suppose. Think."

"What else could it be?"

She shook her head. "You are behaving like the blind-folded man catching sparrows. Study conditions conscientiously and proceed from objective reality, not from subjective wishes." And with that she started up the hill ahead of me.

I was about to continue up after her when I heard shouting from across the stream. Some peasants, two women and a man, were racing up the hill toward the reservoir. I turned just as Yen came hurrying down to meet them with the chairman of the revolutionary committee and several members of our group. After a rapid exchange in Chinese, they headed for a small wooden bridge. I followed them over to the other side of the stream, where a grain storage bin towered above a still pool of water. Floating on the surface beside a jagged rock outcropping was the dead body of a Chinese man.

"He must have fallen from above," Yen said immediately to the shocked Americans who were gathering behind him.

The peasants reached in and pulled the man out of the water. Blood still trickled from a large gouge in his skull where the rocks had smashed his cranium. Nancy Lemon gasped and looked away. Max Freed clutched his stomach. He was turning yellow.

"This is a great shame you should see this," Yen continued, trying to usher us away as the chairman of the revolutionary committee directed the peasants to wrap the body in a blanket.

On professional instinct, I stepped around him for a better look. It was certainly an odd death. From the placement of the wound, it seemed the man would have to have fallen backward off the storage bin, a rather clumsy maneuver for a local peasant. Unless he had a stroke. Or . . .

"The detective inspects the body . . ." said Yen with a half-smile.

"Yeah. It looks like he was practicing his back dives."

"Back dives?" Yen looked confused.

"You know. Like this." I made a gesture like I was diving back first into the water.

"Oh, yes." Yen forced a dry laugh and looked at me a moment. "It is unfortunate to say, but there have been many such accidents here, especially under the Gang of Four. They preached a bad style of work and peasants and workers did not take safety precautions. This man himself, I am told, was a supporter of the Gang of Four." He indicated the dead man, who was now almost wrapped in a green blanket.

"The Gang of Four?" said Max. "That seems hard to believe."

"I have it on the greatest authority," said Yen. "But we must not linger here." He signaled for us to follow him up the hill.

As I turned, I caught sight of Liu, who was standing a few feet off. She was touching her hand to her forehead and staring at the corpse with that intense sense of loss you associate with relatives at a funeral.

"You knew him," I said.

"What?" She seemed startled.

"You knew this man."

"What? No. Of course not." She stared straight ahead, trying to look definite. I wondered if comradely loyalty turned everybody into a member of the immediate family. But no one else looked that distressed. "Come." She motioned to me. "You must see the commune reservoir. You must not let such accidents ruin your trip to China."

She started up the hill rapidly. In a few seconds she was at the top of the ridge. I walked up slowly, watching the peasants carrying their lumpy blanket downstream. By the time I

64

caught up with Liu she was already translating the chairman's speech on the reservoir, her short black hair unruffled in the blistering wind. I stood with the others and listened.

That night the man's death had faded into no more than an unpleasant interlude. A special event had been planned for us. We were to attend the "Small Dagger Society," a revolutionary dance drama about the Taiping Rebellion of the nineteenth century. The best section of the memorial theater named for Soong Ching-ling, the widow of Sun Yat-sen, was roped off for us and I sat with Sonya, front row center, in an audience of over three thousand. Above my head, a large red banner read SUPPORT CHAIRMAN MAO'S REVOLUTIONARY LINE IN LITERATURE AND THE ARTS! I leaned back and tried to watch the extravagant leaping and the sword dancing, but, although under normal circumstances I would have been fascinated, my eyes kept wandering from the performers to someone else.

"I'm glad you like China so much, Moishe," said Sonya, following my gaze off to the right, where the guides were sitting. "It pleases me very much . . . but remember, whatever happens, you're here to study socialism."

IX BY THE morning of the third day we were all drunk on ideology and in love with China. Even bouts of flu and diarrhea ("Chiang Ching's Revenge") did nothing to cool our ardor. We were only worried that the people back home would not believe us when we returned.

And, as if to erase any possible lingering pall on our trip, Ana Tzu came down for breakfast. She had arrived at the border the previous night and, with Yen's help, a special car was sent to bring her from Lo Wu to Canton. No one seemed disturbed that the doctors in Hong Kong were unable to diagnose her illness and that questions about her present condition were met with evasive responses if any.

The group's euphoria continued as we boarded the bus to visit the ancient ceramic factory in the suburb of Foshan. Only Sonya, sitting by herself in the back, appeared upset. She always had a dark, secretive side of her—the product of more disillusionment than she wanted to admit—and I didn't expect her to open up about it. But we weren't five minutes out of the hotel when she leaned over my seat and whispered to me as if Goebbels had just been elected mayor of Philadelphia.

"What're we going to do about them?"

"Who?"

"The Gang of Two."

She nodded ever so slightly to the front, where Fred Lisle and Nancy Lemon were jammed tightly in a jump seat, laughing and rubbing thighs as they bounced along on the bumpy Chinese roads.

"Oh, come on!" I said.

"Don't think the Chinese haven't noticed."

"How do you know?"

"They always do. . . . Besides, last night after the play Yen mentioned it to me."

"What'd he say?"

"That it was up to us."

"What's up to us?"

Just then Mrs. Liu stood up to point out the Peasant Movement Institute, the former Temple of Confucius, where in 1923 Mao first battled the Russian representative Borodin over whether the industrial proletariat or the peasantry should make the Chinese Revolution.

"What's up to us?" I repeated.

"How to handle them."

"But what have they done?"

Sonya gave me a look.

"Sonya . . . how're we supposed to handle them if they haven't done anything?"

"How do *you* know?"

"That's right. I don't know."

"Then how am I supposed to know?!"

"Well, ask Natalie Levine, for crissakes. She's been her roommate for two nights!"

"Hey, what's going on?" said Harvey Walsh, turning around. "Anything I can mediate?"

"Nothing. Bullshit. Forget it," I said.

Before he could respond, we arrived at the ceramics factory —a bright, airy structure built around a courtyard and seemingly untouched by such political cataclysms as the Cultural Revolution and the struggle against the Gang of Four. After

67

another Brief Introduction, we toured the workshops. Attractive Cantonese women sat at well-lit tables shaping little fish and dragons for export or, occasionally, more ambitious ceramic statues of model workers and barefoot doctors. Upstairs, a few men sat under skylights modeling large hunks of dark clay. They had exceptionally long, graceful fingers and winning, easy smiles. These were the designers.

Natalie Levine wondered why none of them were women. Later, at the question session, we found out only twenty per cent of the factory revolutionary committee were women although the factory had nearly eighty per cent women workers.

It was just like home. I sat there, a vaguely guilty male, while the women in our group got more and more steamed up—all, that is, except Nancy, who at the moment didn't seem like anything could faze her.

"What's going on?" Harvey repeated to me as we left the meeting room and entered the crowded factory store to purchase souvenirs.

"Don't worry about it," I said.

"Look, I'm a professional group leader and when something's going wrong with group dynamics I have a sixth sense about it."

"Yeah. And I'm a professional eavesdropper and I know the smartest thing to do is keep my mouth shut when something's only gossip."

"It's Nancy and Fred, isn't it?" he said.

I didn't reply, searching the shelves for some trinkets for my kids. Some little pandas caught my eye, but farther down I saw something I immediately wanted for myself—a magnificent three-foot-high ceramic of Mao, Chou En-lai and Red Army General Chu Teh standing atop Chingkiang Mountain.

"How much is that?" I asked the nearest of the Canton guides.

A back-and-forth with a clerk brought a quick answer—one hundred and forty yuan. Seventy dollars American. Not bad, I thought, considering, and decided to buy it when I saw another clerk slide it off the shelf and into the greedy mitts of Max Freed.

"For the board room of *Modern Times*," he grinned, lording it over me. A row of abacuses behind us clicked away as members of our group bought out the store. I purchased the pandas and left.

Outside, all we proud owners of revolutionary Foshan ceramics climbed onto the bus with our new possessions. Yen walked up and down the aisles, inspecting them. He passed Reed Hadley, who was clutching a fragile bouquet of ceramic geraniums—the most expensive item in the store—and stopped at Ruby Crystal, who had bought a large, handsome sculpture of three women workers—one black, one white and one Oriental.

" 'Women hold up half the sky,' " said Yen, translating the Mao quote on the base. "How much was it?"

"Two hundred and eighty yuan," said Ruby.

"Very nice," said Yen. "Your friends will admire it."

She looked embarrassed. We had just learned the average worker at the factory earned forty-six yuan a month, barely enough to buy this particular ceramic with six months' wages. To Ruby, I imagined, it was less than an hour's work.

Yen turned away.

"When do we see the duck?" Reed asked him.

"The duck?"

"Yes. The Han Dynasty Duck. The one they didn't send with the archaeological exhibition."

"I have never heard of such a thing." He looked questioningly at Mrs. Liu. She didn't respond.

The bus pulled out, taking us to our last two stops in the Canton area—a silk factory where several hundred looms spun out twenty thousand meters of fabric daily, and a Taoist temple from the Ming period, now a people's park.

The temple was in the same district as the ceramic factory and was ornamented with glazed figurines made there several hundred years ago. But the workmanship was more exacting in the old days and the quality of the glazes richer. I edged my way through dense crowds of curious Chinese to a room filled with bronze gongs and yin/yang symbols. The decor reminded me of a macrobiotic restaurant I used to know in Berkeley, where three graduate students had to be hospitalized for food poisoning. Some dioramas illustrating what I took to be the evils of religion during that period lined one of the walls. One showed a Taoist priest eating a banquet while people outside starved, another a monk-overlord whipping the workers who were building the temple. In a glass case on the opposite wall were a series of cartoons of more recent villains—the Wang–Chang–Chiang–Yao Gang of Four. The men were shown as traitors, hiding black cloaks or being pelted with tomatoes, their devious faces secured firmly in the stocks. Chiang Ching was portrayed as a kind of 1890's hussy, adjusting her black nylons while addressing a group of people who appeared to be foreign journalists.

The cartoonist had done his or her best to portray Chiang Ching in the most repulsive light possible, but the cartoon's effect on me was peculiarly erotic. An association with the subject of the Gang of Four had been made in my mind. I couldn't resist it.

I turned around, half expecting to see Liu standing there. But she wasn't, of course. In her place was a group of retired Australian social workers I recognized from the hotel. I nodded to them and walked past, determined to find her. I looked through the various rooms of the temple and headed down the steps into the courtyard. A line of smiling Young Pioneers obscured my view, their clean minds and bodies following their teacher in even steps. I waited for them to pass and then saw her. She was standing by an acacia tree, talking with Sonya. When they noticed me watching, they separated immediately, as if somehow embarrassed to be caught together. Liu started walking in my direction.

"I was looking for you," I said when she reached me. "I wanted to ask you about those cartoons of the Gang of Four."

"Yes?"

"One thing's been troubling me . . . Chiang Ching was married to Mao for over thirty years, wasn't she? How come he didn't know she was so bad?"

"Oh, but he did. In 1974 Chairman Mao told Chiang Ching, 'It's better we don't see each other.' And after the Tenth Party Congress he said, 'Chiang Ching has wild ambitions.' "

"That's not much compared with most marriages I know."

"What?"

But I let it pass. I looked over at the Young Pioneers, who were sitting down en masse to eat their lunch. Beyond them, Ana Tzu was walking rapidly across the courtyard.

"Let me explain Red and expert," said Liu. "You are a detective. You fire a gun, do you not?"

I nodded.

"Do you fire it well?"

"Sometimes."

"When do you shoot best?"

"When I need to."

"That is the meaning of Red and expert. If you first learn to serve the people, if you learn to *need* to serve them, then you will be an expert at what you do. You will do it better because you do it for the right reason."

There was a loud shriek. I turned around to see Ana Tzu doubled over on the steps of the temple. I ran toward her as fast as I could.

"What happened?" I shouted, arriving at the steps a few feet ahead of the group and a gathering crowd of Chinese.

"My stomach . . . burns."

"Burns?"

"Yes. Burns. You must tell everyone. Tell everyone."

She barely got the words out through a series of unceasing screams. Yen pushed his way through, barking commands in Chinese which sent people scattering in various directions. I looked up at him. First the dead man at the commune, now Ana Tzu's strange illness. I wondered if there was a connection.

I crouched down and scrutinized her carefully. There were no external wounds. Her face was beet red, but that could have come from the screaming. Her eyes seemed clear.

"What's the matter?" said Sonya, squeezing my shoulder.

"I don't know."

"We leave for Shanghai in an hour," she said. "Goddamn Hong Kong doctors—they can't do anything but make money!"

I looked up at her. "Don't jump to conclusions."

A pair of men in white uniforms appeared and, forming a chair with their arms, bent down toward Ana Tzu.

"Who are they?" I asked.

"Public Security," said Yen. "Do not worry. She will be well taken care of."

I could still hear her shrieks as they carried her off through the crowd.

X THE IMPACT of Shanghai is like a time bomb exploding in the consciousness. It exists on three levels at once and probably more. First there is the mythic past—a Dietrich movie directed by Josef von Sternberg, mysterious figures pushing back a beaded curtain and descending into the ballroom of a grand hotel, a lifetime of Mah-Jongg games played in a brothel. Then there is the real past—the words NO CHINESE AND DOGS affixed to the gate of the park along the Hwang Pu, coolies (the "bitter strength" of China) slaving on the wharves, the German Club, the Russo-Asian Bank, the Customs Building built by the English in Tudor style, the massacres of Chiang Kai-shek's "White Terror," the miles of slums, the starvation and disease. Even this is difficult to comprehend, but not half as difficult as the third level—the Shanghai of today, commercial heart of Communist Asia and the most populous city in the world.

The three levels danced in my head that evening as we drove in from the airport over the Rainbow Bridge, where the Red Army and the Kuomintang battled for control of the city in 1949. Now thousands of bicycles, more bicycles than I had ever seen, streamed in an unceasing flow from the factory suburbs into the central core. The streets were jammed with pedestrians, competing with the bicycles or pushing through at the wave of a hand from one of the white-uniformed men from Public Security. This was a city of density and movement, like New York or downtown Chicago. It made Canton look like the provincial outback in some struggling banana republic.

We were put up like sahibs in a place called the Jin Jiang in the old French Concession. Nixon had stayed there, Spitzler informed me, and I could just see the creep playing snooker in the paneled billiard room off the lobby.

I reclined on the chaise longue in the suite I shared with Li Yu-ying, sipping Jack Daniel's and staring out at the red neon sign reading SERVE THE PEOPLE which dominated the nighttime skyline of Shanghai, when Max Freed and Harvey Walsh burst in looking pretty ripped.

"Hey, let's go, boy. Let's boogie!" said Max. "This is Shanghai!"

"No time to waste," said Harvey. "Let's get on the capitalist road!"

"Very funny." I looked over at Li Yu. "Want to come?"

He shook his head. Ever since we had crossed the border, Li Yu had been strangely quiet. I had been looking forward to finding out why, but a night on the town, particularly this one, was hard to resist.

"Come on, Li Yu," I said. "We need you . . . we need a translator. 'Sailing the seas depends on the helmsman.' "

"Lin Piao said that," he replied, "and he's dead."

"Hey, don't worry about that. You've got a dick with you," said Max. He turned to me. "Don't forget your gat."

Half against his will, Li Yu followed us into the corridor, where Mike Sanchez and Ruby Crystal were delivering their dirty laundry to the hall attendant. For someone who almost never had to spend time dealing with the proletarian details of life, Ruby was handling herself very well. We told her and Mike what we were doing and the attendant stared as the six of us teamed up and started down in the elevator.

Outside, the temperature was lingering in the nineties—the "Tiger Heat." From the steps of the hotel, I could see people sitting on curbs, gossiping or playing cards. The streets of Shanghai were still crowded although it was after ten o'clock at night.

We started up toward the Nanking Road, the main drag of the city, which was only a few blocks off. The sidewalks were lined with newly planted trees, but the streets were surprisingly underlit for a downtown district. The local people did not appear disturbed by this, however, nor were they overly curious about us, the way they had been in Canton. This was Shanghai, after all, home of events far more amazing than a half-dozen sightseeing foreigners. It was here, in this most revolutionary of cities, that Chairman Mao turned to ignite the Cultural Revolution when the political mandarins of Peking proved too conservative.

We made a right on the Nanking Road, continuing on against the constant tingling of bicycle bells and the intermittent roar of cicadas—a violent, onrushing hum that has a startling effect even when you realize it is just the scraping front legs of a million harmless insects.

The walls were covered with large billboards commemorating the fiftieth anniversary of the People's Liberation Army, and smaller posters urging participation in public health campaigns. I was fascinated, though apprehensive. We had never asked permission to make this excursion. But I walked on anyway, looking from the walls to the faces in the stores and the noodle shops until I realized that Li Yu was not with us. I stopped and turned around. He wasn't there. I walked swiftly to the corner. Still nothing. I was about to call out when he appeared from behind a building a couple of blocks down. I hurried over to him.

"I think I found the Great World," he said. "My father told me it was off the Nanking Road."

"The Great World?" I remembered Spitzler mentioning it back in Malibu. And Nancy Lemon writing it on her preference form.

"Puppets, dancing . . . spectacles!"

"An amusement park?"

"More than that. Tearooms, classical opera . . . something for all ages. It was the soul of Shanghai."

I followed him around the corner. The other members of the group hesitated, then followed after us.

"My father used to take me when I was a boy," he continued. "The Communists kept it open after Liberation, changed the content of the shows . . . but even that ended during the Cultural Revolution. . . ."

"Is your father alive?"

Li Yu shook his head. "He owned some factories. I'm surprised they let me back."

We arrived at a large frame building built with a terrace around a central court. The windows were double-boarded with thick plywood sheets and the walls covered with layers of whitewash. A padlock the size of an elephant's foot fastened the gate into the central court. It indeed looked as if it had been the victim of massive social change, but there remained the odd presence of another era.

"That's where the main attraction was," said Li Yu, pointing into the court. "There were other buildings too, with an underground passage between them."

Frustrated, I strained for a better view through the gate, looking for concrete proof another civilization had once been there. The courtyard was empty and all the doors were shut and painted over, but on the back wall, beneath a peeling political poster, I thought I could just make out the leg of a tango dancer. It was like an archaeological discovery.

Looking for more, I put my eye to a crack in one of the window boards. I don't know if I expected to see Anna May Wong reclining on a divan, a long cigarette holder in her hand, or the insidious Fu Manchu himself, resplendent in his dragon robes, but it was pitch dark.

"You know what this town needs?" said Max, coming up behind me. "A good opium den."

I hated to admit it, but I could see his point and was about to tell him so when a brick smashed into the curb at my feet.

I spun around to see where it came from, but no one was there.

Then another brick landed.

We jumped backward.

Three muscular Chinese youths emerged from behind a truck, pointing and yelling at us with tremendous anger. They wore bright pink tank shirts and held rocks and sticks in their hands. We continued backing toward the wall, but their shouting only increased.

"What're they saying?" I asked Li Yu.

"It's Shanghai dialect." He looked frightened.

"You don't understand?"

"Something about . . . foreign devils."

"Well, tell them we're all right," said Ruby. "Tell them we're friends."

But Li Yu didn't say anything. Or couldn't.

"Come on, Li Yu," said Harvey. "Relate to them."

One of the youths shook his stick angrily and the three started down the street in our direction, yelling louder. For a split second the image of that dead man projected in my head, the gaping fissure in the back of his skull.

"Now what're they saying?" I found myself grabbing Li Yu's arm and shaking him.

"I don't know . . . foreign devils ruin China—something like that. . . . Go back to the hotel. Imperialist, go home!"

A rock flew over our heads. Then another fragmented in front of me, one of the pieces careening into my left shin. I saw a knife glint under a street lamp.

"Tell them we'll do it," I said. "Tell them yes!" I didn't want to get into a fight, not then, on the corner of Nanking Road and Yenan Boulevard.

But I could see Li Yu wasn't going to say anything. He was trembling.

Just then another rock flew, smashing into the pavement and rebounding sharply into Ruby's leg. A trickle of blood started running down her pale calf.

I reached for a handkerchief but she stopped me immediately. "It's all right. Don't worry."

I looked over at the youths. I had no choice but to pick up a rock of my own now, in self-defense. But before I could move, they took three steps backward and disappeared, just as quickly and mysteriously as they had come. It was as if they'd vanished into a rabbit hole. The six of us stood there, staring after them into the darkness.

Five minutes later we were back at the hotel. We couldn't wait to barrel through the revolving door into the safety of the lobby. But once inside, we all stopped and shuffled around. Our encounter had depressed us all and no one was sure where to go next. Ruby's wound was hurting, and she, Mike and Li Yu excused themselves and went up in the elevator, leaving Max, Harvey and me behind.

"Christ," I said, "where's the bar?" knowing there wasn't any.

"Drink me," said Max, thrusting a joint in my hand. It was housed in one of those odor-proof metallic holders we used to use before California went legal. I hesitated a second before taking a good hit. The cannabis went straight to my brain, scrambling the synapses in one easy jolt, the way only the best weed can do it. And Max Freed, of course, had the best weed. Under the circumstances, it definitely called for seconds.

I had thirds and followed the others into the hotel library, plunking myself down on one of those overstuffed chairs I had come to associate with the People's Republic. In my present condition, it took me a few seconds to realize Mrs. Liu was sitting opposite us with a book in her hands.

"What're you reading?" I asked.

"Engels' *Anti-Dühring*."

"Oh." I searched through my addled brain for a connection. Schorske's class at Berkeley began to suggest itself, but it was—as the man said—all Chinese to me.

"Well," said Liu, "you have all taken a walk through Shanghai. What have you discovered?"

"China isn't all it's cracked up to be," said Max, his tongue loosened with dope.

"Cracked up?"

"It isn't paradise."

"Nobody said it was."

"You know what happened to us?" He was beginning to sound belligerent.

"No. Of course not," said Liu.

"Some punks started throwing rocks at us," he said. "Calling us imperialists."

"How do you know that? Did they speak English?" I could see Liu staring down at the holder in Max's hand, but she didn't react.

"Li Yu-ying was with us," I explained. "One of them hit Ruby."

"Is she all right?" Liu sounded alarmed.

"I think so."

Liu nodded. "This is unfortunate," she said. "In our society there are still bad elements."

"Oh, that explains it," Harvey said sarcastically.

"What's a 'bad element'?" said Max.

Liu didn't reply.

"Yeah. What *is* a 'bad element'?" said Harvey.

She didn't say anything.

"Come on. What is it?" said Max. "What's a 'bad element'?"

She still didn't answer.

"I'll tell you what it is," Max continued. "It's Chinese jargon for punks. They're punks. Maybe they work for the state, but they're punks anyway!"

"Unresolved conflict," said Harvey. "Repression's all over this society."

"Sick, sick, sick . . . Fascist and sick."

"Acute social paranoia. The outside world is a threat just because it exists!"

Liu still remained silent. She held the book in her hand

and just looked at them. I wondered why she didn't respond. They may have been behaving like stoned assholes, but a couple of words of explanation would have shut them up. And even I, somewhere in the cannabis haze that passed for a memory, had some dim recollection of the meaning of the phrase "bad element," which had started all this in the first place.

"I bet she approves of them," said Max. "They throw stones, but they talk jargon just like she does!"

"Oh, come on, Max. Can it," I said.

"Coming to her defense, huh? Weren't you the one who said on the way back a society that closes its amusement parks is in deep trouble?"

"Look—"

"Didn't you say that?"

"So what if I did? Besides, you know what a bad element is anyway," I said. "It's self-explanatory!"

"So were the Spanish Inquisition and the Star Chamber!" said Max. And he stood up and left the room.

A moment later, Harvey joined him. Liu and I sat there facing each other.

"You went to the Great World," she said.

"Yes."

"I used to go there when I was a girl. They had beautiful puppets."

I smiled sardonically. "A good Communist?"

"You do not have to be sarcastic. I live in Shanghai. I grew up here. My father taught school by the Yu Garden and my mother was a musician."

"What does your husband do?"

She hesitated. It was a normal question, but under the circumstances seemed strangely bold.

"He is an engineer in K'unming, Yünnan Province."

"A thousand miles from here. . . ."

"More."

"You must not see him very often."

"Three or four times a year."

She sat there a moment. I thought I detected a hint of embarrassment before she went back to her book.

When I got back to the room, Li Yu was waiting up for me. He was sitting nervously on the edge of the bed with an envelope in his hand.

"It's for you," he said, handing it to me. "It was under the door."

I looked at the envelope. It was hotel stationery with the flap heavily taped. I worked it open and pulled out a postcard from inside. The photograph on the back was described in Chinese but I recognized it immediately as the Han Dynasty Duck from the catalog of the archaeological exhibition. On the back a message was printed in neat block letters: MOSES WINE. YOU WILL BE IN GREAT DANGER. BE CAREFUL AT ALL TIMES.

"What is it?" asked Li Yu, his voice rising.

"My mother," I said. "She's always watching out for me."

XI "WELL, MOSES, how're you enjoying China?" Yen's direct question broke me out of my reverie as we drove through the outskirts of Shanghai to the Number Four Heavy Industrial Plant in the suburb of Ming Hoang. Even though it was just nine in the morning, the "Tiger Heat" had not subsided and the temperature was already well into the nineties, enough by itself to put me in a stupor if the events of the previous evening had not kept me up all night, brooding.

"Fine," I said. "Considering."

"Yes. I understand you met up with some 'bad elements.'"

I nodded. Everyone in the rear part of the bus leaned in our direction.

"You must understand that these people are not representative of our society. We welcome foreign guests in China."

"Not always," said Staughton Grey. "In sixty-seven, British diplomats, their wives and children were paraded in the streets of Peking and made to wear dunce caps while their legation building was burned to the ground."

"Nonsense!" said Sonya.

"What do you mean?"

"It's a lie and you know it!"

"It is not." Grey looked taken aback.

"A lie and a distortion. All your life you've been lying and distorting things!"

"What're you talking about?"

"You know perfectly well what I'm talking about!"

"No. I don't."

"Pretending you were some kind of Movement leader while the whole time you were undermining the people you loved!" Sonya was livid. I couldn't imagine where the anger was coming from, but it was there all right. I glanced back at Liu, who was looking very unhappy.

"Mr. Grey is substantially accurate," she said. "But past excesses have been corrected."

"You too have bad elements in your society," Yen added. "Lumpen proletarians and others of the wrong class background who have not yet learned to serve the people."

"He's right," said Harvey, whose attitude had changed from the previous night. "What right do we have to criticize their society until we've policed our own?"

"Yes, we all have much to learn and can improve ourselves," said Yen. He was staring directly at Nancy and Fred, who were seated as before on the favorite jump seat in front.

Our bus drove into the driveway of the heavy industry plant, where the usual sign reading WARMLY WELCOME U.S.–CHINA PEOPLE'S FRIENDSHIP STUDY TOUR NUMBER FIVE awaited us. But despite the applause of the "leading members" of the factory, I was beginning to feel increasingly unwelcome in China. And I didn't like the feeling. It made me angry—at them for betraying me and at myself for being so easily betrayed. I tried to fight it, but at the Brief Introduction I was more dismayed than usual by the photograph of Stalin on the wall beside Marx, Engels and Lenin. Whatever one thought of communism, the former three were at least idealists of one degree or another, but Stalin was a butcher unfit to gaze down upon a room where civilized people drank tea, munched peanuts, and listened to the latest figures on the rise and fall of production.

I didn't care much about the Gang of Four either. They couldn't be to blame for all the ills of a society of eight hundred million and it was painfully obvious all these charges and countercharges were just a masquerade for a vicious power struggle at the top, cynical jackals in gray cadre suits picking over the bones of Mao's carcass.

From the expression on their faces, others in the group must have felt the same way.

"But it *was* the Gang of Four," I heard Liu tell Ruby as we passed a drill press of umpty-ump kilotons' capacity. "They fomented anarchism in the workplace. They told workers they shouldn't listen to any regulations and to run the factory themselves. Since the workers owned the factory, they could report to work late if they wanted to, and leave early. Or not work at all!"

"Well, it is their factory," said Ruby. "That's socialism, isn't it? The means of production in the hands of the working class."

"But don't you see? That's metaphysics. Of course the workers control the means of production, but they still have to work. China is a developing country. If the factories don't produce, the people will starve!"

Ruby and Liu stared at each other a moment before Ruby spoke: "You mean to tell me this 'gang' stopped people from working all over the country?"

"Not all over—but in many places."

"Then why weren't they stopped earlier?"

"People tried." Liu's voice dropped very low. "And we were scared."

Ruby smirked skeptically.

That afternoon, the atmosphere improved. It was the children of China who did it. We visited a Children's Palace in the center of Shanghai, in a handsome old mansion which once had housed the most lavish whorehouse for the potentates of the local underground. Now it was an after-school center, a jewel of socialism run on the principle of "friendship first, competition second."

Who could resist when each of us was greeted by an individual child, called "aunt" or "uncle," and led through a series of rooms of choral singing, ballet, science labs, workshops, calligraphy, paper cutting and on and on? We heard "Turkey in the Straw" played by an orchestra of young fiddlers, and an elegy called "Fishing Song of the East China Sea" played on a traditional instrument resembling a zither. Then, in a small theater, a group of four-year-olds performed a puppet show of some hard-working bees who, through cooperative action, overcame a lazy, individualistic bear who wanted to steal their honey. This was followed by a relay race in which the fastest returned to help the slowest finish, and a tug-of-war in which nobody won.

We all clapped and clapped and I thought about my children. I wished they were there, wished children everywhere could grow up in a world where, from the age of two, they were taught to share and to love each other as much as themselves. Here—in these children—was the beauty and the glory of the New China. How could we have been so foolish as to let our minds be swayed by the hostility of some malcontents, some 'bad elements'?" China might be an emotional roller coaster, but there were more ups than downs, and the final destination was worth whatever minor pain might befall our tender behinds. Friendship first, competition second. It was good to be back in paradise again.

I almost did not hear Sonya when during the final dance show the children put on for us—multicolored flags swirling to the tune of "All the National Minorities Love Chairman Hua"—she leaned over to me and said, "You've got to come with me."

The two lead girls, exquisite twins in red-and-white dresses, carrying golden tambourines, danced back to a braided cord, pulling it down to reveal portraits of the two chairmen, Mao and Hua. The music swelled. "What?" I asked.

"I need you to go with me," she repeated. "Mr. Hu's going to take us."

"Where?"

"I'm not sure," she said. "Something's come up. The Chinese usually only deal with one person at a time, but I insisted."

"Insisted what?" But everyone was standing now, applauding each other.

Moments later, I was sitting in the back of a gray Red Flag limousine honking its way through a stream of bicycles. I glanced from Sonya through the rear window to the rest of our group, standing by the bus in front of the Children's Palace and looking as baffled as I felt. To my left, Mr. Hu appeared nervous. He looked younger than his twenty-six years, about ten years younger.

"What's up?" I asked him.

"I do not know," he said.

"Well, where're we going?"

"I . . . do not know."

"But I thought you were taking us."

He shrugged. I would have asked him a more pointed question, but I had the distinct impression his English was about to fail him.

The limo continued honking, pushing its way through the dense traffic of central Shanghai. A man balancing a dozen steel drums on his bicycle almost crashed as he hurried to get out of our way. We turned onto the bund and drove another couple of blocks until we pulled up at a large office building.

"Once German bank," Mr. Hu offered shyly.

A functionary opened the door and we entered the former bank. It was now a giant bureaucracy filled with a staggering number of offices. I looked through one door where the desks appeared to go on forever. Hundreds of clerks were seated behind them and, as in offices the world over, most of them seemed to be doing nothing.

We were ushered up in the elevator to the ninth floor and out into a reception room with a view commanding the port of Shanghai. There we were met by a man in his fifties and a woman approximately the same age. Although they were dressed in slacks and simple white shirts, something about their directness and confidence indicated they were high officials. As soon as Mr. Hu left, they introduced themselves as Mr. Chao—director of the China International Travel Service, Shanghai section—and Mrs. Xu of the Shanghai Bureau of Public Security.

"Won't you sit down?" said Mr. Chao, pointing to a heavy sofa. "You have had a very busy schedule. You must be tired."

We sat down, followed by the two Chinese.

"Not so bad," said Sonya. "The last time I was here we visited seven cities in twenty days. Half the group had bronchitis and the other half spent the whole time on the—" she stopped herself, remembering the prudery of the Chinese "—washing their hands."

Mr. Chao smiled, but Mrs. Xu did not react. Evidently she didn't speak English. As an afterthought, Chao turned to her and translated. She nodded her head.

"Well," said Chao, "perhaps you are wondering why you are here."

"Yes, we are," said Sonya, trying hard to sound disingenuous. It wasn't her forte.

Chao said something to Mrs. Xu and she took out a folder and handed it to him.

"At 1245 hours today a member of your group attempted an illegal entry into the offices of the *Liberation Daily*."

"What??" said Sonya.

"According to the comrade responsible, he climbed over the walls of the newspaper office five minutes after being refused admission at the gate."

"Who did that?" I asked.

Mr. Chao consulted his file. "A Mr. Nicholas Spysler."

"Nick Spitzler?" Sonya and I said simultaneously.

"Yes, Spitzler," Chao corrected himself.

"There must be some mistake," said Sonya.

"Why should there be a mistake?" said Chao.

"Mr. Spitzler would never do a thing like that."

"But that was the report of the comrade responsible."

Sonya and I looked at each other.

Then Mrs. Xu talked for some time in Chinese, staring at us with deadly seriousness, as if we were supposed to have complete understanding of what she was saying. When she stopped, Chao picked up again, his jovial manner suddenly gone.

"You realize, of course, the seriousness of this accusation. It is just this kind of adventurism that the Gang of Four tried to promote in our country. Under normal circumstances, we would ask your group to leave China immediately. The comrades at the newspaper have had a struggle-meeting and demanded no less. In fact, a final determination has not yet been made on this matter."

He stopped and eyed me pointedly. The hand-printed warning of the previous night suddenly popped into my brain—MOSES WINE. YOU WILL BE IN GREAT DANGER. BE CAREFUL AT ALL TIMES. It seemed ridiculous, but somehow I couldn't smile.

Chao turned to Sonya before continuing. "But since you are an old acquaintance of the Chinese people . . . and since we are attempting to make better relations with our American friends—even though they have violated the spirit of the Shanghai Communiqué and continue to support the reactionary clique on Taiwan, occupying a province of China with their own troops—we have decided to excuse this one occurrence. But you must make certain, as Responsible Person of U.S.–China People's Friendship Study Tour Number Five and as a leading member of that group, that it happens not again."

"It won't," I said.

"We'll see to it," said Sonya.

Chao nodded, indicating our interview was over. We stood as he reported what he had said to Mrs. Xu. Then he turned back to us.

"There is one other thing that is not a public security matter. A comrade worker at the Jin Jiang Hotel tells us he had a request from a Mr. Fred Lisle to change his accommodations to share a room with a Mrs. Nancy Lemon."

"Oh, no!" said Sonya.

"They are both married, are they not?" said Chao.

"Yes," said Sonya.

"We do not care what bourgeois things these people want to do in their own countries. But they are the guests of China and must act accordingly."

"We'll see that it doesn't happen again," said Sonya.

She was trembling. This wasn't exactly the kind of thing to deal with at sixty-four years of age.

XII It must have been a little of the old chauvinist pig-gery, but I made Sonya let me deal with Fred Lisle myself. I caught him in the corridor before dinner and pulled him back to my room.

"Sit down, Fred," I said, pointing at an armchair in a rough imitation of Mr. Chao's interrogation methods.

He stared at me irritatedly before complying.

"Tea?"

"No, thank you."

"Look, Fred, there's no sense beating around the bush. This is a trip to China, not two weeks at the Asian branch of Club Méditerranée!"

"What?"

"Don't play dumb with me. We all know what's been going on between you and Nancy."

"What's been going on between me and Nancy?"

"I don't know about the sleeping hours, but everyone on the trip knows you two have been spending every waking hour together."

"Nancy and I are just friends."

"Hey, I'm not a gossip columnist. I don't give a shit

whether you and Nancy are just friends or what you are . . . but the Chinese are starting to get concerned."

"Oh, God, the Chinese are such prudes!"

"You're in Rome, Fred. Do as the Romans."

"Well, I do."

"I bet."

"What do you mean—we shouldn't sit together on the bus?"

"According to the Chinese, you asked to have your room switched so you could share one with Nancy."

"Good Christ!"

"That wasn't very clever, Fred."

"What do you take me for—an idiot?"

"I don't take you for anything. Just cool it or we'll all get in trouble."

"Trouble? For what? Don't you see what's going on? These Chinese are crazy. Crazy. They see people fornicating behind every bush."

"Fred, asking to have your room changed isn't every bush."

"I've had it. I've had it up to here." He jumped to his feet. "My father was right. It was a tragedy for the people of the world when we lost China!" He bounced impatiently on the balls of his feet, staring out the window at the "Serve the People" sign, then he turned back to me. "And you, you're their dupe. It's all happening right in front of you and you don't even see it. And you call yourself a detective. It's incredible!"

"Just stick to your own room, Fred. That's all I ask."

"Anything you say, comrade."

He left the room.

Dealing with Nick Spitzler was more complicated. It called for a group meeting to explain where Sonya and I had gone after the Children's Palace and a thorough exploration of the ramifications. The hotel people offered us the main meeting room downstairs, but we decided to meet in Sonya's room for privacy. So, after dinner, all fifteen of us gathered in her room, filling up the chairs and spilling over onto the beds and the floor. Sonya got to the point right away. What we didn't count on was Nick's reaction.

"It's a lie," he said. "I never climbed over the wall."

"But you weren't with us," said Sonya. "You missed lunch."

"I wanted to go shopping," Nick said. "I saw a department store from the bus and remembered where it was because it was near the bund."

"And you went to the *Liberation Daily?*"

"I guess that's what it was. It was across the street from the store. It looked very official and had a lot of newspapers displayed in glass cases along the front wall. I made some hand signs asking the guard to let me in, but he shook his head."

"And that was all?"

"That was it."

"Nick," said Natalie Levine, "you can be honest with us. We all know you're an impetuous guy."

"What're you talking about?"

"You didn't take no for an answer when Moses, you and I saw that old prison on the island. You pushed the gate open yourself before we could stop you."

"Are you calling me a liar?"

"I'm not calling you anything, but we all know the thing you most wanted to see was a newspaper. You told me yourself you put it down first choice on the request form."

"This is ridiculous!"

"Why don't we calm down?" I said. "Nobody's making any accusations around here. The point is the Chinese think you tried to break in there. Now, why don't we just try to de-escalate the whole thing and make sure it doesn't happen in the future."

"But somebody's lying around here," said Mike Sanchez.

"We can't sweep this under the rug," said Harvey. "This is a group problem that must be dealt with fully or the functioning of the group will be fatally impaired."

"I'm telling you," said Nick, "I didn't go over that wall."

"Then the Chinese are lying," said Nancy.

"I don't believe that," said Mike.

"Why not?" said Nick. "You think everything they do is perfect?"

"I thought you were a friend of progressive peoples."

"Now, Mike—"

"Well, either the Chinese are lying or somebody else is lying."

"Maybe it was an accident," said Sonya. "An error."

"What kind of error?" said Mike. "A mirage? Or did somebody dressed up like Nick Spitzler climb over the wall of the *Liberation Daily*?"

"Why'd you have to get us into trouble?" said Reed Hadley. "This is a Communist country."

"Holy shit!" said Nick. "I can't believe I'm actually hearing this!"

"Why don't we ask the detective?" said Ruby. "Maybe he can tell us what happened."

All the eyes in the room turned to me. Offhand, I couldn't remember a time I wanted the responsibility less. "Look, uh, like I told somebody else before I left: I'm not here on a working vacation. . . . Besides, I don't have any more idea what's going on here than you do."

"What do you think, Max?" asked Sonya. "You haven't said anything."

"I'm scared the room is bugged."

"Jesús y María," said Mike. "One little mishap and the whole petit-bourgeois crowd starts jumping off the side like rats off a sinking ship."

"He's not jumping off the side," said Fred. "He's only talking common sense. You don't have to be Sherlock Holmes to see what's going on here."

"What *is* going on?" said Mike.

"Just what Reed was good enough to point out to us. This is a Communist country. Also, this is the Orient. What happens here can never be fully comprehensible to those of us with the Judaeo-Christian sensibility."

"The what, *pendejo*?!" said Mike. He took a couple of

93

steps, as if he was about to march across the room and slug the guy.

"You heard me," said Fred. "You'll never understand the Chinese mind."

"I think I could have something to say about that . . . as an inscrutable Chinese." It was Li Yu speaking. His quiet voice suddenly had the most weight in the room. "When I was in high school, I was the only Asian-American in my class. Everyone thought I was strange and no one ever talked to me. They called me Chop-Chop. After a while, I got the reputation of being silent, mysterious, inscrutable. But I was simply alone. Under my skin I am the same as you are—a human being. The myth of the inscrutable Chinese would be funny to me if it weren't such horrid racism, pure and simple."

"*Exactamente, amigo,*" said Mike. "*Exactamente.*"

There were murmurs of approval around the room.

"Well, I guess that takes care of me," said Nick. "Now that we know the Chinese are saints, I have to be the sinner."

"Not exactly," said Staughton Grey. "Perhaps you are both sinners."

That inscrutable remark cooled the temperature down somewhat. It was agreed that we were never going to settle this argument with the means at our disposal and the best solution was to put it behind us. For the rest of the trip, no one would invade forbidden territory or climb over walls without the group's permission. If they did, the group would insist on that person returning home, even if the Chinese never discovered it.

"All right," said Nick. "I'll accept that. But this is still pretty weird to me. Just for the record—and as long as I'm in my right mind—I want you all to know I never did try to climb over that wall."

Who knew whether to believe him?

Moments later, the group broke up before frayed nerves and exhausted bodies combined forces to turn us into a gaggle of squabbling geese. The members returned to their rooms. Tomorrow would be another full day of friendship and study.

But that night, for the second in a row, I was unable to sleep. I got up and, leaving Li Yu asleep in the bed next to mine, went for a walk in the corridors of the Jin Jiang Hotel.

Something was disturbing me and I couldn't figure out what it was, but I knew that in some way it was triggered by what Li Yu had been saying. I knew he was right about the nature of Chinese inscrutability, that it was a myth rooted in racism, but my perceptions of this society—and the experience of the group—were clouded at best. It was like the old metaphor of the Chinese box, one inside another inside another. The Gang of Four made a Cultural Revolution, yet now they were the enemy. Nick Spitzler was a friend of China, yet he broke into the *Liberation Daily*. And then he denied it. And what did the *Liberation Daily* have to hide in the first place? And then there was Ana Tzu, sick in Hong Kong, then well, and then sick again in Canton. And the corpse at the commune, another victim of the Gang of Four, at least according to Yen. And Nancy Lemon and Fred Lisle, seriocomic lovers out for a last fling in a land where all lovemaking was kept as shadowy as possible, a land where "bad elements" attacked us as imperialists when we had come as friends. Or had we? And why did these things trouble me anyway? Was it just professional habit, a detective unable to turn off the switch? But I was anxious not to involve myself in a professional way, especially here in a country where the distinctions between amateur and professional had been blurred for serious philosophical reasons.

And then there was Liu—the most radical of our guides and yet the most human. Or was it the reverse?

I had no answers. I thought of that strange postcard with the Han Dynasty Duck, as I stood at the window at the end of the corridor, the neon light blinking on and off: SERVE THE PEOPLE. SERVE THE PEOPLE. SERVE THE PEOPLE.

XIII THE NEXT day began innocently enough with a visit to a residential neighborhood on the west side of Shanghai. Fifteen thousand families lived there—a total population of sixty thousand people. After having our Brief Introduction, we split into groups of five to visit the apartments of the workers. They were small but clean. All the rooms except the bathroom and kitchen were called bedrooms because they had beds that were covered during the day so they could do double duty as living areas. An older woman told us about the "bitter past," and a member of the revolutionary committee explained how the Gang of Four had sabotaged production at the neighborhood handkerchief factory. Later the children at one of their several nursery schools put on a performance for us. They wore ethnic costumes for the finale and did dances from the Tibetan Autonomous Region.

We returned to our hotel for lunch and then went for a visit to the Shanghai Industrial Exhibition Hall, a building, our local guides were eager to point out, whose heavy Russian design was inappropriate to China. No one could argue. It had ten thousand square meters of floor space and over four thousand articles on display, all made in Shanghai. The wall case filled with about fifty different kinds of thermoses amused me, but basically the endless corridors of trucks, Ping-Pong paddles and toilet seats were about as depressingly dull as the average trade fair at the L.A. Convention Center.

I was about to fall asleep on my feet when I noticed the bad elements again. There were six of them this time, loitering around the display of proletarian handicrafts, three from the previous night and three others. I didn't try to notify our guides or the other members of our group, but slipped behind a turbine instead to observe them. They slouched against the museum columns, nasty sneers on their faces, in the international pose of second-rate juvenile delinquents. Any minute I expected them to pull some coins out of their pockets and start to pitch pennies. In the flat fluorescent light of the exhibition hall, they were about as menacing as a group of Mouseketeers on Halloween—until I noticed a bulge under one of their shirts that could only have been a shoulder holster. For a split second, I had the distinct sensation it was meant for me. It was then that Mike Sanchez recognized them. He was so astonished that he cried out for Yen at the top of his lungs.

One of the bad elements reached into his jacket. Before I could move, he had aimed at Mike. I thought he was going to kill him, but he had gone for a can of spray paint instead of his gun and squirted it all over Mike's shirt.

Then they started running, yelling out at members of the group, pushing them over, and hitting a few more with spray paint. I saw Natalie Levine crash against a hydraulic lift. One of the bad elements swung something resembling a wrench and slammed it hard into Max Freed's ribs. I saw him stagger and then crumple, falling backward in a daze onto the marble floor.

I don't know what possessed me, but I bolted after them as they headed for the giant doors of the exhibition hall. I was out on the wide plaza in front of the building before I had a chance to realize how stupid I was to be following them, or that I was truly terrified. I could see them running across the concrete two hundred feet ahead. I plunged after them and would have continued had I not lost them completely when they disappeared down a narrow side street. I turned around to see a hundred Chinese gathering around me, staring at me like I was a creature from the second galaxy to the right. MOSES WINE. YOU WILL BE IN GREAT DANGER. BE CAREFUL AT ALL TIMES.

The ride back to the hotel was filled with apologies. Yen, for one, was beside himself, acting as if he took it as a personal humiliation.

"I don't know how we can make this up to you. It is a gross insult to you as guests of the Chinese people. If you wish, we will return you to your country immediately."

"Not a bad idea," muttered Fred Lisle under his breath.

"Just catch the creeps," said Mike Sanchez, somewhat louder. He was clutching his shoulder, where one of the bad elements had clipped him on the way out.

"Public Security is looking into it directly," said Yen.

"I hope they're better than the FBI," groaned Max. His rib cage had already been heavily taped by a pair of barefoot doctors assigned to the exhibition hall.

"They will find them before the day is out," Yen replied. "And when they are caught, you can be sure they will receive life imprisonment."

"Life imprisonment?" Ruby was astonished. She herself had gotten off lightly with an original Jackson Pollock spattered across her white blouse. "For this?"

"Does that surprise you?" said Max. "Look where we are."

"I don't think it will be necessary," said Liu, reassuring her.

"It better not be."

"Well," said Nick, "at least none of us will be making the mistake of Lincoln Steffens. I can't see anybody from this tour going home the way he did—bragging that he'd seen the future and that it worked!"

"Amen!" said Natalie. She was toweling a glob of blue paint off her yellow crepe skirt.

98

I looked over at Liu. The expression on her face was noncommittal, but her eyes had a sadness that was unspeakable.

She was the first to disappear when we arrived back at the hotel. I saw her walk swiftly through the lobby and pass through a side door. I had been wondering where our guides stayed and supposed this was the door that led into their section, an austere counterpart to the lavishness under which we foreigners were kept.

Yen moved directly to the front desk, picking up the telephone and making a series of quick calls.

"Do not leave the hotel," he told those of us who were still in the lobby. "We are trying to make this better for you."

I headed upstairs. Back in the room, Li Yu's sadness seemed to be as profound as Liu's. I respected his feelings and we didn't speak for quite a while, sitting with our own thoughts in the fat easy chairs, drinking tea.

It was Li Yu who finally broke the silence: "I wish Nick hadn't said that."

"About Lincoln Steffens?" I asked.

Li Yu nodded.

"Nick's like that," I explained. "Back in the sixties he was on television all the time. He still is. You get used to making pronouncements."

"What do you think he'll say this time?"

I shrugged. There was no use belaboring the obvious, but then I added, "I hate to think what Max is going to say. Every jerk teenager in the country reads his paper."

"And what about Natalie?" said Li Yu. "She seems to be on the six o'clock news every time I see it."

"And Ruby."

"Maybe we *should* go back."

I nodded. A morbidity was setting in. I was surprised I even cared. I wanted to stick my head under a pillow, but Li Yu had one more question before we shut up.

"Do you think he did it?"

"What?"

"Break into the newspaper."

"Oh, hell, I don't know."

Then we fell silent again. The conversation would only depress us more. And I didn't feel like telling him one of the bad elements had a gun. I poured another round of tea and stared out at the skyline. This was the first time we were back in the room in the daytime and I hadn't realized how much smog they had in Shanghai. It was like staring into downtown Los Angeles from the Dodger Stadium bleachers on an August afternoon.

I don't know how long we were sitting there, but my mind was far off when Hu came to the door. He knocked lightly and I got up to open it, forgetting that it had no lock.

"Please pack quickly," he said. "We are going."

"Going? Where?"

"To Peking."

I turned back to Li Yu, who looked as astonished as I was. We were supposed to be in Shanghai for two more nights.

Yen gave us the full explanation less than a half hour later, when we assembled in the hotel meeting room.

"It is for your own protection that we are going to Peking immediately," he said. "We do not want anything to happen in case these bad elements insist on continuing their unfortunate behavior. You see, Shanghai was the stronghold of those counterrevolutionary capitalist-roaders, the Gang of Four. Yao Wen-yuan, Wang Hung-wen, Chang Chun-chiao, even Chiang Ching—all of them came from Shanghai. And it was they who created confusion among the people and told them to distrust all things foreign. Here they still have followers—and we cannot allow you to suffer if they insist on pursuing their Rightist tactics."

So it was the Gang of Four. I knew it all along.

XIV The airport in Shanghai is like La Guardia in the early fifties—one large building with a plain waiting room and one simple board announcing a handful of arrivals and departures. You still feel like a pioneer in the age of domestic aviation.

The sun was setting when we got there, reflections glinting off the hull of a solitary CAAC Boeing 707, by-product of the slight thaw in U.S.–China relations after the Nixon visit. Parked over to the side were a pair of PLA transport planes of prewar vintage, hardly the heavy-duty armament with which to liberate one's brothers and sisters on Taiwan.

We headed directly into the plane, without undergoing any formalities. I could see why, once we were inside. Almost all the seats were already filled. They must have been waiting for us.

We took seats in a block near the front, straining for a look at our fellow passengers. Most of them were military people or cadres of various sorts, but in the Chinese fashion, the pecking order was difficult to determine. A stewardess, dressed in loose-fitting slacks and a white shirt, distributed fans with scenic prints on the back. Moments later we were flying over the Chinese countryside, the outskirts of Nanking visible in the twilight beneath us.

For fifteen American tourists headed for their first visit to Peking, the mood of our group was decidedly grim. But I decided I didn't want to hear any more bitching than was necessary and deliberately selected a seat on the aisle. Mrs. Liu was seated catty-corner across from me, staring blankly at the seat in front of her. She appeared not to notice when the stewardess came back in our direction, passing out magazines and gum. I had a malicious desire to tell her about the stewardesses on the route between Frisco and L.A., how their skirts were so short the businessmen would stick their hands up and grab ass while they served them their cocktails, but I decided to ask her something more important instead.

"Are you as depressed as I am?"

"I do not understand," Liu said, looking back at me peculiarly. I was going to argue but it dawned on me this lack of comprehension was not fake or a conversational gambit to avoid intimacy, but the literal truth. In California one "spoke to his emotions" when beginning a serious conversation; in China one spoke to the "material conditions."

"Oh," she said finally. "You are sad about having to leave Shanghai."

"Yes. And about some of the things that happened there."

"So am I," she said. "Conditions in Shanghai were not good. Much disturbance of friendship." She tried to smile.

"Do you think we should have left?"

"It was decided."

"Yes, I know that . . . Liu . . . but, uh, what about you? How do you feel about it personally?"

She stiffened slightly. My line of questioning was perhaps more direct than it should have been. But no one could possibly hear us over the roar of the plane.

"I do not like it," she said.

"You don't think it was necessary?"

"No."

"Why not?"

"It is extreme. Besides, some of the youths were already caught."

"The youths were caught?" I looked up and down the cabin with the sudden suspicion we were being watched. But no one was paying any attention except for Harvey, who was staring at us harmlessly from the front of the plane, with a Cheshire-cat grin on his face.

"What will happen to them?" I asked.

She shrugged. "A few months' hard labor in the country-side."

"Then why?" I gestured to the plane.

"A precaution. . . . Yen wanted it."

"Oh." I sat back.

"But do not worry," she said. "There are many things to do in Peking. You will be glad to have the extra time." And she smiled a smile so beautiful Anna May Wong could never have dreamed it.

The airport in Peking was scarcely more elaborate than the one in Shanghai. An Air Pakistan jet was parked by the terminal and another CAAC 707 was being serviced in a hangar when we arrived, but that was all.

Outside, however, a sleek Mercedes bus was waiting for us at the bottom of the stairs when we got off the plane. The Peking guides who met us were older and apparently heavy-weights in the Travel Service. An effort was being made to make amends. A warning had gone out to the Center that an American group had been mishandled and the Center had responded. We were being given the full diplomatic treatment.

Without formalities, we were loaded onto the bus and whisked into the city, along the same snow-lined route Nixon had taken, with all of us glued in amazement to our television sets. Now those streets were lined with low mud huts, emergency housing constructed after the desolation of the recent earthquake. They would remain until the authorities felt the threat of further tremors was sufficiently diminished. When that would be, nobody seemed to know.

We started craning our necks as we drew closer to the center of the city. Unlike Shanghai, Peking is low and sprawling, a linear city reaching out in all directions, like Los Angeles. But unlike L.A., it has a center worth finding, monuments more impressive than a city hall where they used to shoot *Dragnet* or the biggest taco stand west of Albuquerque. Our first glimpse of the Forbidden City, illuminated at night across the vastness of Tien An Men Square, was at least as astonishing as the first sighting of the Roman Forum or the Eiffel Tower. To its left, at a right angle across the square, squatted the Great Hall of the People, ugly in its proletarian utility, but definite in its insistence that it would not be removed by some more elegant yet less staunchly radical China of the future. Behind us lay the new Mao Memorial and Chien Men, the old South Gate of the city itself, an imposing fragment of the wall that once surrounded Peking.

We pulled up at the Peking Hotel, a large complex bordering on the Forbidden City and rebuilt in three successive stages after its destruction during the Boxer Rebellion. We were ushered into the newest part. It was a slickly modern wing in a dull international style, but there was something reassuring about its electrically operated doors and clean terrazzo floors after the high-tension density of Shanghai. We were even pleased to hear the rooms had keys, carefully left in the custody of a hall man who sat behind a counter on each floor.

That night, although we were all physically and emotionally exhausted, we had another meeting in the room Sonya shared with Ruby Crystal. But it was probably a mistake because before long we had a battle royal on our hands.

"First of all," said Max, "we all know that the Gang of Four stuff was bullshit!"

"How do we know that?" said Mike.

"And secondly," said Max, "I don't want to be involved in some second-rate Chinese propaganda scheme. It's gotta be obvious to all of us that all they're trying to do is cover up. They just don't want us going home and blabbing about what a creepy place this is." He clutched his side as a stitch shot through his bruised rib.

"He's right, you know," said Nancy. "Christ, they invited Nixon back."

"You know, I believe *him* now." Max pointed at Nick. "As far as I'm concerned, this country's so bonkers they probably thought Nick was going to jump over the wall just because he was walking by it!"

"You know what convinced me," said Harvey, shaking his head. "That they flew us up here without working through the problems in Shanghai. You never solve things without working them through."

"I've had it," said Fred. "The Chinese have accused me and Nancy of doing things we just haven't done and turned members of the group against us for no reason . . . I think we should just go home."

"I don't believe what I'm hearing," Sonya said, striking her forehead with the heel of her palm. "What a group!"

"It's a thought, Fred," said Reed. "But how're we going to do it? You don't just hop on a plane around here."

"What? What're you talking about?" Sonya was turning scarlet. "I bet you have something to do with this, you monster!" She pointed her finger at Staughton Grey.

"Sonya's our Responsible Person," Fred continued. "We simply empower her to go to the Travel Service and request that we go home. Moses can go with her, if he wants to. . . . How about it, Moses?"

"I don't think it's a great idea," I said.

"Why not? Assuming we take a vote. . . ."

"Moses is too stuck on Mrs. Liu," said Harvey. "He'd never want to leave."

"Thanks, Harvey," I said.

"I hate to hear myself saying this," said Ruby, "but I suppose they got us out of Shanghai because they're hiding something. . . . It's so depressing. It makes me feel like I want to leave China!"

"I know what you mean," said Nick. "It's a disappointment."

"We ought to get out of here while we've still got a chance," said Natalie.

"Now I've had it!" said Sonya, suddenly jumping to her feet. "What is this? A meeting of the John Birch Society? You, Spitzler, ten years ago you went to jail rather than give away the whereabouts of a priest who was opposing the war; seven years ago you were all over the Northwest defending Indians, with rednecks on your tail; last year you were fighting for the rights of illegal aliens on the Texas border. And now a little struggle in China makes you turn tail and run like a scared fox. . . . And you, Ruby Crystal, you risked a big Hollywood career and millions of dollars for what you stood for. And you, Max Freed, at one time your magazine spoke for the dreams of a whole generation of Americans—"

"All right, all right," said Natalie. "I don't want to hear what you're going to say about me."

Sonya sat down.

We were all silent a moment, contemplating the traffic sounds along the Ch'ang An. But a sense of frustration was welling up in me and I had to speak out.

"Look," I said, "this is my first time in Peking and maybe my last. I don't want to run out of here in one night just because of some incidents that may or may not be important. We'll have plenty of time to evaluate them later. Right now we're in China. Why don't we give this one more day? We'll come together tomorrow night at this time and vote. If a majority wants to leave then, so be it. Sonya will go and notify the Chinese and I'll go with her if I have to. For the moment, I don't know about the rest of you, but I'm tired. I need to get some asleep before I try to decide anything."

I must have made sense. Most of the group muttered their assent.

I went back to the room which I shared with Mike Sanchez. It had a television and I flicked it on while Mike went into the bathroom. A Ping-Pong match was playing on the one channel, but I couldn't figure out how to turn on the sound. I was fumbling with the dials when I noticed a photograph on the table, of a slightly sleazy blonde in a macramé bikini. It was signed "To Mike from La Rubia" and covered the beginning of a letter of which I could just make out the last few words: ". . . so, I don't want to say it's over between us, but if this crazy trip of yours doesn't work out . . ." Doesn't work out? I didn't know what she meant specifically, but it seemed a perfect summation of the whole tawdry affair. For Mike and for the rest of us.

I gave up on the television and lay down on the bed, picking up a *Peking Review* from the side table and flipping through it while Mike continued his shower. Chinese political writing had always had a soothing quality to me, fascinating but distant, like the catechism of another religion. This time it was a lengthy discussion of Mao's essay "On Practice," his pragmatic attack on those airy intellectuals who build theories in the sky. "Whoever wants to know a thing," he wrote, "has no way of doing so except by coming into contact with it, that is, by living (practicing) in its environment. . . . If you want knowledge, you must take part in the practice of changing reality. If you want to know the taste of a pear, you must change the pear by eating it yourself."

XV THE NEXT morning we learned that this knowledge was not to be ours. We were all seated demurely in our bus, waiting to be taken for the requisite tour of the Forbidden Ciy, when Yen clambered aboard, his face ashen and his normally erect posture stooped.

"My friends," he said, raising his hands, "I have something very unfortunate to report to you. . . . You will be leaving China within twenty-four hours."

"Oh, my God!" It was Natalie who said it, but it was all of us who felt it.

"What happened?" Nick shouted, suddenly alarmed by the very thing he had been advocating the previous evening.

"There were many considerations," said Yen. "And I can assure you it was not my decision. . . . There was the new schedule, of course. . . ."

"Oh, come on," said Max. "There must be more to it than that!"

Yen nodded. I looked back at Liu, who was sitting at the rear of the bus, but she was staring straight ahead, impassive. She must have known, I thought.

"I think you owe us all an explanation, Mr. Yen," said Sonya, doing her best to control her emotions under the circumstances.

Yen looked away before answering. "The Revolutionary Committee of the China International Travel Service thinks that . . . the unfortunate experience of this group . . . and their attitude . . . make further travel in China unfeasible at this time."

"Our attitude?" said Nick, fed up.

"We will do our best to see that you enjoy your last day in China. You will visit several of the major sights and a farewell banquet has been arranged for you tonight at Peking Duck Restaurant. . . . We hope we will see some of you again on another trip."

"Thanks a bunch," said Harvey.

Yen shrugged and signaled for the driver to start off. In less than a minute we were pulling up at the gate of the Forbidden City.

"This is the Forbidden City of the Emperors," said Yen, "now called the Palace Museum, because it is no longer forbidden. All the people may come here whenever they wish."

The driver opened the door and Yen indicated it was time for us to get out. But most of us were still too stunned to move.

In actuality, the day was a tourist's dream, a clear and balmy Sunday, not oppressive at all as it had been in Shanghai. Thousands of Chinese were out strolling in the square or come in groups of families or friends to visit the once Forbidden City. A proud papa picked his baby out of a bamboo pram and held him up to the bus windows, waving his little fist to the friendly foreigners. Nobody waved back.

Liu stood up and walked to the front of the bus. "We must go now," she said, and clapped her hands.

We got up and with a surly obedience followed her out. One of the Peking guides picked us up in front of the South Gate.

"Here we are at the Forbidden City," she said, "first built by the Ming sovereign Yung-lo in the fifteenth century. Over the years, many palaces crumbled or burned down, and the entire city was rebuilt by Ching Emperor Ch'ien-lung. Later the Dowager Empress Tz'u-hsi added pavilions in the northern part. . . . This way please."

We followed her through the gate into a vast courtyard with five marble bridges spanning a sea of rippling cement. Another long gate straddled the far side, guarded by two bronze lions. A girl sat on one of them, having her picture taken.

"This is the Golden Water River," said the guide, waving her hand over the expanse of courtyard and bridges, "leading to the Gate of Great Harmony. Eunuchs would carry the Emperor up its twenty-eight steps in a chair. . . . This way to the palaces."

The group continued after her, but I stopped, my attention held by two men in gaily colored skullcaps standing on one of the bridges.

"Who are they?" I asked Liu, who was starting up the steps with Mr. Hu.

"Sinkiang Region National Minority . . . people wish to visit here from all over China. For Mr. Hu this is the first time."

I looked over at Hu, who had the only smiling face that morning. "I have been only one time in Peking," he said. "In 1966 when Red Guards came to see Chairman Mao in Tien An Men. Palace Museum was closed then . . . for . . . for . . ."

"Remodeling," Liu filled in. "Much remodeling always goes on at Palace Museum. Today you will see the Garden of the Western Flowers—not open for many years."

"Wonderful," I said.

"I see Moses does not lose his habit of sarcasm," Liu said to Hu.

"Yeah," I said. "Well, I guess this is sayonara."

"Sayonara?" She burst out laughing. "You speak Japanese to say goodbye to China. You must learn to speak Chinese. Then you will come back and see us again. . . . The word you want is *dzy gen*."

"*Dzy gen*," I said.

"No, no, no," she said. "*Dzy gen*."

"*Dzy gen,*" I repeated, not hearing any difference at all.

She burst out laughing again.

"You know," I said, "you're taking this pretty well, considering what's gone on. Does this happen on tours all the time?"

She hesitated briefly, thinking back. "Only once before. But that was several years ago—when Mr. Hu was still in language school. . . . Now, come along. Don't you want to see the Forbidden City? You will feel bad when you get home if you miss it."

She tapped me on the wrist and started up the stairs. For a moment I thought she was going to take me by the arm. But of course that was impossible.

We caught up with the group on the terrace of the T'ai Ho Tien—the Hall of Supreme Harmony—the largest of the front palaces, where the emperors and empresses presided over official gatherings, the eighteen provinces of China symbolized by eighteen bronze tripods arranged along the steps. Fred and Nancy were posing for Fred's time-release Nikon by the statue of a dragon-turtle and I thought how easy it would have been to have made a little cash, something concrete from this trip at least, if I hadn't been so self-righteous back in L.A. Her husband was probably good for megabucks.

We continued on through the Hall of Complete Harmony into the Hall of Persevering Harmony, where the Emperor would receive students who had passed official examinations. Only children of the ruling class were permitted to take them, we were reminded. I had a suspicion I would have failed them anyway, my mind was already so beclouded by the events of the past few days and by the staggering wealth of Chinese art I had virtually no background to comprehend.

We crossed under another gate—Resplendent Purity—to the area of the private palaces, the dynastic living quarters. They were smaller, less imposing, more on the Bel Air scale, yet decorated with a mixture of extravagant beauty and bad taste no one in Bel Air could match even in their wildest flights of chinoiserie. The first of these was the Palace of Heavenly Purity, where the Dowager Empress presided over the mysterious death of her son and heir. Nearby was the Palace Where the Masters Are Honored, dedicated to Confucius and his teachings, and out of vogue at the moment, as was the Palace of Intellectual Honors, where sacrificial rites were held in praise of philosophers and leading artists.

A few days before, the wretched excesses of the Chinese court would have turned my stomach or simply amused me, but now I wasn't so certain that that epoch had any monopoly on wretched excess. A feeling of sympathy for the Chinese people, exploited for centuries by rulers in mandarin robes or gray cadre suits, was developing in me.

"Now, please. Come." Our Peking guide was urging us onward. She was a brisk woman of about forty, with high cheekbones and thick round glasses. "This is the Garden of the Western Flowers, reopened only this month after many years of remodeling." She was pointing at something that was clearly not a garden, but a building of some grace and proportion. It had been recently painted, with bird designs in Chinese red and blue across the transom. A trompe-l'oeil scene of a woman's bedroom decorated the front door. "Much of the Manchu treasure was housed in this pavilion," she continued, "until it was burned to the ground in 1927 and looted. Many of the relics contained there at that time disappeared only to turn up years later in Chiang Kai-shek's museum on Taiwan. Others, however, were returned to the state and have now been restored to their original places precisely as they were during Manchu rule. As a gesture of friendship to the members of U.S.–China Friendship Study Tour Number Five, we now invite you to be the first foreigners to view the restored collection."

"How interesting," said Yen, who looked more pleased than we were.

A gateman unlocked the trompe-l'oeil door and we entered.

Inside, the light filtered through the lattice onto a meticu-

112

lously ordered room of tables and screens, with a relatively small number of examples of Chinese art, yet it was clear even to my lay eye that these were among the best.

Chou bronzes stood against one wall, along with celadon vases and a Chang Dynasty wine amphora identified as belonging to Chen Fei—"The Pearl Concubine" of the 1890's. A life-sized jade suit, the funeral shroud of Tou Wan, the wife of Prince Ching, occupied a place of honor in the corner.

"Here we have a Tang horse," said our guide, leading us around a screen, "of the three-colored type that is much appreciated. At one time experts considered this one of the finest examples in the world."

"How much would you say it's worth?" asked Reed Hadley.

"I do not know," she answered. "I have not tried to buy it. But I am sure it could feed many thousands of people."

"What's this?" said Max, moving ahead of the group with the avidity of a collector. He was pointing to an object occupying a pedestal by itself although it was only three or four centimeters high.

"No, no. That is different," said the guide, attempting to move in another direction. "Not one of the treasures of the Manchus." But the group had gathered around the pedestal, forcing her to stop.

"Look at it," said Ruby. "It's fantastic."

"Where'd it come from?" asked Harvey, who was moving a hand across its back as if trying to detect a field from the object.

"One of the great discoveries of the Cultural Revolution," said the guide, "unearthed in 1968 at Mancheng, Hopei Province."

"It's the duck!" said Fred.

He was right. We were staring at the same artifact that appeared on page thirty-four of the guide to the Chinese archaeological exhibit, the one that never left China—an intricately crafted miniature duck of luminous gold body with carved carnelian feet and delicate white jade feathers extending from its back. It was extraordinary.

"Where'd they find it?" asked Natalie, who was studying the statue with the practiced eye of someone who'd spent many leisure hours combing through the rare antiquities at Gump's in San Francisco.

"The Tombs of Liu Sheng," explained the guide. "It was the wedding gift of Prince Ching of Chingshan of the Western Han Dynasty to his wife, Tou Wan. At least two thousand years old."

"It's priceless," said Reed.

"You can say that again," said Nancy, who was peering over his shoulder. "I know a curator at the L.A. County Museum who would give his eyeteeth for this." She turned to the guide. "Why don't you sell it and help build more of those factories you claim you need so badly?"

"That is not my decision."

The group all crowded in for a better look. Even the most radical of us, like Mike and Nick, seemed transfixed by the animal, its emerald eyes reflecting all the glory of Imperial China from the overhead lamp. From across the room I could see Mrs. Liu watching us, her worst suspicions confirmed about the materialistic obsession of foreigners.

"You are now free to examine the pavilion and the other palaces at your leisure," said the guide abruptly. "Please be ready to return to the bus in forty minutes."

She looked over to Yen for confirmation, and he nodded his approval.

I walked over to Sonya and put my arm around her. Nothing had worked out as she had planned—a lifetime of struggle for progressive causes, on every picket line and sit-in from Seattle to South Carolina, only to wind up here in Jerusalem, being beaten by the Pope. And to make matters worse, her charges were being fed sugar-coated candy, dumped in a room filled with enough material goodies to fluster even the most resilient radical heart before the return home. Poor Sonya.

She started to lead me out, but I stopped to take a last look at the duck. It was indeed beautiful, far more so than in the catalog or on the warning I received in my hotel room in Shanghai. For a moment I considered telling Sonya about that postcard, but I thought better of it. It could have been somebody's idea of a gag anyway, the kind of practical joke someone like Max Freed would love to play on a detective. We left the pavilion instead and I turned to see the members of the group straggling out one by one.

I wasn't surprised when they decided to spend their last afternoon shopping. On the way back to the Peking Hotel for lunch, the decision was practically unanimous. Only Staughton Grey and Li Yu-ying disagreed with it and arrangements were made for them to visit the Museum of the Revolution, with Yen as their personal guide. I was torn myself, but I did have my promise to the kids to consider, and I did want a few hours to walk the streets of Peking, just to see.

Mike Sanchez said he would go with me. We decided to skip the formal lunch and with a certain amount of finger-pointing and head-shaking managed to purchase our fill of steamed dumplings in a little workers' café on a side street. Later, on our way to the Friendship Store, we were followed down the sidewalks by a large number of curious Chinese. I thought Mike's brown face was the attraction, but then I smiled, realizing that in Communist Asia we were equally exotic.

When we got to the store, at first it seemed none of the others were there. But then I noticed Harvey Walsh, off in a corner, addressing a large crate of foodstuffs he was shipping back. He turned away from me. To his right, behind a row of coats, Nancy Lemon was folding a silk robe into an oversized cardboard box. I saw Ruby Crystal heading swiftly out the back door of the building with an armful of packages. Spitzler was down in the basement buying propaganda posters, stuffing dozens of them in tubes and mailing them home. Max Freed was blowing a couple of hundred bucks on green and gold kites from the Tangshan Kiteworks, rewrapping them with little notes to his myriad publishing connections. Everyone was separated, into their private worlds. I waved to

Natalie Levine but she did an about-face when she saw me and Mike slipped off at the same time in the direction of the mail room. Alone, I finally ran into Reed Hadley, who was buying enough jade to fill a medium-sized jewelry store in Dubuque.

"See this?" he said, holding up a largish carved piece. "Only three hundred and twenty yuan. What do you think that would cost in San Francisco?"

"Fourteen dollars," I said.

"Ah, c'mon. You're pulling my leg."

I grinned and he took me by the arm into a corner.

"You know," he said, "I thought I was going to have trouble on this trip . . . me, with all those radical-liberals . . . but it worked out just fine, didn't it?"

"Yeah, Reed, just fine. You're going home two weeks early."

XVI By FIVE o'clock I was back in my room, swacking down Mike's Jack Daniel's with Mike and Harvey.

"You know what my old lady said before I came here?" Harvey was saying. "That I shouldn't bother—politics was a sixties trip." He finished off his glass and Mike poured him another. "I guess she was right."

"Might as well finish the sucker off," Mike said. "We'll be back where we can get all we want before we need a refill. . . . Shit, it ticks me off I spent all the money on this tour and look what happened."

"What happened?" I asked.

"Who the fuck knows?" said Harvey.

"Well, it's going to be one hell of an expensive dinner at the Peking Duck," said Mike.

"You don't have to worry about it," said Harvey. "You got a scholarship, didn't you?"

"Hey, boy," said Mike. "I don't know about you, but I work for a living. They dock my pay when I go away . . . and I got five kids."

"Five kids?" said Harvey, amazed.

"What's the matter?" said Mike. "They don't let anybody with five kids inside the Santa Barbara city limits? You know, I've been meaning to talk with you ever since this trip started. With all your encounter groups and your . . . your human potential, you need a little education in the real world. Not everybody's living on your spiritual plane."

Harvey was preparing a halfhearted counterattack when the door opened. It was Natalie, dressed up for dinner in one of her wide-brimmed hats and tailored suits, just like on the campaign trail.

"Hey, everybody," she said. "I've got another surprise." We all held on to our seats. "Ana's back."

An audible sigh of relief came from all corners of the room.

"And she's fine. She's got a good idea too. She thinks we should all apply to the Chinese government for refunds right away."

"Hey, that's a great idea," said Mike. "Count me in."

I had to smile. The idea of Natalie Levine in her eight-hundred-dollar outfit worrying about refunds had just a touch of the absurd. She must have read my expression, because not more than two minutes later she was reminding us how her campaign was over a hundred thousand in the red.

Nick and Max dropped in and pretty soon most of the group was in the room. Everyone was dressed up, or dressed up as you can get in the People's Republic, and I felt a little sentimental that our first night out together would be our last. I was getting to like the bunch, for all their foibles. Even the arrival of Reed, Fred and Nancy didn't bring me down. Staughton and Li Yu came in next, and finally Sonya entered, followed by Ruby and Ana. Some of us got up and embraced her. It was good to see her safe and sound.

The group descended in the elevator en masse, overruling the operator, who was disturbed we had gone over the limit of twelve. Our guides were waiting in the lobby and we followed them onto our waiting bus.

The restaurant was not far, only ten minutes away on the other side of Tien An Men, just south of Chien Men Gate.

For the most famous restaurant in China, it had an unprepossessing exterior, a simple door into a decaying townhouse. The interior too was of no consequence. In fact it resembled a soup kitchen in the skid row of any large American city—well-lit and austere to a fault, yet meticulously clean, as if constantly scrubbed by a crew of hard-working Christian Soldiers.

We were led upstairs into a private dining room with two round tables set for the meal and a separate area with the usual armchairs and sofas arranged in front of coffee tables with tea and cigarettes. We were directed to the sitting area, where the senior of our Peking guides, a corpulent gentleman of about sixty whom we had seen only at the airport, took a seat on the center sofa, next to Sonya. Hot towels were distributed and we wiped our hands and faces while a round of tea was poured.

Then the senior guide spoke: "We Chinese have an expression that I think this group should find most fitting—'There is great chaos under the heavens and the situation is excellent.' I realize your stay in China was not what you expected, nor was it what we expected, but be assured that whatever discomfort you have suffered while here we are doing our best to rectify, and other groups to come here in the future will have profited by your unhappy experience. . . . Normally we take this occasion for lengthy speeches and toasts expressing the friendship between the peoples of our two countries, but considering what you have gone through, it does not seem appropriate. Therefore we will dispense with the formalities and go directly to the dinner." He nodded toward the dining tables. "Please eat."

The man's concern seemed sufficiently genuine for our group to break into applause, the guides applauding back. We got up and headed for the dinner tables, Sonya and the senior guide taking seats at the nearer of the two. The rest of us shuffled about a moment, realizing no formal seating had been planned. Hastily, Liu started to seat everyone, sending

Mike and Staughton over to the other table, then Ana, Ruby and Natalie. Yen joined them, sitting between Ruby and Staughton.

"Why don't you go?" she said to me.

"No, no," Nancy interrupted, winking. "Moses sits next to you."

Liu seemed embarrassed.

"He thinks you're cute," said Nancy.

"Cute's not exactly the word for it," I mumbled, but by this time we were sitting together at the first table, opposite Sonya and the senior guide.

"What's his name?" I asked her, indicating the guide, who was peering around with a benevolent smile.

"Comrade Tseng Ssu-yu—Chairman of the Revolutionary Committee of China International Travel Service and former Ambassador to India. He was personal guide of Kissinger in Shanghai and Hangchow."

I took another look at him, impressed. He seemed so earthy and unassuming, a favorite uncle who would crack jokes with the kids at a family reunion while the others were inside watching the football game. He opened his arms with pleasure as plates of shredded scallions and cucumber were placed on the table with bowls of a deep brown sauce.

Liu identified it for me. "Hoisin. You have not had Peking Duck before?"

I shook my head. "In the Chinese restaurants back home you have to order it a day in advance and I never remember."

"Yes. It takes much time. You must inflate the skin with a tube and pour boiling water over it five or six times, leaving it hanging by the neck for several hours before roasting."

A shy young waiter appeared with our duck, holding it out on a platter for us to inspect before they cut it up.

"What do you think?" said Liu.

"I feel like a convict about to take my last meal."

She laughed. "Do not overeat. Sometimes what we think is our last meal is not necessarily so."

I gave her a long look as another waiter entered with a

120

plate of hors d'oeuvres. A waitress was filling our glasses with plum wine and mao tai.

Comrade Tseng stood, hoisting his mao tai. We all followed suit.

"*Gambei,*" he said, downing his in one gulp in ritual fashion.

"*Gambei,*" said Sonya, downing hers with equal alacrity.

We all cheered, Tseng observing Sonya with amazement.

"It's just like slivovitz," Sonya explained while her glass was being refilled.

Tseng hoisted his second glass into the air. "May there be great friendship in the future."

"I'll drink to that!" said Sonya. And they downed them.

Then we sat down to eat, first the platter of p'in pan— Chinese hors d'oeuvres—followed by the duck. It was sliced and cut into pieces with the different parts arranged on different plates. The heart, a delicacy, was served in a separate bowl and eaten by itself. The rest was eaten with steamed sesame buns or thin pancakes. Liu showed us how to make sandwiches with them, placing a crispy square of duck on the pancake with scallions and cucumber, smearing it with hoisin, and then rolling it all up like a burrito.

I don't know how many of them I ate or how much mao tai I drank, but I was starting to see the world through filtered glasses. Across the table, Sonya was getting sloshed with Comrade Tseng. I hadn't seen her looking at a man like that in a long time. It made me think of those family stories, about the old days when she was an organizer in the Bronx Co-ops and about the boyfriend, whoever he was, that she never married.

"I don't know what I'm going to tell Mr. Bittleman," I heard her saying, referring to someone entirely different.

"Who's Mr. Bittleman?" asked Tseng.

"A friend of mine at home. He says the salvation of man is through God and I say it is through man."

"Man *and* woman," Tseng corrected her.

"Right on, brother," said Sonya, knocking down another mao tai. The event was getting maudlin.

I swigged some mao tai myself, but found my glass was empty and reached for the plum wine instead. Usually it's too sweet for me, but under the circumstances, it tasted all right. In another minute I would be totally anaesthetized.

That being the case, it must have been my deep-seated conditioning about the police, a wary distaste that transcended all bounds of country or class, that allowed me to be the first to sense their presence. At least I think it was. To begin with, it was just a case of white on white, white-jacketed waiters talking with white-jacketed Public Security officers on the landing. The officers must have been confused, thinking the group of Swedish labor leaders in the next banquet room was our party. But then, all white faces look alike, if not all white uniforms.

And then it seemed the waiters were arguing with them, prevailing on them to wait until we had finished our meal. But their voices were hushed, they were practically whispering to each other, and still, I think, I was the only one to notice.

More duck was brought out and Liu looked at me. "Why have you stopped eating?" she asked. "You are not another of those Americans on a diet?"

"I go to a place in Tecate every year," I said, checking by reflex to see if the room had any other doors, not that it mattered.

"Tecate? Where is that?"

"Mexico. They put you on eight hundred calories a day and run you around the block a few times. That way I can eat like a glutton for the other eleven months of the year. . . . What're they here for?"

"Who?"

I nodded toward the Public Security officers, who were just concluding their discussion with the waiters. The waiters stepped aside and admitted them into the dining room.

Smiling politely, one of the officers walked over to Tseng and spoke with him.

"What's he saying?" I asked Liu.

"That they have inspected all the bags and it is not in them."

"What bags?"

"Your bags."

"Our bags?"

She put her finger to her lips, straining to hear the discussion between Tseng and the officer.

"What's not in them?" I asked, my mind immediately flashing on Max's stash. What an idiot! Couldn't he lay off for three weeks in China?

"Don't worry," she said. "Nothing serious will happen . . . as long as it is returned."

Tseng stood and walked to the door with the other officers. Now Yen was joining them. By this time everyone in our group realized something was up; their heads were swiveled toward the door.

In a moment, Tseng returned to his place, standing behind the chair until he had our undivided attention.

"Friends of U.S.–China Friendship Study Tour Number Five—I regret to announce that you may have to experience yet another change in plans. As you know, your flight out of Peking for Tokyo was scheduled for tomorrow at noon. But due to circumstances that have been reported to us only this afternoon, this may prove to be difficult."

I glanced over at the Public Security officers, who were standing at attention by the door.

"We delayed making this announcement as long as possible, to make every effort to clear up this small matter quickly, but it seems that will not be easy."

What small matter? What was this about? I looked over at Liu but her eyes were directed straight at Tseng.

"It is all in your hands, of course," he continued, "and we realize that it is the work of one, or at the most two, members of your group, and that a certain amount of group discipline may resolve it in a matter of hours—who knows?"

"Oh, Jesus, what is this?" blurted Nancy, suddenly unable to contain herself. Tseng did not even look at her.

"We are not interested in disciplining the member or members of the group involved. We seek only restitution or definite proof that restitution is imminent, whatever that may be. Until that time, you must remain in Peking."

"*What* is all this about?" said Nick, using his best courtroom diction to command Tseng's attention. The Chairman of the Revolutionary Committee of the Travel Service looked at him, then turned to all of us.

"A member of your group removed a state treasure from the Garden of the Western Flowers sometime between eleven-thirty and eleven-forty-five this morning."

"How do you know that?" asked Max, his voice rising belligerently.

"You were the only ones there. After that time, the pavilion was closed."

"How do you know it wasn't the people who worked there?" said Fred Lisle, asking the next-most-obvious question. Tseng looked prepared for it.

"The rate of crime, as you may have heard, is very low in China. Bicycles are taken, of course. Household items. Radios. Small amounts of money. But as you may have noticed, there were no locks on the doors of your hotels in the cities you visited before you came to Peking. That is, in part, because our people have a cooperative ethos. But it is also because it would be foolhardy for one of us to steal from a foreigner. In an egalitarian society, what could one do with a Nikon or a mink coat when nobody has such a thing? He couldn't use it and he couldn't sell it. He could only be caught with it. The same would apply to a state treasure from the Garden of the Western Flowers—only more so."

"What was it?" I asked.

"A gold duck."

XVII It was like the old joke: Everybody who's leaving China please stand up. Not so fast, Friendship Study Tour Number Five.

The people sitting near me on the bus must have thought I'd gone over the edge, chuckling away on the ride back to the hotel. Everyone else seemed in a distinctly less humorous mood.

I could understand why, but on the face of it the Chinese were being entirely reasonable. When Max Freed jumped up and demanded to call the U.S. Liaison Office, Comrade Tseng placed the call for him himself, even though, according to Tseng, that office had already been notified, a decent courtesy, all in all, considering our country did not yet officially recognize Red China.

And it could not be considered a surprise that the man at the Liaison Office said there was nothing they could do, given that the Office's contacts with the Chinese government were indirect at best and that, after all, even the U.S. Ambassador to France could not do much if such a situation had occurred in Paris, given a *prima facie* case of this dimension; though, of course, the office would do their best and we should, if we wished, make a full report in the morning.

And it further seemed entirely reasonable, even generous, that the Chinese were not restricting us to quarters, before dark, but allowing us the full daytime run of Peking up to its diplomatic boundaries, where unauthorized traffic is stopped anyway, although, admittedly, a white, black or brown American would have considerable difficulty escaping in the hyperdisciplined organization of modern China. But still and all, it *was* a courtesy, and Ana Tzu and Li Yu-ying *were* with us.

Unless, of course, the Chinese were lying and the duck had never disappeared. But why would they do that? Weren't we alienated enough as it was?

"I know why you're smiling," said Nick, leaning over my seat. "This is your big chance. *Murder on the Orient Express* meets the Bamboo Curtain!"

"Starring Ruby Crystal."

"Right."

"I don't think it'll sell," I said. "The people are too weird."

"Maybe we can get Max Freed to serialize it!"

I was glad at least one other person wasn't ready to jump off Chien Men Gate as we pulled up to the hotel. Despite the general state of terror and exhaustion, Sonya had insisted we all meet in her room immediately to decide how we were going to proceed. I didn't see a lot of options. In fact, I didn't even see one.

"We still have twelve hours," she reminded us as we shuffled into the room. "If someone returns that duck, we can still be on the plane home tomorrow."

"You know what I don't understand," said Mike, "why the Chinese think we have it when they've checked our bags."

"Because you had a whole afternoon, sweetie," said Natalie. "You could have hidden it thirty places in Peking or gift-wrapped it and mailed it anyplace in the world in that time."

"The main post office is only a couple of blocks up Ch'ang An," said Harvey.

"How do you know that?" demanded Reed.

"I had to buy stamps."

"You can do that right here in the hotel . . . and mail all your letters!"

"Are you making some kind of accusation?"

"No, but—"

"I don't think you're in touch with where you're really coming from, man. If you work through your emotions, you—"

"Shit!" said Mike. "Are we gonna have to listen to that garbage? Let's find that duck and get out of here fast!"

"Easier said than done," said Fred.

"Well, where were *you* this afternoon, Señor Don Juan!?"

"Hey, hey. Now wait a minute!"

"And what about your buddy, Reed?" Mike continued. "He's got about as healthy a taste for jade as the Dowager Empress herself!"

"That wasn't jade. It was gold!" said Fred.

"White jade inlay! Remember?"

"No, I didn't," said Fred, eyeing Mike with an irony broad enough to be visible in the next country. "But I didn't spend about half an hour in the mail room of the Friendship Store!"

"Time out," I said. "This is the quickest way to get us nowhere. It's obvious if any of us has that duck, he or she's not going to reveal it here."

"You got a better idea?" said Max.

"We could leave someone's door open tonight."

"And . . . ?"

"Let whoever it is leave the duck by the entry and tomorrow morning we'll all go see if it's there. If it is, we return it en masse to the Chinese."

"If it's not?" asked Nick.

"Welcome to China," I said.

The idea was accepted for lack of a better one. The room we were in was selected, the one Sonya was sharing with Ruby, and we went to bed.

I don't think it surprised any of us in the morning that nothing was there. We crowded in around one table in the large dining room of the Peking Hotel and stared at each other's haggard faces while they served us what they called a "Western breakfast"—burnt bacon, cold toast and overcooked eggs. It was a sad comparison to the meal of the previous night, but no one was hungry anyway. We watched as diners of various nationalities straggled into the room, businessmen preparing for the day's negotiations or members of other tour groups, rubbing their eyes and adjusting their cameras as they readied themselves to meet their guides for another day of friendship and study. I wondered what they would say if they had any notion of the bizarre circumstances that had befallen Friendship Study Tour Number Five.

"Well, Sam Spade, strike one," said Nick.

I shrugged.

"Got any other bright ideas?"

"I don't know. We could all make a beeline for the ocean and swim for Taiwan."

Nobody laughed.

"Well, I don't think there's any use beating around the bush," said Sonya. "We're all in your hands, Moses."

"Why is that?" asked Staughton.

"We don't have a choice." She stared angrily back at him. "He's a detective!"

"Oh," he replied, "so the great progressive opts for individualism. . . . I don't see why we need a detective. We're responsible adults. We can deal with this in a group, democratically."

"Oh, yeah? Where'd you get that idea?" said Max.

Natalie broke in. "I don't know about you, but—"

"Wait a minute. Wait a minute!" I said. "I already made it clear I'm not on this trip in a professional capacity and that still holds!"

"You'll be paid," said Max.

"Are you trying to insult me or what?"

"Well, how're we going to get out of here? I've got a magazine to put out!"

"Sit tight, buddy. You wouldn't be home for ten days anyway!"

Max was leaning over the table, about to yell back at me, when a group of tall Africans in tribal robes came over to us.

"Excuse me," one of them said. "You are Ruby Crystal?"

"Yes, I am," said Ruby, slightly embarrassed. The African turned to his mates with the equivalent of "You see?—I told you" in his native language.

"You are liking China?" he asked.

"More or less," said Ruby.

"We are having fine time." He indicated his mates. "National Volleyball Team of Ethiopia. Play tonight at Workers' Stadium. . . . You wouldn't mind?" He placed a paper and pencil in front of Ruby.

We all watched as she signed a half-dozen autographs.

"See you at the bar," he said, smiling, and he and the other Ethiopians returned to their table.

"They *are* large," said Nancy.

"Now where are we?" said Max.

"Back where we started," said Sonya, "trying to persuade Moses to be a detective."

"I'm against it," said Fred.

"So am I," said Natalie.

"Why?" Max asked her.

"I think Staughton was essentially correct. We've started as a group and we have to function as a group. We can't let one person go snooping into our affairs, individually."

"And how do we know he's any good?" asked Reed.

"He's good," said Max.

"How do *you* know?" Reed pursued.

"We did an article on him."

"Oh," said Reed, looking at me as if I were some kind of strange bird.

"That's not the point," said Staughton. "I'm sure he's good. We're all good. But we might as well take our cue from the Chinese—although they may not be the most popular people on the block at the moment—and learn to work together as a unit."

"What do you think, Ruby?" said Sonya. "You've been pretty quiet signing autographs."

"Right," said Nancy. "Ruby was on a detective series before she got her start in films—weren't you? *A Girl Called Sam.*"

"Leave my career out of this," said Ruby. "Besides, you learn about as much about being a detective on a television series as you do about cars making Chrysler commercials. But if you want my opinion, I don't think we're ready to leave ourselves in Moses's hands, however good he is. I think we should try it as a group for at least one day."

"Sheer madness," said Max.

"Look," I said, "I don't have any more idea how to solve this than you do, so don't get yourselves overexcited. It's not worth the argument."

At that point, Yen arrived. With him was another man in a gray cadre suit, who weighed about a hundred pounds and might have been five feet tall in his Mao cap, but the severity of his expression gave him a weight that more than made up for his slight build.

"Good morning," said Yen. "Have we enjoyed our breakfast? . . . I would like to introduce you to Comrade Huang of the Bureau of Public Security. Comrade Huang will be responsible for the criminal aspects of your case, although your guides, Mr. Hu, Mrs. Liu and myself, will remain at your disposition to assist you whenever necessary."

Comrade Huang spoke several words to Yen in Chinese.

"Comrade Huang wishes you a good morning and a speedy conclusion of the case."

A rubbery piece of fried egg dangled on the end of my fork.

XVIII

"HELLO, DAD. . . . We just got your first post-card. It sounds great!"

"Yeah, uh . . . will you get your mother on the phone?"

"Can you hear me?"

"Yes. I love you, Jacob. Now please get your mother."

"Sure."

"Hello, Moses. . . . Is that really you . . . in Peking?"

"Yup."

"How is it?"

"Not good."

"Not good? I can't believe it! Do you have any idea how difficult it's been for me to—"

"Suzanne!"

"What?"

"Just shut up and listen!"

"What?"

"Listen and don't tell the kids what I'm telling you!"

"I can't hear you, Moses."

"How's this???"

"Okay. I can hear you."

"Don't tell the kids, but I may be staying in China a little longer than we expected."

"What?"

"Did you hear me?"

"Yes. . . . What happened? Are you defecting?"

"Good God, no! Will you listen?"

"Okay. Okay."

"The Chinese have put us under a kind of house arrest. We can go around Peking but that's about it. They think somebody on the tour stole a gold duck."

"Jesus! How long has this been going on?"

"Since yesterday. . . . Now, the reason I'm calling is so you don't get alarmed if anything shows up in the press because of Ruby Crystal and Natalie Levine and the rest . . . and so you can reassure the kids that I'm okay and they don't get panicked. . . . Now, put them on—no, wait a minute. Wait! Call Seymour Bittleman, Sonya's friend, and tell him. But for godsakes be careful—don't give him a heart attack. . . . Now put them on."

"Hi, Daddy."

"Hi, Simon."

"Did you see the Great Wall yet?"

"No, I didn't."

"Oh."

"Hi, Dad."

"Hi, Jacob."

"What's Mom so upset about?"

"Oh, you know—it's your Aunt Sonya. You know how she is. She wanted to move to Shanghai, but I talked her out of it."

"Good, Dad."

I talked with them a while longer before hanging up and staring down at a paper on the desk of my hotel room. For my own amusement I had written fourteen names out: Li Yu-ying, Ruby Crystal, Mike Sanchez, Harvey Walsh, Reed Hadley, Max Freed, Nancy Lemon, Nick Spitzler, Fred Lisle, Ana Tzu, Staughton Grey, Natalie Levine, Sonya Lieberman and Moses Wine. I also had written down a list of motives: money, revenge, anger, frustration, sabotage. The only one that made any immediate sense was money and I looked up at the list again, crossing out Ana Tzu, who was not in Peking at the time, and Moses Wine, assuming I was not suffering from amnesia. Some of the names seemed more likely suspects than others and I was about to put checks after them when there was a knock on the door. I got up and answered it. It was Max.

"Where's Mike?" he asked.

"Down in the bar. We finished off the Jack Daniel's, remember?"

"Good . . . I want to hire you. What's your fee nowadays?"

"That depends. A hundred and fifty a day plus expenses."

"I'll double it. I'm desperate, Moses. I need to get this fucking thing solved."

"Don't we all."

"Come on. Name a price. You know I'm good for it." He took out a checkbook.

"You're getting vulgar, Max."

"I don't want to get blamed for something I didn't do."

"Who's blaming you?"

"I've got enemies on this trip."

"Like who?"

"Like Natalie Levine, for instance. We ran an exposé on her two months ago, three weeks before she lost."

"I haven't been keeping up with the magazine, Max."

" 'Natalie Levine—Limousine Liberal.' It went down the list of her backers: oil executives, land developers, some industrialists who own three tin mines in South Africa."

"Tch, tch, tch," I said.

"So?" Max fingered the *Peking Review*, waiting for me to respond.

"Forget it, Max. You know what the others would think if I worked for one individual on this tour."

"You wouldn't have to tell them."

"You don't think they'd figure it out?"

"Shit, Moses, I'd think you owed me something for all the free publicity I gave you!"

"You want payola."

"I don't want payola. I just don't want to wind up in a Chinese prison for something I didn't do. . . . Oh, fuck you!" And he stormed out, passing Reed Hadley, who was coming the other way.

"What'd *he* want?" said Reed, staring after Max until his steps receded down the corridor. Then he closed the door.

"I think he's scared."

Reed nodded, pacing around the room. He looked pretty on-edge himself. He finally stopped and looked at me. "I don't know how to say this without sounding like I'm talking out of school, but I think it's Ruby."

"Ruby?"

"You saw how the eyes went out of her head when she saw the thing."

"She and a lot of other people."

"Well, she really wanted it. I know what it's like—when I take a customer out to see a piece of land in Palm Desert and Rancho Mirage and they have to have it at any cost. You stick it to 'em!" He couldn't suppress a grin as he looked at me nervously. "Besides, you know that museum in Pasadena?"

"Norton Simon?"

He nodded. "They had a show last fall from the biggest collections of Oriental art on the entire West Coast . . . and you know whose was biggest of all?"

"Ruby Crystal's?"

"You see!"

"We all know Ruby's an art collector." I could have added that the exhibition catalog on her coffee table had a bookmark on page thirty-four.

"Yes, but we don't know where she went with all those packages when she left the Friendship Store yesterday. She was gone the rest of the afternoon . . . and she pretends she gives all her money to social causes. . . ." He spun around and looked at me. "Well, what're you going to do about it?"

"About what?"

"What do you mean about what? About Ruby!"

"There are other suspects, Reed. As I recall, someone wrote 'Han Dynasty Duck' as his first choice on his preference form back in Hong Kong."

"That has nothing to do with it!"

"What do you mean, it doesn't?" The voice was Mike, who was standing in the doorway. He must have heard Reed halfway down the hall. "You're trying to tell us it has nothing to do with it when—"

"I'm just a tourist!"

"I'll bet!" Mike turned to me. "We all know he's the one who did it. He's the likeliest suspect on the whole tour!"

"Who says?" Reed blurted.

"What do you mean, who says? Everybody says, *carajo!*" Mike leaned into me. From the smell on his breath, I guessed he'd been making a determined search for the best Chinese brandy. "What're we wasting our time for? We should be searching his room!"

"The Chinese already did that. Besides, we have an appointment at the Liaison Office in half an hour."

"Big goddamn deal! What do you think they're going to do? They all think we're commies anyway! Well, what kind of a detective are you? Do something!"

"I can't do anything now, Mike."

"Jesus, he's going to get away with it and we're all going to be stuck here in Peking!"

"Without La Rubia."

"Hey—now, just a second. . . ."

"I don't think there's anybody on this tour without *something* to hide, Mike." I stood, slipping my list into my pocket, and waltzed past the two of them into the corridor.

On the way to the elevator I met Ana Tzu. She was smiling and humming to herself and looking the most relaxed I'd seen her since the start of our trip.

"How was Canton?" I asked.

"I feel much better," she said. "They treated me with acupuncture."

"What was wrong?"

"They didn't want to tell me."

"What?"

"It was very complicated," she said. "A lot of needles."

"Did you see your relatives?" I asked her.

Ana smiled.

XIX The U.S. Liaison Office in Peking is in the San Li Tun, an antiseptic diplomatic ghetto to the northwest of the city, with low-slung ranch-style houses backed up against a row of high-rises. It's almost as if the Chinese had created their own enclave of imperialism in reverse, restricting the foreigners to a self-contained suburb of supermarkets and tennis courts, a kind of miniature Los Angeles without freeways and billboards.

The Liaison Office itself called to mind Southern California when we drove up in three taxis commandeered for us by Yen. A pair of potted palms stood by the front gate of a two-story cinder-block building with a large picture window and a lanai. A kid's Big Wheel stood upended, overlooked by the groundskeeper, against the garage wall. It could have been a nice, upper-middle-class tract in the San Fernando Valley.

Dan McGraw, the Liaison Chief, was taking his Chinese lesson when we arrived, and we were met at the door by Mr. Karpel and Mr. Winston, two foreign service officers. They ushered us in with the polite condolences of morticians who are about to sell you the biggest plot in the cemetery, seating us on early-American antique chairs in a comfortable American-style living room with modern American paintings on the wall.

"Thank God we're here!" said Nancy Lemon as "real American coffee" was poured for us from a silver service by a Chinese servant in a white smock.

"Yes. You people are having quite an adventure," said Mr. Karpel.

"You could call it that," said Natalie.

"Too bad you're not in office at the moment, Mrs. Levine," he replied. "Then we might be able to kick up a diplomatic fuss and finesse the whole thing."

"You folks sure picked a winner," interjected Winston. He was smoking a pipe. "That duck of yours was in the original group of archaeological discoveries the Chinese have been showing off in museums all over the world."

"No, it wasn't," I said. "They wouldn't let it leave."

"That's right," said Karpel. "Even worse." He smiled. "Next thing you know they'll be asking you for a self-criticism."

"I don't think so, Bill," Winston deadpanned. "But it's too bad they can't blame it on the Gang of Four."

"We're here to find out what you gentlemen can do for us," said Sonya.

The men looked at each other.

"Frankly, ma'am," said Karpel, "not a great deal. As I told Mr. Freed on the phone last night, our hands are tied on this matter for a variety of reasons. Above all, I'm sure you know we're engaged with the Chinese in some ticklish negotiations at the moment, concerning normalizing our relations with China while protecting our legitimate interests on Taiwan."

"So where does that leave us?" asked Mike.

"In a difficult position," Winston admitted. He leaned toward us, gesticulating with his pipe. "What the Chinese are trying to do," he explained, "is engage you in their own peculiar legal process. And odd as it may sound, what it comes down to is making you police yourselves."

"But how can they do that?" asked Reed, growing belligerent.

"By breaking down into small groups on the neighborhood level and discussing the problem. You can do that in a to-

138

talitarian state. Group sanction is so important hardly anyone would dare go against it."

"And don't expect any help from lawyers," added Karpel. "According to one book I've been reading, there are more lawyers in Oakland, California, than in all of China. The Chinese distrust them altogether."

"You see, the Chinese are addicted to a kind of militant amateurism," Winston explained, "whereas we Americans want professionals to do our jobs."

Several members of the group nodded. I realized we were being treated like the audience at some low-level State Department briefing.

"Help yourselves to more coffee," said Karpel, pointing to the silver service, which had been left on a Chippendale table.

At that point Dan McGraw came downstairs. He was an affable man, only recently posted to China, but there was something about the way the State Department guys did not face him, the way they stood when he entered the room, that told me they already didn't like him.

"How extraordinary to think that someone in this room has actually stolen a duck," he said, shaking hands with each of us. "It's like being in an English drawing-room mystery . . . with a famous lawyer"—he looked at Nick—"a politician"— he nodded to Natalie—"a movie star"—he smiled at Ruby— "and the publisher of a powerful magazine"—he saluted Max—"not to mention an intriguing supporting cast. You don't mind being called a supporting cast, do you? Even in egalitarian China. But something does seem to be missing. Where's Inspector Poirot?"

"Right here," said Max, holding up my hand as if I had just won the quarter-finals in the All-China Golden Gloves. "Moses Wine, private detective."

"Amazing," said McGraw.

"Yeah, but our clever little group won't give him power to investigate."

"Does he need it? If he's worth his salt as a detective, he's investigating already anyway."

Suddenly everyone stopped talking and looked at me.

"Don't get paranoid," I said.

"Of course you're all filled with hesitations," McGraw continued. "We all are. . . . Imagine my position when the richest country in the world still hesitates to recognize the legitimacy of the government of the world's most populous nation, although it has been in power for nearly thirty years. Totally absurd, isn't it?"

Karpel and Winston looked like they were about to go through the floor. For a public official, McGraw was surprisingly outspoken.

"I'm sure you people understand Mr. McGraw is speaking to you as a private citizen," said Karpel, "and not in his capacity as a representative of the U.S. Government."

"Oh, get off it, Bill," said McGraw. "This is the modern world, not a meeting of the Old Boys' Club of Kuala Lumpur!"

"And this isn't a union hall in Harrisburg, Pennsylvania," muttered Karpel, making a fairly crude reference to McGraw's previous occupation as a nationally known labor mediator.

"We do this often," said McGraw, trying to make light of it. "That's what happens when you don't promote from within. . . . Well, now, I suppose you've come here to ask us to do the impossible. Unless, of course, you deny that any one of you could have taken that duck. Then we *could* help you."

He looked around the room, but no one was willing to speak up.

"Well, no takers, I see. Group spirit never was our forte." McGraw checked his watch. "I'd like you to stay but this is the day of our first annual Texas barbecue for officers and staff. I'm duty-bound to oversee the occasion."

"We wouldn't have it any other way," said Karpel.

McGraw nodded, extending his arm, indicating it was time for us to leave. "Normally we ask visiting groups for their impressions," he said, leading us out. "We don't get around

China that much, you understand. It's more restricted to us than it was to you . . . but in the present circumstances . . ." He stopped and looked at us. "If I were you, I'd hire this man." He clapped me on the shoulder, opening the door himself. "If you don't, you may be here until Chinese New Year. Next year is the Year of the Horse, by the way. . . . Let me know how it turns out." And he closed the door behind us.

"Year of the Horse!" Sonya muttered, as soon as we got outside. "Wouldn't you know those ruling-class stooges would be up on all the old superstitions?" She stopped and looked at us. "But the bastard's right. We're wasting our time. We can't get together as a group, so we might as well get Moses started right here."

"Goddamn it," said Reed. "We made an agreement to—"

"To what?" said Mike. "I don't know how a reactionary like you got on this trip anyway!"

"I've been a dues-paying member of the Palm Desert chapter for three years!"

"I wish to hell you were back in Palm Desert right now!"

"So do I!"

"Then let him do his work, for chrissakes!"

"Not until I hear from her!" Reed was pointing at Ruby. "I want to know where she was yesterday afternoon."

"Are you accusing me—?"

"I'm not accusing you of anything. I just saw you disappearing into the native quarter—"

"The native quarter?!"

"Call it what you want. It doesn't make any difference to me. I want to know what you were doing there."

He stared hard at Ruby, who seemed peculiarly reluctant to speak. "Well?"

She didn't say anything. Soon we were all looking at her.

"I had the address of an acupuncturist," she said.

"An acupuncturist?" said Sonya. "Something wrong?"

"No . . . uh . . . I . . ." Ruby was turning scarlet. "I heard he had some needles that would stop you from aging . . . that would take away wrinkles."

"*Umbashrayen!*" said Sonya, clapping her forehead with her palm. "Now I've heard everything!"

"It was a mistake," said Ruby. "I feel so stupid."

"Now can we let him do his work?" said Mike, looking from Reed to me.

"All right," said Reed grudgingly. "I'll go along with it if I have to."

"Then no one's opposed?" said Sonya.

She glanced over at Staughton and at Ruby, both of whom had voiced some objections earlier, but neither reacted. Sonya looked relieved. She turned to me.

"How do you want to proceed?"

"I'll need carte blanche to talk to everyone privately. Aside from that, I don't know. It's not exactly the kind of case I've handled before."

"Do you want to be paid?" said Natalie, not trying to hide her sarcasm.

"Yeah," I said. "I want you all to take me out to dinner when we get home. Just no Chinese food."

We climbed into the cabs and headed back to the hotel. I wasn't exaggerating when I said I wasn't sure what I was going to do. In fact, I had no idea at all and no notion of how I might go about it if I did. Moreover, I had no basis to compare the assignment with anything I had done in the past. On the face of it, the whole thing had a quality of the bizarre anyway. Who could do it? Who would want to steal a duck so much they would risk apprehension in the most foreign society in the world?

I leaned against the window of the cab, trying to get inside the psyche of the person who might be capable of committing such a crime. For a while nothing happened. My mind was blank. But then something swam slowly into view. It was the blurred vision of a silver Porsche, careening along Mulholland Drive. And some words of Sitting Bull's I remembered reading someplace: "Be very careful of the white man," said the Indian, "for he is strange. The love of possession is a disease with him."

XX THAT AFTERNOON I went to Harvey's room to interview him. The hall boy had left some hot jasmine tea in a flowered thermos and we sipped some for a while without talking. Finally I broke the silence.

"I wanted to talk with you first, Harvey," I said, "because you're the least likely person to have done this."

"Want me to turn this off?" he asked, referring to a tape recorder which was playing a Randy Newman cassette on his bed table.

"You like that?" I asked. " 'Short People'?"

"I can get into it. . . . Hey, that was flattering what you said to me."

"What?"

"That I was the least likely person to have done it."

"Yeah, with your groups and stuff you probably worked through your material urges a long time ago. . . . Got any Cat Stevens?"

"Nah, I left it home. Want to hear *Paul Horn at the Taj Mahal?*"

"Absolutely," I said.

He ejected the Newman cassette and snapped in the new tape. "Listen to the high part," he said. "It always makes me think of Krishnamurti."

"Been to India?" I asked.

"Uhuh. Twice."

I nodded along to the music.

"You think this is good?" he said. "You should hear it on my home machine."

"What kind of machine have you got?"

"A limited-edition Akai AA-1050 quad driving four Advent studio speakers with a moog."

"Oh, yeah. . . . Where'd you get it?"

"Through a record producer friend in L.A. Of course, I had to have the turntable sent directly from Europe."

"Naturally."

"Bang and Olufsen—you know."

"Right. . . . Videotape?"

"Sure . . . I need it for my work."

"To record your . . . ?"

"Groups . . . yeah. It gives people feedback."

I sat back and sipped my tea. On the table with Harvey's Sony tape recorder was a Nikon FT with a fish-eye lens, a Vivitar strobe, a 100-300mm zoom, a pair of Nikon binoculars, a Casio Computerized Quartz CQ-1 clock-calculator, a Polaroid SX-70 and a Canon sound movie camera with a cardioid mike. Harvey had not come to China unprepared. I wondered if he had bought it all on time or if the Gestalt therapy business in Santa Barbara was as good as I thought it was.

"Who do you think did it?" I asked.

"Oh, gosh, I don't know . . . I mean I could make the same guesses you would, but I wouldn't want to make any accusations."

"Oh, what the fuck," I said. "Go ahead—the door's closed. There's nobody bugging us but the Chinese Secret Service."

He didn't say anything.

"Come on, Harvey, give a guy a break. You people set me up with the task of saving everybody's ass. You've got to help me."

144

He glanced at the tape recorder a moment, then turned it off. "All right," he said. "I think it's Li Yu. The day we went to the Great World he told me his father had been completely wiped out by the Communists. They confiscated his factory and took every penny he had."

"What does that mean?"

"It means he thinks they owe it to him."

"That duck might *be* worth a factory," I said, "for all I know. Well, thanks for your time."

"You're going?"

"That's right," I said.

"Aren't you going to ask me any questions?"

"What could I ask you? Did you take the duck?"

"No."

"That's what I thought," I said, and I exited. I believed him. Harvey may have been greedy, but he was the same kind of equipment freak I was. We would have both chosen a ten-speed Motobecane in a minute over an antique duck from any dynasty.

Out in the hall I debated dropping in on Li Yu right away, but decided against it and knocked on Fred Lisle's door instead.

"Come in."

I pushed it open. Fred wasn't there, but Staughton Grey, his roommate, was seated in the easy chair, reading the same *Peking Review* I had glanced through the other night.

"Where's Fred?" I asked.

"With Nancy, I assume, wouldn't you? Were you going to interrogate him? He would seem a natural suspect—a missionary's son and all, born in China."

"Is that what he is?"

"And it is pretty godless around here nowadays, isn't it?"

"I think that's a safe assumption," I said, starting to edge my way out again. "Sorry to disturb you."

"How's your aunt taking this?"

"She'll be all right."

"We old people have to stick together."

I stopped and looked at him. "I imagine you two must have run into each other before . . . back in the old days."

Grey laughed. "You'd be surprised what she was like. Very attractive but obstinate as a—" He broke off. "So when're you going to interrogate *me*? You are going to interrogate me, aren't you?"

"I wouldn't know what to ask."

"What about what I was doing that evening in Hong Kong?"

"You already told me—visiting an old friend in the British diplomatic corps."

"Yes, quite. . . . What were you going to ask Fred, then?"

"You explained it—why Yen welcomed *him* back to China."

"Because he's a missionary's son," said Nancy, entering. She was alone.

"Where *is* Fred?" I asked.

"Out getting a haircut, if you can believe it. A Chinese haircut. I hate to think what it's going to look like." She plunked a bottle of mao tai on the table in front of Staughton. "Somebody's waiting for you anyway," she told me, "down in the lobby."

I checked my watch. It was only seven o'clock. She was certainly quick. I had only left a message a half-hour ago.

"See you all later," I said.

"Remember the penalty for sabotage of the family," said Nancy, giving me a big wink.

I started out the door but then stopped myself. "I do have a question," I said to Staughton. "After the Garden of the Western Flowers, you went to the Museum of the Revolution with Li Yu."

"Yes."

"He stayed with you the whole time?"

Staughton nodded.

"Then he wouldn't have had a chance to mail anything or hide anything."

"Not to my knowledge."

146

I nodded and left.

I didn't realize how nervous I would be as I crossed the hotel lobby five minutes later. It was a feeling I hadn't experienced in a long time, but I recognized it right away as that titillating queasiness you feel as a teenager just before you knock on the front door of your date's house—the terrible, delicious pain of adolescence. Under the circumstances, it was completely absurd, but it was definitely there when I saw Liu on the other side of the room, staring up at a needlepoint mural of the Great Wall, which she must have seen hundreds of times before.

I came up behind her and spoke before she noticed me. "Back home I would offer you a drink."

"Bourgeois habits," she said without turning around. "A meeting between a man and a woman in your society can never be simple. There must always be some . . . complication."

"Then don't have a drink."

"I will have an orange soda." She turned and smiled puckishly at me. I signaled to a waiter who was taking orders from other hotel guests. We sat opposite each other beneath the mural.

"You wanted to see me?" she asked.

"Yes. I have a few questions—and this time they're not about the Gang of Four."

"Oh, but you must not neglect to put politics in command. Remember what I told you about 'Red and expert'?"

"I hope I can remember."

"And you must always discriminate between contradictions among the people and contradictions with the enemy."

"Contradictions with the enemy, eh? I don't know about that one, Ninotchka. We're down to the short strokes here in Peking. Some foreign friends aren't feeling as friendly as they used to."

"That is too bad. But someone has taken a duck. Have they not?"

"Yes. And I've been elected to find it."

"Ah. The detective has his case."

"I was wondering if you could help me."

"But how?"

"I talk to a lot of people during an investigation. I'll need someone to translate for me."

"Perhaps Mr. Hu can do this for you."

"His English isn't good enough . . . and Mr. Yen will be busy attending to the needs of the group."

I looked at her, but she didn't say anything. On the other side of the lobby, a couple of the Ethiopians were cornering Ruby by the book stall.

"Also, I'll need permission to see things and go places I might not normally be allowed," I continued. "To begin with, I want to be readmitted to the Garden of the Western Flowers tomorrow morning."

"This may not be possible."

"And I'd like the help of someone from your Bureau of Public Security, someone who knows how to use white powder and ink pads."

"But there were no fingerprints," she said. "We already checked."

"Thanks for telling me."

"You did not ask."

We sat there looking at each other. She had bright hazel eyes and a pale yellow complexion that was absolutely exquisite, like a bead of unblemished amber held up to the light.

"This could get distracting," I said.

"What do you mean?"

"Nothing."

"Perhaps you *should* get Mr. Hu to assist you."

"Oh, no. No."

Suddenly she stood. "I will see you tomorrow," she said.

"Wait. One question." I hurried to make one up. "When did you find out about the theft?"

"At three o'clock in the afternoon. The museum authorities informed us."

"We left the museum about one. That leaves about two hours that the duck could have been stolen by someone else. . . . Do you agree with Comrade Tseng that it could not have been taken by a mainland Chinese?"

"Comrade Tseng is a wise comrade."

"Then why do all the bicycles outside this hotel have locks?"

She started to answer.

"Wait a minute—don't tell me. There are still class enemies in China. Even under the dictatorship of the proletariat, the class struggle continues."

She smiled.

"But no Chinese—class enemy or not—would be foolhardy enough to steal an object nobody else had. They'd only get caught. Right?"

"Right."

"Then tell me why there are locks on the doors in our rooms in the Peking Hotel when there weren't any in Shanghai or Canton."

"Because Peking has many foreigners," she said.

This time I was the one who smiled.

"Do you have any other questions?" she asked.

I shook my head.

"Dzy gen," she said, and started away.

She was only a few feet off when I stopped her. "Liu . . . ?"

"Yes."

"I do have one more question."

"Yes?"

"The man who died at the commune near Canton—that wasn't an accident, was it?"

She waited for what seemed like a full minute before answering. "What do you think?" she said.

"I'd bet against it."

"Americans like to gamble. *Dzy gen.*"

"Dzy gen, Liu."

I watched as she walked through the side door into the old wing of the hotel. Then I wandered back through the lobby to the front door. It was a warm night and I thought I'd go for a stroll and try to straighten out my thoughts on how I should proceed. But I hadn't even reached the door when a man appeared as if out of nowhere.

"Friendship Tour Five?" he said.

"Yes."

"It is forbidden for you to leave the hotel after six o'clock." He smiled politely, waiting for me to turn back into the building. He must have been one of Comrade Huang's boys.

XXI ON MY way back to my room, I stopped across the hall at the room Li Yu was sharing with Max. Both men were sitting on their beds, writing letters.

"It's the Grim Reaper," said Max. "Who're you here to see?"

"I wanted to talk with Li Yu for a minute."

"Want me to leave?" Max put his pen and paper aside.

"No . . . you can stay."

"Any news on the duck?"

"No. Li Yu, remember how you told me your father took you to the Great World when you were a boy?"

"Yes."

"You must remember that fondly."

"Yes . . . more or less."

"What do you mean more or less?"

"I liked the Great World. But my father did not want to go. I think he felt it was his duty."

"I see . . . and that made you feel uncomfortable?"

"Yes, of course. I was a little boy."

"What happened to your father?"

"He died."

"Where?"

"In Chicago."

"Did he lose everything? After the Revolution."

"Oh, yes. Everything."

"Specifically what?"

"Two factories, a house in Shanghai, another by the water in Hangchow...."

There was a knock on the door.

"Should I get it?" Max asked.

I nodded.

"Come in," said Max.

The door opened. It was Mike Sanchez.

"There's a telephone call," he said to me. "I think it's for you."

"I'll be right back," I told Li Yu, and walked across the hall to our room. The telephone was off the hook. I picked it up and spoke into the receiver.

"Hello."

"Moses Wine?" said the voice on the other end. It was Chinese.

"Yes."

"Right now go bright and flowery."

"What?"

"Right now go bright and flowery."

"Excuse me, I don't understand."

"Right now go bright and flowery."

"Hey, what is this? Do you speak English?"

"Moses Wine?"

"Yes. This is Moses Wine."

"Right now go bright and flowery."

"What're you talking about. Bright and flowery what?"

"Right now go bright and flowery."

"What??"

He hung up. I turned around and walked back into Max and Li Yu's room.

"Who was that?" asked Max. "Yen announcing we were all going to Tibet?"

"Not exactly. Li Yu, can I ask you a couple of questions more?"

152

"Of course."

"Did the Communists ever pay your father for the factories?"

"Maybe they would have, but he wouldn't admit his mistakes."

"Admit his mistakes?"

"In those days, the Communists would only make payments to the bourgeoisie who admitted they made mistakes and promised to support the Revolution."

"*Did* he make mistakes?"

"He paid the workers in his factory practically nothing and caused them to be beaten. Then he put all the profits into foreign banks."

"How did you feel about that?"

"How would *you* feel," he said, "if you heard that about your father?"

"That's what I thought. . . . Do the words 'bright and flowery' mean anything special to you, in Chinese?"

"They mean bright and flowery."

Obviously. What did I expect?

"Li Yu, could you come with me for a moment?"

"What's going on?" said Max.

"Relax, Max, huh?"

"Maybe I could help?"

"Do you speak Chinese?"

Li Yu and I left the room. Our hall man was standing behind the counter but I deliberately walked past him to the elevator. Li Yu followed.

"Where're we going?" he asked.

But I didn't answer right away. I pressed the second floor and the elevator started to descend.

"I want you to find out what 'bright and flowery' means."

"I don't understand."

"I'm not sure I do either, but a Chinese voice on the phone said to 'Right now go bright and flowery.'"

The elevator opened on the second floor. Li Yu looked at me. I put my foot in the door so it wouldn't close.

"There's a hall man on this floor," I told him. "Every floor has one. I'll wait here while you go ask him about 'bright and flowery.' "

Li Yu didn't move.

"Are you nervous?"

He nodded.

"It's all right," I said. "He won't recognize you. You come from the seventh."

"I don't do things like this," Li Yu said. "I'm a professor."

"You're telling me you never sneaked a peek at the promotions list in the department chairman's office?"

He didn't smile.

"Look, Li Yu, I'd do this myself but none of these guys speaks English. Anyone who does would be too suspicious."

"You remember when I told you how surprised I was they let me back in China? You don't know how bad my father really was!"

"I can guess."

He shook his head.

"Come on, Li Yu, I don't know why I'm saying this, but I have a feeling they're going to like you more because of this . . . and if they don't, they're not worth it."

He bit his lip.

"Li Yu!" I whispered.

Before he could stop me, I half pushed him out and he started down the corridor toward the hall man. In a few seconds I heard them talking in Chinese. But they hadn't said more than a couple of words when Li Yu came hurrying back toward me, looking agitated. He didn't say a thing until the elevator door was closed and we were headed back toward the seventh floor again.

"223 Wang Fu Ching."

"That's an address?"

"Yes—223 Wang Fu Ching."

"But what is it?"

"I don't know."

"He wouldn't tell you what it meant . . . 'bright and flowery'?"

"I didn't ask."

"Oh, crap."

The elevator opened on the seventh and Li Yu bolted out, but he turned around sharply when he realized I wasn't coming with him.

"What're you doing?" he asked.

"Going to find 223 Wang Fu Ching."

"But you're not supposed to—"

I nodded, letting the elevator door shut in front of me. On the way down, I pulled a street map out of my hip pocket. As luck would have it, Wang Fu Ching was the main street running perpendicular to Ch'ang An along the right side of the hotel. Finding the address would be relatively simple, but I had no idea how I was going to get out of the building without being spotted.

The elevator opened on the main floor and I stepped out in front of the red and gold sign reading WE HAVE FRIENDS ALL OVER THE WORLD. The lobby itself was practically empty. I headed across it, trying to look as purposeful as I could, proceeding directly to the book counter on the other side. I stopped there, pretending to peruse the reading material. A collection of Mao's poems in English was on display under the glass. I read a couple of lines—"The Red Army fears not the trials of the Long March, Holding light ten thousand crags and torrents"—and looked up. No one seemed to be watching.

I turned to my left and pushed swiftly through the door into the old wing, passing into the back of an overwrought Victorian lobby. The carpets were threadbare and the furniture was worn at the base. A large crystal chandelier dominated the center of the room, with all the lights lit but one. On the other side a couple of hotel workers were playing a game of cards. They looked at me strangely as I walked toward them, but I simply held up a postcard and waved it at them, pointing at the missing stamp like some idiot tourist trying to find a post office. Before they could come to my aid, I banged through a pair of double doors leading into a kitchen area and continued through it down a set of stairs into a dark, narrow corridor. I had no idea where I was but I decided to duck down under the stairwell and wait to make sure no one was following me. After several minutes, I emerged into the corridor again and headed down it. At the back were a service elevator and a trap door. I opted for the trap door and pushed it open. It opened on an alley behind the hotel. There was a gate at the end of it, bolted with a padlock. In full view of the pedestrians walking past, I took a quick running jump and vaulted over it. I was on the Wang Fu Ching.

The street was busy, although it was almost ten o'clock. I headed down it, looking for 223. I passed the big state department store and a large market already receiving its produce for the next morning. Then I crossed the street to a block of less impressive buildings, little shops tucked in alleyways with noodle joints and dumpling counters. A store selling traditional instruments stood beside a shop displaying cut nameplates with carved tigers on the top. I found 223 on the far corner, a blank exterior with a single wire glass window obscured with steam. There was a Chinese sign hanging above it and more Chinese writing on the door itself, but they didn't help me much.

I backed up a couple of steps, trying to get up my nerve to go in, when someone opened the door to leave. About a dozen Chinese men stared out at me from what seemed like a waiting room of some sort. I smiled as ingenuously as I could and entered. A young man of about sixteen came forward and began speaking to me in very rapid Chinese. I shook my head and several of the men in the room started to laugh. The young man reached his hand into a cash box and held up what appeared to be a ticket. It dawned on me I was supposed to pay for this and I pulled out a handful of change from my pocket. He took the equivalent of fifteen cents and led me through a swinging door. Beyond it was a tile corridor and a series of private rooms with bathtubs. At the far end was a giant room with three larger communal baths, thirty or forty men bathing themselves or reclining on wooden lounge chairs around them. Bright and Flowery was a Chinese bathhouse!

The young man unlocked one of the private rooms for me, but I shook my head and pointed down at the public room. He looked at me as if I were crazy—I must have paid for the private—but shrugged and led me down there anyway. He spread out a towel on one of the lounge chairs, handed me a pair of clogs, and pointed out the changing area. I went over to it and started to strip down. From over in the pools, several of the men were watching me. I must have been the first white face they had ever seen there.

Continuing to strip, I examined the room, wondering who sent me and what I was supposed to be looking for. Nothing made any immediate sense. I finished undressing, slipped on the clogs, and headed over to the bathing area. The three pools were of different temperatures and one toe in the first one was enough to ascertain it was about thirty degrees too hot for any self-respecting foreign devil. A couple of men smiled in amusement as I slipped into the second one. It was still pretty hot, as hot at least as the hot pool in a place I used to go in Desert Hot Springs. And that was a hundred and ten degrees.

This center pool was the most popular and there were about fifteen men in it, sloshing about and soaping themselves in the steam. Someone passed me a thick cake of brown soap and I started to lather up. Most of the men seemed pretty relaxed, workers on their way home from a late shift or students taking it easy after an evening's study. The place wasn't luxurious, but it was clean and friendly and simple. Despite the bizarre circumstances of my presence, I was almost beginning to relax myself when I thought I recognized someone in the far corner of the pool. Perhaps it was just that racist blur with which Western eyes register yellow faces, but he was staring straight at me and at first I couldn't place him at all. Was he someone we had seen at a factory? Or a guide? He was a young man about twenty, not particularly handsome, but with tough, sinewy muscles rippling in the water.

Then I knew—he was one of the bad elements, the very one who threw the rock at us in Shanghai. What was he doing here in Peking? From the intense way he was staring in my direction, I was sure he recognized me. For a split second, I didn't know what to do. Should I rush him? Splash? Duck? Run? Instead, I chose to smile, nodding to him in an innocent fashion and taking the risk that he would assume I didn't recognize him. He frowned back at me. I made a sad face, miming a tourist who was upset that the locals didn't like him. Then I turned away, soaping my arms and chest, pretending to go about my business.

The other bathers regarded me strangely, for the first time seeming aware there was a white presence among them. I nodded to them, trying to remain cool, but my heart was pounding. I fully expected the bad element to attack. But after a short while he climbed out of the pool and walked swiftly to the changing area. I could see him watching me out of the corner of his eye as he toweled off. I didn't look up or alter my behavior in any way. He dressed quickly and headed for the door. I still continued to soap up, waiting to see if he would come back to check that I wasn't dressing to follow him. It was a good guess; he was back in two minutes, standing in the doorway and staring at me. I chose that precise moment to reach for more soap, rubbing it all over my scalp and neck for an incredibly sudsy shampoo. Then I clapped my hands together and started to soap, washing ears and feet. The men in the pool thought it was the oddest foreign habit they had ever seen. The man at the door smirked and left.

I ducked under water, rinsed off, and jumped out of the pool. Then I ran over to the changing area, pulling on my clothes as fast as I could, without bothering to towel off, and to the astonishment of the bathhouse patrons, raced out of the building sopping wet.

I was just in time to see the bad element riding off on a bicycle. I headed after him on foot, jogging along the sidewalk a block behind him. This wasn't my usual inconspicuous tailing method, but I didn't have much choice and under the circumstances I wouldn't have been very inconspicuous anyway. Besides, it was hard to keep track of him in the night light. Fortunately, however, he was not pedaling too fast and his destination wasn't far. We hadn't gone two blocks when he dismounted from his bicycle and walked it across the street through the gate of what seemed to be a park. I crossed after him and followed him through, but by the time I was inside the gate he had disappeared. I stopped and looked around. A series of paths wound off between the trees and bushes in front of me. To my left, the moonlight silhouetted some large brick parapets, reflecting down on a dark, somewhat ominous body of water. If my geography were in any way correct, the parapets had to be the back of the Forbidden City and the water at my feet the moat that surrounded it.

Then, from thirty feet away from me, I heard a plangent cry. A man was standing by the edge of the moat, singing some ancient Chinese song resembling a Spanish *cante hondo*. Farther along the water someone was playing the trumpet, but this music was more modern, almost a cross between thirties jazz and traditional band marches. I walked down a path, as if lured by the sound, when something came at me in the darkness.

I saw a knife flash in the moonlight, a blade plunging toward me.

At the last second, I ducked and rolled forward into the bushes.

I came out on the other side, my whole body trembling. I could see people nearby and I headed for them quickly. At a stone wall, a group of men were practicing martial arts. Some of them had shaggy, Beatlelike haircuts I hadn't seen since Hong Kong. Farther on, bicycles were leaning in pairs against neat piles of construction bricks, four supine legs visible at the bottom, entwined about each other. This was

159

obviously a part of China where they didn't take the tourist.

Staying under a row of street lamps, I continued on to the other side of the moat. There I could see the trumpet player. He was standing on a rock, his horn pointed out over the water. Near him, a couple of men were talking behind a bush. I looked behind me and approached them quietly. The closer of the two was a squat, bald man wearing a yellow T-shirt; the other was the bad element. They were having an argument about something and the squat man started to walk off. The bad element grabbed at him, pulling him back by the shirt and raising his other hand in a threatening chop. Then they exchanged a few loud words that drowned out the trumpet for a moment. I ducked behind the bush and drew closer. Just then the squat man stepped backward, taking out a wad of bills and starting to peel them off for the bad element. From the picture of the workers and peasants on the front, I could tell they were ten-yuan notes, the largest denomination in People's China.

XXII "WHERE THE hell were you?" said Mike the minute I walked into our room.

"Taking a bath," I said. "Give me a second." And I headed into our bathroom to straighten up.

"Well, you're up shit's creek, whether you know it or not. Comrade Huang's been looking for you."

"Comrade Huang?"

"Yeah, he was up here himself an hour ago. Yen was with him, translating. I said I had no idea where you were."

I walked back into the bedroom.

"Did he know I left the building?"

"Not then he didn't."

And after all my efforts to escape detection.

"He wants to see you right now."

"It's a quarter to twelve!"

"That's what he told me. I was to send you up to the ninth floor the minute you came in."

Mike was staring at me with a half-mocking smile, as if he was pleased to see me in the soup.

"You didn't take the duck by any chance?" he asked.

"Absolutely," I said. "And the mask of Tutankhamen."

I left and went to the elevator, pressing the button with a vengeance. The ninth floor was empty when I got there and I walked nearly the entire length of the corridor before I noticed a light shining under one of the doors. I backtracked to it and knocked.

"Come in," came the flat voice from inside.

I pushed the door open on a conference room. Comrade Huang was sitting there at a long table, with Yen, Liu and another cadre I didn't recognize. Aunt Sonya was seated at the far end, looking very upset. Huang gestured for me to sit down, then said a few words and turned to Yen, who translated for him.

"Good evening, Mr. Wine. We had been waiting for you."

"Sorry about that."

"Where have you been?"

"Out taking a walk."

Yen frowned and reported my response to Huang.

"And where have you been walking, Mr. Wine?"

"I don't really know. I can't read the names of the streets."

"You realize, of course, that no members of your group are to leave the Peking Hotel after six o'clock."

"Yeah, well, I kind of forgot."

Yen conferred with Huang once again. This time their conference went on a little longer.

"Comrade Huang says Comrade Soon of Public Security reminded you of this regulation at precisely seven-fifteen this evening. At that time you were attempting to exit the hotel through the main door."

"That's correct," I said. "I, uh, should have known better. It's just my nature—what you call bourgeois individualism. I have to get out and see things for myself." I glanced over at Liu, who did not react.

"And what did you see, Mr. Wine?"

"Oh, you know, the usual Peking by night. People moving about, eating noodles. I looked in the windows of some shops . . . and stopped to admire the Mao Memorial."

Yen frowned again and translated for Huang. I knew it wouldn't sound convincing in Chinese. It didn't sound convincing in English either. Huang took a pen from the pocket of his gray jacket and began to gesture emphatically.

162

"Comrade Huang wishes to remind you a special privilege has been granted your group. You have been treated as true foreign friends."

"I understand."

"He also wishes to remind you you have a special responsibility yourself as the person chosen by the group to find the missing object. You must therefore be exemplary in every way, be above reproach. As Chairman Mao has written, a cadre must be modest and prudent and guard against arrogance and impetuosity. He must be imbued with the spirit of self-criticism."

I looked over at Liu. She was watching Yen closely as he translated Huang's words. Huang paused and reached for an envelope. I glanced over at Sonya. She had a look of dread on her face.

"So will you now please tell us where you have been, Mr. Wine?" said Yen.

I started to fabricate a vague answer when Liu interrupted in Chinese. Yen answered her back sharply. Liu responded, but the conversation was broken off quickly by Huang, who passed the envelope over to Yen.

Yen looked at me. "Unfortunately, there is a matter of greater urgency," he said. "This arrived for you by cable at the Peking Hotel at approximately eight o'clock this evening."

He handed me the envelope. I opened it. There were two pieces of paper inside. The first was a money order made out to me for fifteen thousand dollars. The second was a short note on elegant personal stationery. It read: "Thanking you in advance, Arthur Lemon."

My immediate impulse was to break into hysterical laughter, but one quick look around the room told me no one else shared my sense of humor.

"We hope you have an explanation for this, Mr. Wine."

"Yes, of course. Arthur Lemon is the husband of Nancy Lemon."

"We know that."

"Back in Los Angeles he wanted to hire me to watch her."

"Watch his wife?"

"Yeah, um . . . make sure she wouldn't commit sabotage of the family."

"I told you he did things like that . . . remember?" Sonya broke in.

Yen reported to Huang. I glanced over at Liu but she avoided my gaze.

"And what did you tell him?" asked Yen.

"I told him it was her business. I didn't want to be involved."

"Yet he sent you fifteen thousand dollars. . . ."

"He's rich."

I shrugged. I knew it sounded crazy. A fee like that would have been absurd enough at home, but here in China it must have seemed like a down payment on the Dowager Empress's marble boat.

"Rich enough to purchase a Han Dynasty duck?" said Yen.

"Maybe so."

"Where were you tonight, Mr. Wine?"

"I told you, walking around Peking."

Yen looked at me. It was obvious he didn't believe me but I decided to keep my mouth shut for the moment. After what seemed like an excessive interval, Huang began to talk again. His voice was monotonic and low, almost inaudible. He did not gesticulate with his pen or move in any way. His eyes stared straight in front of him. You could hardly see them blink.

"Our point of departure," Yen began to translate, "is to serve the people wholeheartedly and never for a moment divorce ourselves from the masses, to proceed in all cases from the interests of the people and not from one's self-interest or the interests of a small group."

He paused for Huang to speak. I ran my hand through my hair. It was still damp. I wondered if they had noticed. A dark water stain had soaked through the front of my shirt.

"The masses," Yen continued, "and only the masses are the

real iron bastion which it is absolutely impossible for any force on earth to smash, be they landlords, rich peasants, counterrevolutionaries, bad elements, Rightists, renegades, enemy agents, or unrepentant capitalist-roaders. The Party is the servant of the masses. That is why we must obey the following rules of discipline: One—the individual is subordinate to the organization. Two—the minority is subordinate to the majority. Three—the lower level is subordinate to the higher level. And four—the entire membership is subordinate to the Central Committee. Whoever violates these articles of discipline disrupts Party unity."

He stopped again. I took a deep breath. The rhetoric was depressing me. Across the table, Yen and Huang looked like characters out of a 1950's Red China movie, the Yellow Peril ready to die for their Chairman. Even Liu looked that way. And Sonya, at the end, was their pathetic dupe.

"So, Mr. Wine, the organs of the state must practice democratic centralism, they must rely on the masses and their personnel must serve the people. For those reasons we have decided to make certain changes in our policy. Your group has only one more day to return the duck. Otherwise we have no choice but to place the group under preventive detention and remand this matter to the appropriate branch of the Bureau of Public Security for formal criminal processing and group trial." I looked over at Sonya. "Furthermore, Mr. Wine, you personally are never to leave this building unless in the company of an officer of the Bureau of Public Security or of a guide of the China International Travel Service."

With that, Comrade Huang and the cadre who had not said a word stood up and left. Yen and Liu sat there a moment longer, then Yen got up. For a split second I thought Liu was going to remain behind, but she got up, too, and said good night.

"About my request to return to the Garden of the Western Flowers?" I asked, stopping her at the door.

"Mr. Hu will take you," she said. Then she pointed at my check—"Do not forget that"—and exited.

Sonya and I sat there alone.

"I wish Comrade Tseng had been here," she said.

"What difference would that make?"

"I like Comrade Tseng."

"They're all the same, Sonya. They wear the same things, they learn the same things, they say the same things, and they do the same things."

"But those things are good."

"Sonya, how can you still say that?!"

"You are so young."

"What's that got to do with it?"

"You are so young," she repeated, as if it were a funeral litany.

"Goddamn right, I'm young. And if that's what being young is all about, I want to stay young the rest of my life."

"Where were you?"

"None of your business."

"Oh, it's come to that, has it?"

"You think I'll tell you? You'd probably go running to Comrade Tseng and we'd all be spending the rest of our lives in some forced labor camp!"

"You really think they're all alike?"

"No, you know something—I really don't. Some of them are fascist scum and some of them are just plain scum!"

"Moses!" She looked mortified.

"Okay . . . okay. . . ." I relented.

"You little racist!"

"All right . . . all right. I'm a racist . . . I mean I'm not a racist. At least I don't want to be. But whatever I am, your dear friend Comrade Tseng may have thrown us a curve."

"What're you trying to say?"

"Telling us no Chinese would steal a precious object."

"Well, did one?"

"I don't know. But the bad element collecting a raft of yuans down by the moat of the Forbidden City tonight sure wasn't Jesse James."

XXIII

THAT NIGHT I remembered my dreams. I don't usually, but I was up a lot, staring at the walls, and I forced myself to remember them.

It was years ago, probably in the 1930's, and I was in some Chinese city; it must have been Shanghai. I don't know what I was doing there, I was a reporter of some sort, drinking gin at a long oak bar with a lot of English types in tweed jackets, listening to secondhand gossip and third-rate dirty jokes. A tiny Chinese servant shuffled in and tugged at my sleeve, saying something like "Come on, boss. She here now. Come on, boss." We went out the bar by the back way, where a rickshaw was waiting. The driver tipped his straw hat and I climbed in next to an elegantly dressed Chinese lady. A veil covered her face.

"We must hurry," she said, "or my husband will see us."

She placed her hand on mine as the driver pedaled off through the streets of the city and into the countryside. I can't remember what we talked about, but there was a war going on, convoys of multilated wounded moving back and forth in Red Cross trucks.

We arrived at a villa by a lake, where the woman's maidservant came out to receive us. She held the door for us as we entered a living room decorated with screens and rare antiques. The woman pulled back her veil. It was Liu, of course. I took her in my arms.

The rest of the dream went swiftly. We were eating and then we were making love, on a brass bed with a purple silk quilt. Outside, it was raining. We had made love several times, three or four times at least, when she jumped out of bed and rushed to the window.

"Get dressed," she cried. "They are coming."

"Who? Your husband?"

"No. The Communists. They must not see us."

"Don't be silly."

I smiled and reached out for her, but she was already putting on her gown. I realized she was serious and I got up and went to her, holding her by the waist as she peered through the window shades.

"Is something wrong?" I asked.

She turned to me with a terrified expression and threw herself in my arms.

"Let me take you away from here," I said, holding her close, when there was a dull thud, followed by a crash. She was shot in the back, a violent spurt of blood splattering on the silk quilt. I awoke with a start.

In the second version of the dream, I said, "Is something wrong?" and she said, "No. I am a Communist, too," turned to me with a pistol in her hand, and shot *me* in the stomach.

That time I sat up straight and stared at the inert television set in my hotel room. Mike Sanchez was snoring comfortably in the next bed. I must have remained awake for about an hour, mulling things over, futilely lying down and sitting up again in front of the television, until I had my third dream.

I was a little kid and I was sitting with Sonya and my mother watching the McCarthy hearings on our five-inch Du Mont set. "That man is true evil!" said Sonya, her finger pointing at the tube. "True evil," my mother repeated. "The worst," said Sonya, "the very worst." "The very worst," said my mother. "Worse than worst," said Sonya. "The worstest!"

"Hey, ladies, wait a minute." McCarthy turned away from whoever was talking to him and turned directly out toward us. "Give a guy a break. Some of these people may actually *be* Communists. Then what?"

"Then nothing," said Sonya.

"I'm sorry to tell you this, lady," McCarthy replied, "but those people advocate the violent overthrow of the U.S. Government."

"So big deal!" said Sonya.

"Big deal? You're not kidding it's a big deal. It's your life, sister! . . . What about you, sweetie pants?" He turned to my mother, who was much better dressed than Sonya and about ten years younger. "Do you want people in your government who have sworn their allegiance to a foreign power?"

"Well," said my mother, equivocating.

"See." McCarthy turned back to Sonya. "Sweetie pants over there knows. To be a Communist is to turn away from those you hold most near and dear, to embrace the masses and discard your one true love, to obey a faceless commissar and insult your own parents!"

"Abraham!" my mother called to my father. He calmly walked into the living room, carrying a large law book. "Is McCarthy telling the truth?"

"Yes, dear," said my father.

I woke up in a cold sweat. And thirty minutes late for breakfast.

This was not a disaster, however. Comrade Tseng's new orders had already been promulgated and, as I learned later, my popularity with the group was at a low ebb. Luckily, they had all left the table when I arrived in the dining room. I downed a cup of foul coffee and went into the lobby looking for Mr. Hu. He wasn't there. I left a message at the desk and sat down to read the latest English-language dispatches from the Tsinhua News Agency ("Peasant in East China Achieves Record Wheat Yield," "Small Hilly County Sets Pace in Modernizing Postal and Telecommunications Services Self-Reliantly"). I was deep into an enthralling account of a reception marking the seventeenth anniversary of the independence of the republic of Gabon when I was aware of someone sitting across from me. It was Liu.

"Are you ready?" she said.

"Where's Mr. Hu?"

"Mr. Hu was given the day off. He has never had the opportunity to visit the Great Wall and he has gone with the Ethiopian volleyball team. . . . Are you disappointed?"

"What do you think?"

"Perhaps you are tired of my company."

"Not likely," I said.

She stood and signaled for me to follow her. On our way out, I saw Mr. Yen watching us from the side of the lobby.

A cab was waiting for us at the bottom of the steps but Liu hesitated when she saw it. "Shall we walk?" she said. "It is better for the health."

"Yes, better," I said.

She smiled and we started along the Ch'ang An toward the Forbidden City, keeping a discreet car-length apart as we walked—or maybe it was more like a small bus.

"How will you spend your money?" she asked.

"What money?"

"All that money you received yesterday."

"Oh, that. I'll never cash it. It wasn't mine anyway. I never did anything for the guy."

"Some members of your group may feel differently."

I laughed. "What do you think? Do you think I stole the duck?"

"That is not for me to say." She clapped her hands in surprise as a trio of black limousines whizzed past us. "Look," she said excitedly. "They are on their way to the Great Hall of the People for the Eleventh Party Congress!"

It was true. Across Tien An Men I could see a number of limos lined up in front of the Great Hall, the forces of the People's Liberation Army forming a *cordon sanitaire* between the masses on the square and the arriving cadres.

"This makes you happy?" I said.

"Our country has come through a time of great trouble—

170

the earthquakes in Tientsin and Tangshan, the deaths of three great leaders—yet we are still together. The Revolution continues!"

She turned toward the gate of the Forbidden City. I made no attempt to keep pace. I had spent my adult life considering nationalism one of the most debased human emotions and her Chinese ultrapatriotism made her seem a thing apart.

We passed through the Meridian Gate and continued across the Golden Water River toward our destination, the Garden of the Western Flowers. By contrast to our previous visit, this morning the Forbidden City was practically empty, similar to how I imagined it was during the nineteenth century, a vast open space with decadent courtiers scheming behind palace walls.

No one was near the Garden of the Western Flowers as we approached it. Liu walked up the steps ahead of me and pulled on the door. It was locked.

"We wait here," she said, standing on the top step and surveying the area for the gatekeeper. Her beauty had an exquisite human simplicity against the ornate artificiality of the door. I wanted to reach out and take her hand or touch her or something, but whatever it was—the severe social mores, the fears for her and for me, or just my own shyness—I couldn't bring myself to do it.

"I hope you will not remember China badly," she said.

"I don't know how I'll remember it. It's not over."

"No. It is not over."

The gatekeeper came up the steps to unlock the door and swing it open for us.

"I'll remember you," I said.

"Yes?"

"Yes."

She smiled and looked away. I followed her into the pavilion, the gatekeeper standing by the door like a sentry or a chaperone.

"So this is what a detective does," she said, the sarcastic edge returning to her voice as I walked around in a circle, scrutinizing the empty pedestal where the Han Duck once planted its carnelian feet.

"Bourgeois individualism at its purest," I said. "I work alone and I live alone . . . 'Down these mean streets a man must go who is not himself mean, who is neither tarnished nor afraid. He must be the best man in his world and a good enough man for any world. He is the hero, he is everything.' "

Liu burst out laughing. "Who said that?"

"Raymond Chandler. You find it funny?"

"I feel sorry for him."

"Why?"

"How can one man be everything?"

I looked at her. I was going to say something about Chairman Mao, but I had a suspicion I knew what the answer would be and it was irrelevant anyway. She was right.

"Well," she said, nodding to the pedestal. "What have you discovered?"

"Nothing."

"Nothing?"

"No. And I didn't think I would, either."

"Why not?"

"Something's been disturbing me about this from the beginning." I smiled. "That's a detective line."

"What has been disturbing you?"

"That anyone would steal a valuable object from the Chinese Government—one that was out here in plain view—eighteen hours before leaving China and expect to get away with it."

"I imagine he or she mailed it out of the country."

"A risky procedure . . . but even so, why didn't he or she think the Chinese Government would discover the object missing in time to stop us from leaving?"

"Perhaps they expected the Garden of the Western Flowers would remain closed."

"Perhaps," I said. "But that's a large assumption."

"Then what?"

"I don't know."

172

"So the detective is . . . confused."

" 'Stumped' is the word."

She smiled slyly. "In our society we would have a struggle-meeting."

"In your society I might be sent out for five years' hard labor in the provinces."

"It would do you good. You might learn to identify with the masses of the working people and their problems."

"Now, now."

"You are displeased? Not everyone has the money or the time to travel all around the world studying other people's revolutions. Perhaps next year you will go to Cuba or Vietnam?"

"At least you don't think I stole the duck."

She shrugged, giving me the benefit of the doubt.

"Yeah, well, you're probably right. I am something of a left-wing voyeur. I always have been. And I'm an American consumer too, coming to China so I could buy revolution . . . but I do have one question for you."

"What is that?"

I took a couple of steps closer to her and nodded toward the gatekeeper. "Does he speak English?"

"I don't think so," she said, but I could see she wasn't sure. I started walking to the other side of the pavilion. In a few seconds Liu followed after me. I waited for her.

"Who sent me to the Bright and Flowery?" I said when she caught up.

"What?"

"Who sent me to the Bright and Flowery baths?"

"I don't understand."

"I went out last night because somebody called to tell me to go to the Bright and Flowery."

"Who was that?"

"He was Chinese and he didn't speak English very well."

"Did you go to the Bright and Flowery?"

"Yes, I did . . . and guess who was there."

"I wouldn't know."

"One of the bad elements from Shanghai. He tried to take a slice of my small intestines. I followed him to the moat behind the Forbidden City, where a man deposited a nice, fat stack of yuans in his hands."

"Was the man American or Chinese?"

"Chinese—and don't tell me there are still class enemies in China. If I hear that one more time, I'm going to lead a one-man campaign for capitalist restoration!"

Liu looked over at the gatekeeper. He was turned away from us, facing out the door of the pavilion.

"And you think he took the duck," she said.

"Why not?"

"Did you see it?"

"No."

"Then you cannot be sure."

"Correct."

She glanced down at the gatekeeper again. This time he was faced in our direction, his left hand clutching a set of keys on a large ring.

"Have you seen everything you need to see?" she said. "We must go."

I nodded and we started out of the pavilion. Outside, we did not speak for a hundred yards.

"You must consult with your group," she said finally.

"What for?"

"You must consult with your group. You must learn from them."

"Are you trying to tell me something?"

"It is time for further investigation."

"You *are* trying to tell me something."

She nodded and we continued across the Forbidden City, heading toward the Meridian Gate. I tried to understand what she was saying. Again China was a land of signs, of bombastic rhetoric masking far subtler shifts. And it was ever-changing, from the Politburo to the smallest neighborhood. The Chinese seemed to prefer it that way. To be a detective here, even if they had them, would be a perilous job at best.

174

Just as you thought you had come to a solution, the conditions of your investigation would alter and the results be called in question. One would always split into two. But then, of course, this had its good side. In a world of constant change, you could never be wrong. All you had to do was wait and your incorrect assumptions would turn correct.

I smiled at Liu as we passed through the gate and turned on Ch'ang An. Without paying any particular attention, I started to hum to myself.

"What are you singing?" she said. "Is it an American song?"

"Yes."

"Tell me the words," she said. "I do not know any American songs except 'Turkey in the Straw.' "

I reddened, suddenly realizing what it was. "I don't think I ought to. American songs are pretty strange. We haven't had a cultural revolution yet."

"Tell me anyway," she said, stopping by a wall halfway between the Forbidden City and the hotel.

"I'm not sure I remember them." I ran the words to "On a Slow Boat to China" through my head—something about keeping you in my arms evermore, all to myself alone. Not exactly appropriate to proletarian courtship. "No, I don't remember them," I said. "It's an old song anyway. From the nineteen-forties. You wouldn't like it."

"But I like your old things. I saw a movie once called *Queen Christina*."

"Garbo! Didn't I read someplace that Chiang Ching used to watch Garbo movies in the basement of her villa?"

"I wouldn't know. What are some of the songs people like now?" she asked quickly.

"Most of them are about love, of one sort or another. They always have been. Now they use a wah-wah pedal and a Moog Synthesizer."

"A Moog Synthesizer?"

"Electronics."

"Electronic love. It does not seem natural." A man walked by, carrying a wicker basket on the handle of a shovel. He glanced at us as he passed. "Most of our songs are about the struggles of the working people and about the unity of China. To us they are the most important."

"Love is important, too."

"Yes. But it is only a part of life."

"To us it is everything. Love and success."

"Everything for yourself and little for others."

"For you and the ones you love."

"It seems a private world."

"It is."

We stared at each other. A stiff breeze came up, blowing the first autumnal leaves along the Ch'ang An. She looked away and then back at me.

"Some things are not easy, Moses."

"I know," I said.

She nodded and started walking in the direction of the hotel again. I followed alongside her, my heart beating to the rhythms of some Chinese melody I didn't understand.

"Remember the peasant song I sang for your group?" she said.

"About the Jade Emperor? I don't remember the words to that either."

" 'There is no Jade Emperor in heaven. There is no Dragon King on earth. I am the Jade Emperor. I am the Dragon King. Make way for me, you hills and mountains, I'm coming.' "

"It's not 'On a Slow Boat to China,' " I said.

"The words are important. You must study them." She stopped at the steps of the hotel. "Study them carefully." A group of Arab sheiks were entering a limousine.

There is no Jade Emperor, I thought. It didn't make any sense. I had seen it with my own two eyes. Unless . . . But that was too incredible. I stood there a moment without saying anything, staring at Liu.

"Be careful, Moses," she said, "or we are both in great danger."

She hurried into the hotel ahead of me.

176

XXIV OF COURSE it wasn't just what the words meant, but *when* she had first sung them that was perplexing me. The Chinese were very concerned with that—who said what to whom when. In the words of my trusty *Peking Review*, Chiang Ching claimed Mao told her to "act according to the principles laid down." This meant, I gathered, to carry on the Cultural Revolution, with Chiang and her friends in power. But, as we all knew, Mao had said no such thing. Rather, he had said, "Practice Marxism and not revisionism; unite and don't split; be open and aboveboard and don't intrigue and conspire." In fact, on December 28, 1974, he said, "Chiang Ching has wild ambitions, hasn't she? My view is she has." And then: "Don't carry on factional activities. Those who do will take a tumble. . . . Stop carrying on with your Gang of Four." Later he told then *Vice*-Chairman Hua Kuo-feng, "With you in charge, I am secure."

Or did he? It was a thicket of hearsay as dense as eighteen and a half minutes of twisted Watergate tape—and twice as long.

I was certainly nowhere near unraveling this or any other thicket when I followed Liu past Comrade Huang and his assistant into the lobby. I nodded to her in a dispassionate way and was heading toward the elevator when a man in a tailored tweed suit stepped in front of me.

"Monsieur Wine?"

"Yes."

"Pierre de Bretteville, Agence France-Presse . . . may I speak with you a minute, please?"

"Not now," I said, and edged around him into the elevator, pressing the seventh floor.

Most of the group were in their rooms, skulking about like sailors whose liberty had been rescinded three hours after pulling into port. The first one to notice me was Reed Hadley, who stormed into the corridor with an angry "Did you give it back yet?"

"No, I ate it," I said. "The Chinese are famous for their duck."

"I want you to know I just cabled my congressman—Digby Williamson of San Bernardino—to let him know what's going on here. And don't think I didn't mention your name!" Hadley moved in on me, his finger jabbing. "I'm going to get results, too. I've been contributing to that s.o.b.'s campaigns since he was running for junior college board of education!"

I walked past him into my room. If this Mojave Desert Babbitt was a preview of what Liu meant by consulting the group, I was ready to stuff the ballot boxes for individualism until my arms came off.

"I'm calling a meeting of the group," I told Mike Sanchez.

"You can't do that," he said. "They fired you this morning over breakfast."

"Fine. You call it."

Sanchez looked at me. "Turning yourself in?"

But he knew better, and stood and left the room. Ten minutes later they were all assembled there, regarding me with expressions that ranged from contempt to suspicion. I tried to ignore this and began to reveal what had happened to me the previous evening. Normally, I would keep the details of an investigation private until it was completed, but if I were going to function as a member of a group, be a co-

178

operative detective, then I had no choice but to reveal all—almost all, anyway.

"You're sure this was the same guy we saw at the Great World?" said Harvey when I had finished.

"The Great World and the Industrial Exhibition Hall."

"Where'd he go afterward?"

"I followed him to the railroad station. He got on the night train for Shanghai."

"But you didn't recognize the person who gave him the money?" said Max.

I shook my head.

"Whoever did knows who has the duck," said Ana.

"Don't be so certain," said Ruby.

"That's right," said Fred. "He could just be a fence."

"Three times removed," said Mike.

"Yeah. And why would someone want to tip Moses off?" asked Natalie.

"How do we even know he's telling the truth about *that*?" said Reed. "We all know he just made fifteen thousand dollars. Hell, he could just be making this up to throw suspicion off himself."

"I wouldn't be surprised," said Nancy, who had been feeling defensive since breakfast, when the whole group had been informed of her husband's check.

"I saw him go to the phone," said Max, coming to my defense.

"And I got the address for him," said Li Yu. "That really happened. I promise you."

"Then who's paying the goddamn 'bad element'?" asked Harvey.

"And how do we even know it has anything to do with the duck in the first place?" said Nick.

"It has to do with something," said Staughton.

That silenced everyone for a moment. This exercise in group detection was making me edgy. I was already two or three jumps ahead of the group, but I didn't want to say anything. It reminded me of PTA meetings when I had to

179

wait for someone else to express my idea so I wouldn't seem pushy. Usually, I wasn't very good at this and would sit there squirming in my chair while a couple of bimbos spent forty-five minutes debating whether the kids weren't using too many erasers in social studies class.

"There are three choices," said Nick, jumping into the gap. "One: One of us stole the duck or caused it to be stolen; then he or she could be paying off the bad element. Two: A Chinese stole the duck and is paying off the bad element. Or three: The money had nothing to do with the duck at all."

"I don't follow you," said Harvey.

"Oh, come on," said Mike, rolling his eyes.

"Now, if one of us stole the duck," Nick continued, "offhand, it could be for one of two reasons—personal gain or ideological hostility. Looking around this room, I could see grounds for both of these possibilities. And the individuals involved better be prepared to defend themselves in People's Court."

"But if a Chinese took the duck—" said Max.

"Impossible," said Sonya.

"Oh, get off it, huh?" Max retorted.

"They don't do things for personal gain," replied Sonya.

"You still believe that?" Max turned on her sharply, bearing down. "What do you think that 'bad element' was doing, then, practicing his arithmetic for the Canton Trade Fair?"

"Well, then," said Nick, "suppose a Chinese did take the duck. . . ."

"We've discussed this before, Nick," said Staughton. "They do have their bad elements and all that, but an object like that duck would be useless to them, for obvious reasons."

"Unless they sold it to an American," said Nick.

"But whom?" said Staughton.

"Here we go again!" said Max.

"Wait a minute! Wait a minute!" said Nancy. She was jumping up and down in her seat. "There's another reason a Chinese might have wanted to steal that duck!"

Everyone waited. At last we were beginning to get somewhere. I smiled, feeling like the leader of one of Harvey's groups. Perhaps China and California were not that far apart. At Esalen, we had our own struggle-sessions.

"What is it?" Nick snarled impatiently, as if he expected Nancy to give forth with something about as weighty as the latest recipe from *Woman's Day*.

"To hold us here," she said.

"To what?"

"Hold us here. We *were* going to leave the next day."

"What on earth for?"

She shrugged. "So we could change our minds about China. A lot of people in this group had gotten a pretty low opinion of it."

Nick gave Nancy a withering courtroom stare. "Now you've got to be kidding. You're telling us it's state policy to steal objects and blame it on foreigners, so they can learn to appreciate China *more*?"

"He's right," said Staughton. "That makes no sense at all. Ever since I've been in the progressive movement—from the labor movement on—people have been looking for all kinds of complex reasons for things. But it's usually something very simple."

"Like what?" said Sonya in an accusatory tone.

"How should I know?" Staughton replied, taken aback. "That would depend on the situation, wouldn't it?"

"Wouldn't it," Sonya repeated, more nastiness in her sarcasm than I was used to. "I thought your long experience in the 'progressive movement' gave you insight into the contradictions of every historical epoch!"

"Listen," said Harvey, "if we have any problems here with personal feeling, I think we ought to speak to them directly."

"Forget it," said Sonya.

The telephone rang. I reached for it.

"Hello."

"Hello. Mr. Wine?"

"Yes."

"This is Craig Williams of the *Toronto Globe & Mail*. I'd

181

like to ask you a few questions about your group that was detained by the Chinese."

"Not now, thank you."

"What about Ms. Lieberman? Would she care to talk?"

"You'd have to ask her."

"How about Natalie Levine?" he persisted.

"Goodbye, Mr. Williams."

"I'll be down in the bar if you change your mind," I heard him say as I hung up.

"He's been calling me all morning," said Ruby.

"Him and the Frenchman," said Fred. "The more publicity we get, the safer we'll be."

"You want to bet?" said Max. "Just the opposite will happen!"

"Oh, get stuffed!" said Mike. "You just want to save it for your magazine. I heard you placing a call to them this morning!"

"I was calling my accountant!"

"Naturally!"

"Hold it," I said. "We can resolve this later. Right now can't we discuss what Nancy said? Suppose a Chinese did take that statue to keep us here?"

"Oh, Christ, not that again," said Nick. "That's the stupidest idea I've heard yet!"

"Ditto," said Max.

"Group discussion is a great thing," Harvey added. "But you've got to know when to move on."

"To what?" I asked him.

"To the next subject."

"What's that?"

"How we're all going to get out of here!"

There was a silence. I looked around the room. It seemed tight, claustrophobic. For the first time it was becoming real to me that we might actually be here for a while—for months, even years. The Chinese were patient, after all. Didn't Mao say this was the first of thousands of cultural revolutions?

Didn't the sign read TEN THOUSAND YEARS TO THE GLORIOUS AND CORRECT COMMUNIST PARTY OF CHINA?

"When am I going to see my children?" Mike slammed his fist on an end table.

"Your children?" said Max. "I've got a—"

"Oh, shut up with your fucking magazine!" said Mike.

"Who're you to talk? You spent half the goddamn trip trying to figure out who didn't pay! You probably took the duck yourself to pay off the mortgage company, you dumb—"

"Beaner?" Mike jumped up. "How about greaser? You like that better, *gabacho?*"

Mike took a step toward Max, who threw his hands up in front of his face.

"Hey, let's cool this off," said Natalie, jumping to her feet herself.

"Hey, look to yourself, *hermana*, huh? Who's paying that hundred-thousand-dollar campaign debt of yours?!"

"You think I'd steal a duck to—"

"You gotta prove yourself just like everybody else here!"

"Well, how about the collector over there?" Natalie wheeled on Hadley. "He's been acting like the China representative of every antique store west of New Jersey!"

"I'm not the only collector. Hollywood's favorite Cadillac Communist's got more jade than anybody in this room!"

"You think I came here for more?" said Ruby. "How about our missionary friend from California Lutheran? He's got a lot to answer for."

"Like what, for instance?" said Fred Lisle.

"You're so angry about losing China for Jesus, you'd probably steal the whole Forbidden City if they gave you a chance!"

"Don't be ridiculous! Wait a minute! What about her?" Fred was pointing at Ana Tzu. "She's been acting suspicious with her phony diseases since we arrived in Hong Kong. You can't tell me anyone in this room actually thinks she's been sick for a minute!"

"You've got no right!" said Ana, jumping to her feet, too. By this time, half the group was standing, shouting at each other and waving various limbs.

"Well, show us the medical records," said Fred. "Come on."

"I don't have to show you anything if I don't want to."

"I don't care what you want, sister. We're talking about getting our asses back to the U.S. of A.!"

"And we're getting nowhere fast!" said Max, who pulled a joint out of his pocket and started to light it with a fresh book of matches.

"Holy shit," said Nick, "this guy wants to get us stuck in China forever!"

"Put it out!" said Sonya.

"Come on, Max," said Harvey.

"Oh, fuck you all!" said Freed, and marched out of the room.

The group fell silent. The brooding anger which had once been focused on me was now diffused, a dozen or more vectors shooting out in different directions, canceling each other out and stabilizing the atmosphere at a prevailing level of undifferentiated hostility. Whatever experiences, however many years, these people had had in group situations, they could not function as a structured unit or even as a loosely knit ensemble. They were Americans. *We* were Americans.

Without making any comment, I stood up and left. No one was in the corridor. I walked down it the few yards to Max's room and pushed on the door. He was inside, sucking on the joint and staring up at the ceiling.

"Where'd you get those matches?" I asked him.

"What matches?"

"What matches? The matches in your hand, turkey."

"Oh. . . ." He opened his clenched fist and a book of matches fell out. "How should I know?"

"They're your matches, Max. You light your joints with them. Who else is going to know where you got them?"

"Well, uh . . ." He revolved the book in his hands. "I don't remember."

"Did you get them in Peking?"

"Probably."

"They're from Hong Kong."

"Uhuh."

"But you got them in Peking?"

"Yup," he said, smiling a dope-crazed smile at me. "The plot thickens, huh?"

"How do you know you didn't just stick them in your pocket in Hong Kong and carry them for a few days without knowing?"

"First of all, I never went to this place." He pointed to the label on the matches. "Secondly, I was out of matches the night we flew into Peking. I know that because I went crazy trying to light a J in the bathroom. I finally had to send the hall boy downstairs for a light." He laughed to himself. "Think of that—first night in Peking."

"So you don't remember where you got the book?"

He shook his head, offering me the joint, but I waved it off.

"Think, Max. Focus that wierded-out brain of yours and try to remember. If it were some café-society question, you'd know it in a minute. You could probably tell me the last restaurant where you took Gore Vidal to lunch in half a second."

"The Caravelle in New York."

"Good. Now remember where you got the fucking matches."

"The Embassy."

"What?"

"You know . . . the U.S. Liaison Office, where we met all those foreign service creeps. I picked it up from the table next to the coffee urn."

"You're sure about that?"

"Sure, I'm sure." He sat up. "But why're you making such

185

a big deal about some lousy matches from the Peninsula Hotel anyway?"

"Because it's a clue, shmuck."

"I know that. Of course it's a clue. What do you take me for—some deranged dope fiend who can't follow the simple logic of a cheap detective investigation? But what's it a clue for?"

"I don't know," I said. I picked up the matches and left.

Back in my room, the group was already breaking up. I checked my watch. It was still early afternoon—four or five hours until Comrade Huang would or would not make good his threat and place the members of Friendship Tour Five under preventive detention, remanding their case to the appropriate branch of Public Security for formal criminal processing—but that didn't give me much time. I fingered the matches from the Peninsula Hotel, stuffed them into my pocket, and walked down to Staughton Grey's room. Through a crack in the door, I could see that Staughton was undressing, an elderly man slipping into his pajamas for a midday nap, but I knocked on the door anyway.

"Come in. . . . Oh, it's our retired detective."

"Easy come, easy go," I said.

"Yes . . . well, what can I do for you? As you can see, I was about to take a short rest. Older people like your aunt and myself need to take it easy once in a while."

"Sorry to bother you. I was just wondering if I could bum a cigarette."

"I don't smoke."

"Oh, yeah," I replied, starting to back out of the room. "I forgot."

"I didn't think you did either."

"Sometimes," I said. "When I'm under pressure."

He regarded me strangely as I shut the door.

Out in the corridor again, I hurried to the elevator and pressed the down button. I got off at the main floor and walked through the lobby to the bar.

"Craig Williams?" I said, directing my voice to one of four

men ponied up to the rail. The shortest of them, a roly-poly blond man in a brown corduroy jacket, turned around.

"Moses Wine," I said, extending my hand. "Sorry I was so abrupt with you on the phone, but things have been getting a little tense around here lately. . . . What're you drinking?"

"Gin and tonic."

"Two," I said to the bartender, who poured out a couple of smallish gin and tonics and passed them over to us. I paid for them, the equivalent of twenty cents for the pair, and carried them over to a private table with Williams.

"Canadian?" I asked him.

He nodded. "They don't let Yank reporters stay here. Normalization, you know. I'm the only North American at the moment. Couple of French, though. And others."

I sipped the gin and tonic.

"Not bad, is it?" he said. "Shame there isn't more. The only decent bar in China and they roll the bugger up at ten-fifteen on a Saturday night. These people are puritanical with a vengeance."

"You could say that. . . . There's some of your competition." I nodded through the doorway where de Bretteville of Agence France-Presse was pursuing Nick Spitzler across the lobby. From what I knew of Nick and reporters, the Frenchman didn't stand much of a chance.

"Oh, yeah, him," said Williams. "Lucky Pierre . . . he'll do anything for a scoop."

"It's dog eat dog for a story, even here in People's China?"

"I'll say. This place is like one nasty ingrown toenail as far as the foreigners are concerned. And gossipy—it's the most incestuous small town this side of Manitoba." He swallowed his drink in two gulps and looked around him.

"You must have a lot of trouble getting the news."

"It's impossible. These people are so closemouthed they won't even tell you how many dumplings they ate for lunch."

"Do you speak Chinese?"

"No."

"You get around the country much?"

187

"When I want to—but who wants to? It's the same everywhere you go . . . except for Kweilin. Beautiful scenery there. . . . Of course, I have my sources." Williams glanced into the lobby again, then leaned in toward me. "Well, Wine, tell me the long and short of it. I can't tell you how bizarre it sounds. Did someone on your tour actually steal that bird?"

"I wish I knew."

"You have no idea?"

I gazed down at my drink and pursed my lips, trying to look like someone who knew more than I really did. "I think I'm on to something now," I said.

"What is it?"

"I'm not ready to say."

"Come on, old boy. Out with it. You know the old saying: 'I'll scratch your back if you'll scratch mine.' "

"Has there been any news on this yet back in the States?"

"I would imagine. I sent a dispatch over the mojo wire last night. Everyone picks that up. Should be a pretty hot item too, what with Ruby Crystal on board and all that." Williams had a strange smile on his face, a pathetic need written all over it. So this was a China watcher, I thought—one of those men we read over our morning coffee to find out the real truth about life behind the Bamboo Curtain.

"What do you think you could do for me, Craig?" I asked.

"Well . . . I could tell you something about what goes on in the underworld here."

"Like what?"

"Like the Counterrevolutionary Assassin Group of Honan Province." He nodded his head several times, emphasizing its importance. "They were robbing banks all over Honan and the authorities finally had to put up big-character posters with rewards for their capture. Only they never got caught."

"When was that?"

"Oh, uh . . . five or six years ago."

"Anything else?"

"Well, uh, you know. You hear stories."

"For instance?"

"A German diplomat was propositioned by a prostitute last year only three blocks from the Great Hall of the People."

"She was Chinese?"

"That's what I heard. Of course, I don't want to be quoted on this. It would be hearsay."

"Oh. Look, uh, Craig, eighty-six on the underworld. But there *is* something else you could do for me."

"What's that? What's that?"

"And in return I'd promise you any scoop coming from this story. You'd have to trust me, of course. And wait for it. But it'd be yours first."

He scrutinized me a little longer than I had hoped he would. "Okay . . . shoot."

"How do you get permission to go to Shanghai?"

"I call up the Travel Service and tell them I want to go. If it's a big city like that, it's usually no problem. They'd probably assign a guide."

"How quickly can you do it?"

"I don't know." He looked at me. "What're you driving at?"

"Could you get permission to go tonight?"

"Tonight?"

"Yeah, you know, there's a train leaving around seven, isn't there?"

"*You* want *me* to go to Shanghai?" He stared at me, incredulous.

"No, I don't, Craig. No." I waited a moment while the bartender walked by. Across the lobby, I could see the Ethiopian volleyballers striding past. They looked pretty slick in orange and black warm-up suits.

"Then what *do* you want?" he asked.

"I want *me* to go to Shanghai, using *your* papers."

"Jesus, Mary and Joseph!"

XXV WILLIAMS DIDN'T think it was funny when I offered him my VISA card as a guarantee. In fact, it took an exhausting forty minutes to persuade him to go along with me. What finally convinced him was my promise to say I had stolen his papers if I was caught. After all, I explained, it wouldn't make any difference to me at that point. My goose would be cooked either way. He didn't have a response to that, but I could see he still wasn't sure. I wouldn't have been surprised if he reneged when I looked for the envelope behind the celadon planter on the seventh floor later that afternoon.

When I left him, I walked into the lobby and picked up one of the house phones near the desk.

"English-language operator, please."

A couple of beep tones followed a prolonged screech as connections were made.

"Yes?"

"Hello . . . English-language operator?"

"Yes?"

"I'd like to be connected with the room of one of the Travel Service guides—Liu Jo-yun."

"The guides do not have telephones in their rooms, please."

"Well, uh, is there some other way I could speak with her?"

"Yes?"

"It's rather an emergency . . . uh, very important business for our group."

There was no response. The silence on the other end bespoke a kind of impatience. Private telephones were relatively new in China and of a questionable bourgeois nature anyway. They were mostly used by foreigners in the diplomatic quarter. Almost no Chinese citizens had them. There wasn't even a telephone directory for Peking, the desk clerk had told me the previous day, although he could not tell me why. I was about to buzz again and repeat my request, when I heard more beeps and then a familiar whirring noise suspiciously like the sound when I used to man the phone at the SDS office in Berkeley in sixty-seven. We used to play games with that one. Once I dialed a local number and left the entire five acts of the Royal Shakespeare Company's *Timon of Athens* on the tape as a cultural improvement program for the FBI.

"Hello. Who is this?"

"Hello, Mrs. Liu. This is Moses Wine."

"Oh." She sounded doubtful.

"Friendship Tour Number Five. . . . It's about those Chinese stamps you promised to help my buy for my children."

"Stamps?"

"Yes, you remember, surely. I want to bring them a collection of stamps fom the People's Republic."

"There are many stamps."

"I know . . . you were going to help me select."

"Select?" On the phone her English seemed to be failing. Perhaps my ruse was confusing her.

"You were going to pick them out. Five o'clock today. That would be good, wouldn't it? Five o'clock today," I emphasized. "I will meet you in the lobby . . . all right?"

There was silence.

"In the lobby. At five," I repeated. "For stamps."

"I do not know," she said. Then there was a click.

I looked up at the desk clerk, who was standing a few feet away from me.

"Stamps over there," he said, pointing toward the book stall. I nodded my thanks and headed in that direction.

But once I was on the other side I sneaked out of the building again. It was easier this time. A large delegation of Algerian steel workers was crossing the lobby and I pretended to follow them into the elevators, slipping around the bar at the last moment and disappearing through the door into the old section. Before anyone had a chance to notice me, I was down the back stairs again and in the alley behind the hotel. This time the gate was open and I walked straight out into the Wang Fu Ching.

The Chinese, accustomed to foreigners in this area of town, paid me no special attention as I walked swiftly down a couple side streets and then doubled back to the Ch'ang An a few blocks away from the hotel. There I climbed on a bus headed east, toward the diplomatic quarter. The bus was crowded, passengers wedged between the seats and spilling onto the rear platform. I was holding on tight when a young man got up and offered me his seat. I had no choice but to take it, everyone around him was so smilingly solicitous of their foreign guest. I sat down and stared out the window as we continued along Ch'ang An, passing a couple of blocks of lovely old Chinese residences, workers busy repairing the masonry in the warm afternoon sun. A woman rolled a baby in a bamboo pram past a group of schoolchildren, kindergartners probably, who were seated around their teacher on little chairs placed right in the middle of the sidewalk. Suddenly I felt angry. Whatever was happening, I had been deprived of my trip to China—at least the conventional part of it—and I wanted it back. I had the distinct desire to stop this nonsense, jump off the bus, and make contact with these people immediately. Or launch into a conversation with the passengers around me on the bus. But I couldn't and neither could they.

All we could do was smile at each other and point. I sat there instead and brooded. We reached the diplomatic quarter, I nodded to the young man who gave me the seat, and got off, watching the bus as it drove away.

The Liaison Office was only a block and a half away. I tried to walk slowly to devise a strategy, but I was at the door too soon, pretending to ignore the gateman, who was giving me the once-over, undoubtedly disturbed that someone would arrive at the building on foot, without benefit of limousine or, at the very least, taxicab.

I pressed the bell and a maid came to the door. She was dressed in traditional black with a white apron and I had a momentary culture shock that jolted me out of China. For a split second I thought I was back home, doing some routine investigation in Van Nuys or North Hollywood, maybe a child custody case in Woodland Hills.

"You seek someone?" said the maid in carefully enunciated English.

"Yes. I'm looking for either Mr. Karpel or Mr. Winston."

"Who is asking?"

"My name is Mr. Wine. From Friendship Study Tour Number Five."

She disappeared into the house. Through the window I could see her speaking to someone in the living room. She returned immediately.

"Mr. Karpel and Mr. Winston not here."

"Where are they?"

"On visit. Far away."

"I see. Do you know when they'll be returning?"

"Excuse?"

"When are they coming back?"

"I do not know."

"Is there someone else I can see? How about Mr. Mc-Graw?"

"Must have appointment see Mr. McGraw."

"This is pretty important."

"You leave name. You get appointment."

193

"I already gave you my name."

"What?"

"I said I already gave you my name. Moses Wine. Friendship Study Tour Number Five."

"Yes. Leave name, get appointment."

She closed the door in my face. Across the lawn, the gateman's dubious expression had segued into outright suspicion.

"See you later, Chuck," I said, giving him the high sign and waltzing past him with a casual wink. I turned up my collar as I headed up the street, keeping one eye cocked to my side and the other on the road before me. I had dropped into the role of L.A. dick. It must have been partly because of the seeming familiarity of the diplomatic quarter, but more likely it was because I had never felt so out of my element in my life. Indeed, I had never *been* so out of my element in my life.

Going on instinct, I crossed behind the Friendship Store and doubled back on the next street. A wrought-iron fence guarded the rear of the Liaison Office. I looked around and then climbed over, lowering myself behind some poinsettias near the garage. I was about to make for the back door, when I heard a series of strange guttural noises not more than twenty feet away from me:

"*Wǒ yào liǎng gè zùo wèi* . . . A table for two, please. . . . *Wǒ yào liǎng gè zùo wèi* . . . A table for two please. . . . *Wǒ dě měi guó dà xiǎo shǐ* . . . My size in America is . . . *Wǒ dě měi guó dà xiǎo shǐ* . . . My size in America is . . ."

I peered around a branch to see McGraw tromping around the backyard in his shirtsleeves, practicing his Chinese from flash cards.

"*Wǒ yào dai zhè gě* . . . I will take it with me. . . . *Wǒ yào dai zhè gě.*"

"Sounds like you're making progress," I said, emerging directly from behind the poinsettias.

For a moment the Liaison Chief seemed taken aback but

194

he recognized me quickly. "Oh, the detective. . . . How're things at the Peking Hotel?"

"Not so hot. The way things are going, you may be fluent in Tibetan before we get out of here."

"Don't be so sure. They're starting me on ideograms and I haven't even mastered this phonetic alphabet yet." He showed me a flash card. "Take a look at that. You pronounce all the X's like sh, the Q like ch and the C like ts in hats!"

"The only thing I know is *dzy gen*."

"Oh, I know that one—see you again!" He stacked the cards and shoved them in his hip pocket. "What can I do for you?"

"For one thing, you can tell me why your maid's running this place like the tsar's palace."

"Chin?"

"I guess that's her name."

"She doesn't usually do that."

"I don't know what she does, but according to her, Karpel and Winston are on vacation and getting to see you is like earning first audience with the Pope on Easter Sunday."

McGraw looked disturbed. "Winston *is* away," he said slowly. "What's on your mind?"

"I don't know, really. Just a vague connection."

"Surely you must have some reason you climbed over the fence of the Liaison Office. That's how you came in, isn't it?"

McGraw looked at me a moment, then picked up a wheelbarrow that was sitting by the side of the lawn and started wheeling it toward the tool shed. He was obviously the outdoor type with a rugged distaste for idleness. No wonder China appealed to him.

"Where'd Winston go?" I asked, following him along.

"Hangchow . . . he and his wife."

"Funny. I thought he went to Hong Kong."

"Why'd you think that?"

"The Peninsula Hotel. Doesn't he go there all the time?"

"Not that I know of . . . why?"

"Oh, I heard it was popular with your staff."

He turned and looked at me again. "I wouldn't know about that. I've only been here a month."

"Hey, what's going on?" A sharp voice came from across the lawn. It was Karpel, striding toward us. "You can't be here," he said, looking me up and down like a sergeant. "You'll get us all in trouble."

"What's the problem?" asked McGraw.

"He's been restricted to quarters at the Peking Hotel, unless in the presence of a guide."

"How do you know?"

"Public Security informed us. There's a memo on your desk." Karpel looked distressed.

"I guess I missed it."

"Well, we can't have him here, that's certain. Under any circumstances. Something like this could jeopardize all sorts of complex negotiations."

"I suppose so," said McGraw.

"I told Chin to keep him out." Karpel put his hand behind my back and started to push me forward. "Come on, you. Let's go."

"Easy, pal, huh?"

"Easy? You're lucky we don't turn you in to the Chinese."

Karpel gave me a nasty shove. I glanced back at McGraw, who was standing by the wheelbarrow, looking nonplussed.

"I wish you had made an appointment," he said.

Yen was walking up and down in the lobby when I arrived back in the hotel. I didn't think he had seen me come in, but to be on the safe side, I bought a drink at the bar and drifted out into the lounging area with my head buried in another dispatch from the Tsinhua News Agency. Halfway across, I sank into a chair, sipping and reading. It wasn't long before Yen sidled over and sat down alongside of me.

"Well, Moses," he said, "I hear your friends have given you the sack." He sounded pleased with his mastery of American slang.

196

"Wasn't the first time and it won't be the last."

"I was looking for you. Where were you?"

"Reading. Over in the old building." I motioned vaguely in the direction of the other wing. "Anything special?"

"No. I was just wondering if you had any ideas about the duck."

"No, I don't," I said, scarcely looking up from the dispatch.

"You know, speaking personally, I wish you the best of luck."

"Thank you, Yen."

"I would like you to leave China as quickly as possible."

Across the bar, I could see Liu entering the lobby. She was right on time. It was five o'clock. But when she saw me with Yen, I saw her visibly stiffen. I wondered if she was going to turn around and leave.

"I'm very surprised a member of your group would do such a thing," Yen continued. "Unfortunately, your group will soon be restricted to quarters and without doubt your investigation will be greatly impeded. That being the case, I offer you my personal assistance. You may call on me at any time to deal with matters that may be beyond your reach within the confines of the hotel."

I looked at Yen. What did he know? Had Liu told him about the bad element? How sentimental of me to have trusted her. How foolish. I looked over at Liu, who was standing near the hotel desk facing the other direction, and back to Yen again.

"Thanks anyway, Yen," I said. "But you said it yourself—I got the sack."

I stood and started walking toward Liu, but I continued right past her into the elevator, holding the door open with my toe for a while until I heard footsteps. Then I let it close and pressed the button for the third floor. When the door opened, I headed straight for the hall man. "Do you speak English?" I asked. His blank expression was my answer.

It didn't change much when he saw me walking back

toward the elevator and standing there, staring up at the number panel like it was the sacred relic of some arcane religion. The dial didn't move. I estimated the chances that Liu would follow me up at one in ten, and my own ability to persuade her to come with me at less than that, but I couldn't see the sense of going if she didn't.

Someone entered the elevator at the main floor and I watched the numbers move—one, two, three . . . four, five, six, seven, eight. That took care of it. Whatever initiative I had drained out of me in an instant. This wasn't my affair anyway, any more than it was any of the others'. If they had no use for me, then I had no use for them. I would go into retirement and let nature or dialectical materialism—whichever ruled—take its course.

The hall man continued to regard me as just another of those odd foreigners as I stepped forward and pressed the up button. I watched the numbers come down again—eight, seven, six, five, four, three. The doors parted. I walked forward.

"Go up to four," said the voice behind me.

I nodded and entered the elevator.

She had come up the stairs.

"What was wrong with three?" I asked her when we met again on the floor above.

"Nothing," she said, "but you were there first."

"Yes. That's true." She was more careful than I.

"What do you want?"

"Shanghai."

"Shanghai?"

"Yes. I want to go to Shanghai tonight."

She looked at me as if I were crazy.

"I want you to come with me."

Liu threw back her head and laughed, saying something in Chinese I imagined was an ancient proverb like "Beware of lunatics in white skin" or "A man from the West will come and drown you in the Yellow River!"

"I understand I'll need a guide," I explained.

"That is not all you need. You need permission to leave Peking."

"You mean officially?"

"Yes, officially. That would be impossible for you."

"Yes, for Moses Wine. Not the way Comrade Huang is feeling these days . . . but how about for Craig Williams of the *Toronto Globe & Mail?*"

I produced an envelope and handed it to Liu.

"He does not look much like you," she said, examining the document inside.

"I thought we all looked alike."

"That is not funny."

"Yeah . . . you're right. I'll wear a hat."

She folded the paper back into the envelope and returned it to me. "It does not matter. It is impossible."

"Impossible?"

"Yes. Impossible . . . and I do not know why you wish to go to Shanghai anyway."

"To catch a bad element."

"How do you propose to do that?"

"I don't know. Look, Liu, we don't have time left for games. Your Public Security people are restricting us to quarters and about to put us on trial. Some bastard down at the U.S. Liaison is treating me like a leper, and practically everyone in our group hates each other's guts—all because some duck disappeared. Meanwhile, there's a bad element down in Shanghai who might, just might, be able to put it all together for us. I'd like to go see him."

"Then go . . . You are so good at getting in and out of places, you could sneak on the train, hide in the baggage or something."

"And how would I question him, in Greek or in Italian, assuming I could find him?"

"How were you going to find him in the first place?"

"You're from Shanghai. I thought you could help me."

"There are ten million people in Shanghai."

"And according to what you've been telling us, they're all

meticulously organized into factory brigades, production teams, Young Pioneers, Red Guards, three-in-one committees, PLA platoons, Face-the-Sun Courtyards and what-have-you, except for a minuscule handful of misguided bad elements who run around at ideological random like wild roosters in the commune eggery. They shouldn't be hard to find."

She turned and headed for the elevator.

"What're you doing that for?" I said.

"I was wrong."

"What?"

"You have no hope to understand China."

"Now what the—"

"Your mind is so warped by bourgeois ideology you will never be able to see anything objectively."

"Hey, now wait a minute, comrade." I took hold of her arm before she could press the elevator button. "There's some question about who's the one not seeing objectively!"

"I don't think so."

"And the only thing warping my mind around here is you."

She turned and looked at me. I let go of her arm.

"Then there is another reason I should not go to Shanghai."

"That may be," I said," but you don't have a choice."

"I don't?"

"No."

"Why is that?"

"Because I will tell Comrade Huang the truth."

"What is that?"

"You know better than I."

"Do I?"

"Yes."

"What?"

"That you took the duck."

The hall man came by wheeling a load of towels.

XXVI THAT EVENING Tien An Men had the appearance of a military encampment. Thousands of people were gathered in small clusters across the vast square, talking or playing cards on stools temporarily erected on the cement. There was an air of hushed expectancy, related, I assumed, to the meeting of the Eleventh Party Congress inside the Great Hall, which was reported to be drawing to its conclusion. From where I stood near the foot of the Mao Memorial, the number of PLA troops guarding the door seemed to have doubled at least since I saw it earlier. A row of black Red Flag limousines were tightly parked along the curb behind them, a half-dozen armed half-tracks flanking the limousines on either end.

It was not difficult to guess the reasons for these precautions. For a society seemingly so placid and organized, China was still convulsed by revolution only inches beneath the surface. The Cultural Revolution may have occurred in the mid-sixties, but as recently as 1975 Tien An Men itself had been the scene of violent confrontations, supporters of the beloved Chou En-lai demonstrating against the temporary eclipse of their hero. At any moment it could happen again. Because of whom . . . ? The Gang of Four?

I checked my watch. It was six-twenty-five. I had agreed to meet Liu at six-thirty, here at the Mao Memorial instead of at the hotel, so we could go to the railroad station together without arousing suspicion. I could already see a figure I thought was she, making her way toward me across the immense square. She was carrying one of the black vinyl bags the Travel Service guides seemed to take with them everywhere and staring at the ground in front of her as she walked. When she was a hundred feet away from me, I knew that it was she. I admit I had considered turning her in. It would have been the simplest thing and would have been peculiarly Chinese, sacrificing this one individual to the needs of a group. But I knew there was more involved here, that she had done all this on purpose, and that I would have to see it through to the end. And then there were the strange feelings I felt for her.

Just then she turned left, veering onto the Fan Ti Lu, which runs along the ancient city gate. I followed along it a steady distance behind her, reasonably certain our presences would not be connected by the masses of bicyclists and pedestrians returning home from work. In a couple of blocks, the railroad station came into view, a strange amalgam of socialist realism and traditional Chinese architecture. In another block I could hear "The Internationale" playing from loudspeakers attached to the eaves of the roof. As ambivalent as the lyrics of the song had made me feel all my life, the unabashed romanticism of its melody always got to me. I wondered how it made Liu feel, leading this latter-day revisionist to the steps of the Peking Station.

When I entered the building, she was waiting in the lobby, half-hidden behind a column.

"Wait here for me," she said, and crossed to the other side toward the ticket kiosks. There were perhaps a dozen, but only two of them were open. I could see her gesticulating to the man inside, passing over my phony papers and the wad of yuans I had given her. He scrutinized it all carefully, recording the information on elaborate forms. On the other side of

202

the room another group of foreigners—they looked Slavic—waited patiently for their guides while the loudspeaker announced the departure of a train in that shrill high-pitched style that is characteristically Chinese. I could see people filing through the back toward the gates.

Liu signaled to me and I followed her, heading along the side of the lobby to the door. She moved quickly, reaching the ticket taker and showing him my papers before I was close enough for him to see the discrepancies between my face and the picture on the papers. He nodded to me and I passed through to the top of the boarding platform. In front of me was the Shanghai Express, a gleaming green diesel with a red star on it and thirteen or fourteen passenger cars behind. For a moment I lost Liu among the crowds of people pushing and shoving, waving to each other or saying goodbye. I finally caught a glimpse of her six cars down, just as she was reaching up to pull herself on. I rushed forward, bumping into a pair of PLA officers, who eyed me curiously as I slipped past them and moved down the platform halfway between a walk and a run.

I could see Liu edging her way down the corridor when I reached the steps and climbed on. It was a first-class car with the posh appointments of another era—wood-paneled walls and individual compartments in the European style. The first few were occupied by the Slavs and the next by four cadres who were already buried in some heavy paperwork. The two after that were empty. I continued on to the last compartment, where I saw Liu seated inside, across from an older gentleman who was smoking and drinking tea. I sat down next to her and poured myself some of the tea from a white ceramic pot. There were two short whistles and the train pulled out of the station. We were on our way to Shanghai.

I didn't know if I was supposed to speak to Liu or to acknowledge her presence in any way, but we were hardly two minutes out when she spoke to me directly.

"You must keep these," she said, handing me back my "papers" and what I guessed was my ticket. The old gentleman smiled at me and asked Liu a question. She gave a brief reply.

"What'd he want?"

"He wanted to know who you are. I told him you are a journalist from Canada."

I nodded to him and he launched into an impassioned speech, sawing the air with his cigarette and then spitting into a spittoon at his feet as he concluded.

"What was that?" I asked.

"Be very careful when you feed the bear or he will turn around and bite you."

"What?"

"He means the Canadians should not sell wheat to the Russians. Soviet social imperialism is the greatest threat to world peace today."

"Tell him I couldn't agree more."

"That's not true. You do not care."

"What's that supposed to mean?"

"You are a cynical, self-serving person."

"Hey, now wait a minute—"

"You have no need to serve the people of any country. You think only of yourself."

"How do you know?"

"Because I have observed you."

"Observed me? Where the hell do you get off—do you see inside my head?"

She said nothing.

"Just tell that dude what I said!"

"Dude?"

"Him!" I pointed emphatically.

Liu glared at me and reported what I had said to the man, who bobbed his head approvingly. The train rattled on, picking up speed as it headed through the outskirts of Peking.

"Maybe we should get him out of here," I said.

"What for?"

"Just to be on the safe side. The next couple of compartments are empty."

"You are not a good person," she said.

"Oh, come on—not that again!" I slammed my hand on the table for emphasis, jarring the tea. The old man looked up, startled. "Listen, I know I forced you into this, but you're as responsible for what's going on as I am, maybe more so. And if you want to fight about it, we sure as hell *better* get him out of here!"

"I don't want to fight about it," she said, and took a book out of her black bag. I looked out the window. It was almost dark and I could only make out the silhouettes of what must have been farming communes beginning to dot the urban landscape.

"How long is this going to take?" I asked.

"Sixteen hours."

"I'm sorry you didn't tell me. I've been meaning to read Proust for years."

"You are lucky. Last year, before the diesel, it took twenty-five."

"What're you reading?"

"The fifth volume of Chairman Mao's works."

"Naturally."

She looked up at me flatly. "There is much to study. I'm sure *you* like detective stories."

"No, I don't, actually. They usually sacrifice everything to the plot."

But she wasn't listening to my answer. Her head was buried deep in the pages of Volume V. I wondered how many times she had read it before, how much of it she had memorized, and how many study sessions she had attended to discuss it. It all took a peculiar sort of discipline. I marveled at it the way I marveled at friends in graduate school who had to read *The Faerie Queene* or *The Epic of Gilgamesh* dozens of times to satisfy their thesis advisers.

A porter opened the door of our compartment and leaned his head in.

"It is time for dinner," said Liu. "You must go."

The old man got up and left.

"You're not coming?" I asked her.

"No. I will read."

"You won't be hungry?"

She shrugged. I saw the group of Slavs moving down the corridor. They looked like a convention of trade union officials from Newark.

"It's too dangerous, huh?"

"Everything is too dangerous. It was too dangerous to come, too dangerous for me to be here, dangerous for you, dangerous for your group . . . dangerous for China and America."

"For China and America?"

"We live in a world of great-nation chauvinism."

"What does that have to do with it?"

"There is a poem by Mao: 'Ants on the locust tree assume a great-nation swagger/ And mayflies lightly plot to topple the giant tree./ The west wind scatters leaves over Ch'ang An,/ And the arrows are flying, twanging.' "

"Will you, uh . . . speak English?"

"But I am Chinese."

"I hadn't noticed."

"Ah, the famous sarcasm of Moses Wine."

"Not exactly famous."

"But that is not so. We have read much about you here in China. Leading members of the translation section study every issue of *Modern Times* magazine with great care."

I looked at Liu. So my media reputation had preceded me to China. I was not just an index card of vital statistics transferred from brief entries on a visa application, but MOSES WINE—GUMSHOE OF THE SIXTIES GENERATION! I wondered what that could have meant to the Chinese. But it must have meant something to Liu.

"That's why you took the duck, isn't it?" I said.

"Yes and no."

"What other reason could there be? Nancy Lemon was right, wasn't she? The person who stole the duck didn't do it

206

to get rich. He—that is, she—did it to keep us in China . . . keep me in China."

"But how did you know I was the one?" she said. The whistle blew as the train rattled across a bridge. In the black window, I could see the reflection of the white-jacketed porter walking back up the corridor.

"Well, I told you before, I didn't think anybody in our group would be that foolish . . . and you were always trying to tell me yourself."

"I was?"

"Only I wasn't listening. Like when we were in the Forbidden City just before the duck was taken and you were so casual about our leaving China. And later at the restaurant, when I said this was my last meal in China and you hinted it wasn't so. And then the peasant song about the Jade Emperor not existing—you sang that the first day we were here. It's as if you had planned the whole thing from the very beginning."

"In a way. . . ."

"You're not a very good criminal, Liu."

"Perhaps I did not want to be."

"No. You were hiring yourself an American detective. But what I can't figure out is why."

She stood up. "Let us go to dinner."

"Not until you explain it to me."

"There are some things it is better we do not know about each other." She slipped the hinge and slid open the compartment door.

We started out. "And by the way," I said, "thanks for the warning."

"Warning?"

"On the postcard you left in my room in Shanghai. It kept me on my toes."

"You're welcome."

I followed her up the corridor to the dining car, which was already filled with a couple of foreign groups and a scattering of cadres. The car was in the same imperial style as the compartments, with paneled walls and tables set with white linen and flowers. I started down the aisle, when I saw the members of the Ethiopian volleyball team, who were joking and drinking mao tai. I quickly averted my eyes, pretending not to notice their stares of recognition, and hurried behind Liu to the last table, sitting down immediately with my back to the rest of the car. The train rounded a bend. Through a crack in the curtain, I could see through the window to the next coach, where a large number of Chinese were seated on benches, crowded together in the equivalent of second class in this classless society.

"You know them?" Liu asked, sitting down opposite me.

"The Ethiopians? They were at the Peking Hotel. Some of them took a fancy to Ruby Crystal."

"I think they recognized you."

"Does that matter?"

She did not answer as a waiter came by with orange soda and Tsingtao beer. I chose the beer. Liu hesitated a moment, then took the beer also. I hoisted a glass.

"What do we say—to friendship?"

"Yes. To friendship," she said.

We drank. The waiter returned with hors d'oeuvres and plates of kung p'ao shrimp and Szechuan pork. Liu smiled when she saw me gobbling them down. They were followed by a plate of something viscous, almost slimy, which I couldn't swallow.

"Sea slugs," she explained. I watched as she trapped a piece in her chopsticks and lifted it to her lips. "You must try it," she said. "You must always experience for yourself."

"Did Chairman Mao say that?"

"No. But he did say—"

"I know—'If you want knowledge, you must take part in the practice of changing reality. If you want to know the taste of a pear, you must change the pear by eating it yourself.' I'll hold you to that one."

"Chairman Mao always advised the revolutionary to be selective."

"Right."

I gritted my teeth and gulped down a chunk of the slug, following it up with a healthy dose of Tsingtao. The waiter came by and refilled our glasses and Liu and I swilled down more of the beer. By this time the Ethiopians were getting boisterous. A couple of them were standing in the aisle, drinking. I could hear some mention of a match with Peking Number Two Workers Team and a score, but I couldn't tell who had come out on top and I wasn't sure the Ethiopians cared.

One of them stumbled down to our table with a bottle of plum wine in his hand.

"Friendship first, competition second," he said. "You know that is what they say here in China—'Friendship first, competition second!' "

"Sounds good to me," I said. "I never won a game in my life."

The Ethiopian laughed and poured some wine in my glass. "She is beautiful Chinese girl." He motioned toward Liu. "How you get such beautiful Chinese girl in this place?"

"I don't have her. This is China. Nobody *has* anybody here."

"No. But you with her. First time I ever saw foreign man with Chinese girl. How you do that?"

"Lucky, I guess."

"Where you from, brother?"

"The world."

"Oh, come on, brother. I from Addis Ababa. Where you from?"

"Canada," I mumbled.

He stared at me, leaning back with an eye cocked doubtfully. He must have been six feet four. The train rattled across a bridge. I could just make out the silhouette of a boat on the river below.

"You are American," he said.

I shrugged. He turned and said something to the others in what I assumed was Amharic. Someone answered back.

"You are American," he repeated. The rest of his group had swiveled in their chairs and were looking at me with stern expressions. "American," he said again. The word echoed in my brain as I gazed into his eyes, which were suddenly filled with the bitterness of the Third World. I'm not responsible for it all—not responsible, I wanted to tell him. And besides, it wasn't so bad as they thought. It had its good sides, its redeeming features. But somehow I couldn't get the words out.

"What are you doing here?" said the Ethiopian.

The Slavic group had now turned and was also staring at me. I looked at Liu. She was worried, staring down at her plate, her chopsticks frozen to the rice.

"Business," I said.

"Business?"

"Yes, for an American company, exporting from Shanghai."

"But where is the rest of your group?"

"Back in Peking."

"And why do you say you are Canadian?"

"Well, I—"

"This is not necessary," Liu broke in. "If you demand an explanation, I will tell you. He is an undesirable foreigner and I am escorting him out of China."

"Oh, I see," said the Ethiopian, exchanging glances with his countrymen and turning back to Liu. "What has he done?"

"Activities offending the morals of the Chinese people. They cannot be discussed." The Ethiopian looked at me in amazement. "And now if you will excuse us . . ." Liu nodded to me and we stood. "I must make sure he returns to his compartment." She dropped some yuans on the table and escorted me out. I could hear the Ethiopian whispering behind us as we pushed through the door into the next car.

The Pullman beds were already down when we got back to our compartment. The old man, who had returned ahead of us, was unzipping his overnight bag. Liu walked around in front of him and, putting her hand on the bed he had selected, began to speak with him in Chinese. The man appeared angry. He started shouting at Liu, who shouted back at him. The man lifted the bag onto the bed. Liu pushed it off. He started to pull out his pajamas. Liu grabbed his hand. They yelled some more at each other, the argument intensifying. Finally the man threw up his hands, zipped his bag, and walked out of the comparment, yanking the door hard behind him.

"What was that?" I asked.

"He wouldn't leave."

"I gathered."

"I told him Canadians had many bad dreams and snored all night like horses."

"Thanks." I smiled.

"I did it for security. Don't get any ideas."

"Who, me? I didn't say anything."

She shrugged. "Americans are obsessed."

"How do you know?"

"There was a man on a tour in May. He sat next to me on every bus from Canton to Mongolia, whispering in my ear while trying to push his hand under my bottom. Then he would rub my thigh and whisper I was the prettiest Bolshevik since Trotsky's second wife."

"Who was that?"

"A Marxist historian from the University of Chicago."

She smiled slyly and hoisted her valise onto the upper berth. Then she turned away from me and started to undress.

I took out my pajamas and began to unbutton my shirt. The train was swaying from side to side and I was feeling peculiarly short of breath. I had that same tugging in my stomach I had when I was a little boy in dancing school. Or back in Berkeley, when I went to eat dinner in Chinatown.

211

"You are a strange man, Moses," she said. "You do not seem to be the nephew of Sonya Lieberman."

"Why not?"

"She is committed to a better world. Sometimes this is difficult for you."

"Sometimes."

I caught a glimpse of amber skin as she slipped out of her blouse into a nightshirt.

"But you are good."

She climbed into the upper berth and flicked out the light.

"Be careful of these bad elements, Moses. They study martial arts."

"And they carry guns."

"Good night."

"Good night."

I stood there a moment in the darkness. Outside, China was rolling by. It was hard to conceive that I was really there, halfway around the world, riding through the night on a mission I only barely understood, for reasons that were even more elusive. It appeared to me that what I had done was automatic, that I was an investigator by compulsion and that the ambivalence I had had about my occupation back home had actually been a form of self-pity, what they would call here in China "petit-bourgeois vacillation," the kind of luxurious emotion the masses could ill afford. And that, finally, to look for the truth beneath surfaces was an honorable profession, a worthwhile endeavor given the choices we have—even in the tawdry clothes of the private dick.

But this compulsion is not simple. It comes in several different guises at once, some of them potent and others evanescent. But it was clear to me that in this case the most powerful of them was the woman in the bed six inches away from my forehead—this dragon lady in a Mao suit, without a stitch of makeup, who had stolen a duck in order to force me to perform tasks of which I had only the slightest inkling and for reasons of which I knew less.

I slipped into the berth beneath her and lay there for a

while, swaying with the train and staring up at her bunk. Her presence was very real to me. I knew she was awake. I could hear her breathing, moving. The air of South China was thick and palpable. I wanted her so badly I could almost taste her thighs through the bed platform.

"Liu . . . ?"

". . . Yes?"

"I . . ."

"Yes?"

I didn't say anything.

"Is something wrong?"

"No."

The train screeched, pulling into a station.

"Where are we?"

"Lin Nan."

"Are you able to sleep?"

"What?"

"Can you sleep?" I repeated.

"I do not know. I have only been in bed two minutes."

The train lurched forward, relocating itself along the platform.

"What does it matter?" she said.

"I don't know. . . . I guess it doesn't."

"Do you have any other questions?"

"I suppose not."

"If you want to sleep with me, you must say so."

I sat up straight. "Of course I want to sleep with you."

"Why?"

"Why???"

"Yes, why?"

"Why? Because . . . it must be obvious, Liu. I think you are a very attractive woman."

"So?"

"Well, that means something, doesn't it? Beautiful, attractive, brilliant—exceptional in every way. In America, I'd say I was crazy about you."

"What does that mean?"

"I just told you what it means."

"In China we choose our mates by their politics."

"I know, Liu."

"Your politics are not right. Whatever your sympathies, you are still a member of a reactionary ruling-class elite."

"I know, Liu."

"Your mind has been infected by the disease of individualism."

"I know."

"And materialism."

"Yes."

"I understand why you want me even if you do not."

"Why is that?"

A conductor walked past our window, urging some passengers down the platform. Most of them seemed like farmers, country people. I could just make out the form of a peasant woman, hurrying under the lamp with a basket of scallions for her departing husband.

"Speaking bluntly, I am what you do not have."

"That's for sure."

"No. I do not mean that. . . . I mean to say I represent something to you."

"What?"

"A kind of object."

"An object?"

"For Moses Wine, a simple souvenir of China would not mean much—even a jade duck of the Western Han Dynasty. But to have slept with a Chinese Communist guide!"

"Oh, come on!"

"You think I am joking?"

"I hope you are."

"Then what am I? You cannot know me. I am only a symbol to you."

"Of what?"

"The Orient . . . the New China . . . something. A story for your friends when you return."

"That's all, is it?"

"Not all."

"What else?"

"You are attracted to me because you think you cannot have me . . . because I come from a society so much more moral than your own."

"Maybe."

"We must make sacrifices for the new society, give up our personal pleasure for the betterment of all."

"I know that."

"But you do not know what that means! You do not know how hard it is!"

Her voice was suddenly painful—an accusation and a cry. "How could I, Liu? What're you trying to tell me?"

"You are divorced?"

"Yes."

"In your country all you do is snap your fingers and you are separated."

"More or less."

"For me, it is not so simple."

"For you?"

"My husband and I do not get along. We have not had children and for many years we have not even slept together. Four years ago I made an application. . . ."

"And?"

"So far I have heard nothing."

The train jolted to a start. I looked up at Liu's berth. I wanted to ask her a lot of questions but I knew I shouldn't. I lay there in silence as some people moved down the corridor, looking for their compartments.

"You realize how difficult this would be for me," she said.

"Sabotage of the family?"

"Yes . . . I would lose my job, perhaps worse . . . perhaps. . . ."

"But you have already risked that."

"Yes."

The train whistled and raced into a tunnel.

There was another long silence as the compartment seemed to close in around us.

The train emerged from the tunnel. A dim shaft of moonlight illuminated the room. I could see the washbasin and mirror and the narrow clothes closet by the door.

Liu draped her hand over the side of her berth.

I reached out and took it.

A pair of legs slid over the edge beneath a large cotton nightshirt.

China, China, China.

XXVII   "THEY ARE looking for us."

I opened my eyes to see Liu, fully dressed, standing beside me. We were riding an elevated platform between narrow streets. Plots of land had been cultivated between the buildings, three- or four-story housing complexes of recent vintage.

"How do you know?"

"I heard someone speaking to the conductor in Nanking. The Ethiopians were with him. I don't think they believed my story."

"Where are we?"

"Shanghai . . . the northern district."

I jumped up. "They'll be waiting at the station. When can we get off?"

"Two miles—the train slows by the Huang Pu."

I pulled on my briefs and went to the window. Outside, the train was rounding a bend into the city. I could see the river in the distance, the first beams of the rising sun filtering through the haze onto the austere German facades of the bund. I felt Liu against my side. She looked haggard, exhausted. I doubted she had slept all night since she left my bed. I moved to put my arm around her, but she backed away, avoiding my glance.

I turned and opened the door into the corridor. One of the Ethiopians was standing by the W.C., smoking. The train whistled twice, heading into a more populated area. But it wasn't slowing down. I envisioned Comrade Huang and his cohorts waiting for us at the Shanghai station, a couple of black limousines parked by the platform, shades drawn, ready to take us on a long drive to a concentration camp in Manchuria with commissars and barbed wire out of bad Korean War movies. But to jump was madness.

I turned back to Liu. In her face was a resignation that startled me, a frightening Oriental calm I was not able to comprehend, as if the adrenal glands secreted some strange tranquilizer instead of adrenaline.

Then the train began to slow, approaching a dirt embankment rolling down into what appeared to be a wrecking yard. A series of alleys shot off between brick warehouses with an odd resemblance to the mill towns of Massachusetts.

"Is this it?"

Liu nodded and slid past me down the corridor. I followed. The Ethiopian eyed us suspiciously, then came after us. I could hear him calling for us to stop. Halfway through the door, I made an abrupt turn and slammed into his chest, sending him sprawling backward into the corridor. Then I spun around, pushing Liu through the door ahead of me, locking it with a bolt as it shut.

The solitary waiter in the dining car looked at us with a startled expression. Liu started to reason with him, but I grabbed him by the collar and threw him into the car behind. We ran forward and opened the door onto the rear platform. Outside, the train suddenly seemed to be moving twice as fast. Liu looked at me doubtfully.

"Jump forward and roll."

"How do you know?"

"I saw it in the movies once."

"Always jokes," she said, and turned back to me.

"Please, Liu. We don't have any choice."

I squeezed her hand and she turned away again. The wind was blowing across the side of her face.

Then she leaped off the train, leaving me staring down at

218

the ground beneath me. It was whirling before my eyes, the features blurred like the words on the label of a 78 RPM record.

I glanced back at Liu, who was bouncing down the embankment like a tin can coming off a conveyor belt. Then I stepped off. The ground flew up at me. I crashed into it and bounced, sliding down the side on my stomach. Gravel tore at my shirt and hands. I felt something sharp go into my knee. Then I dragged to a halt by an upended wheelbarrow. I looked over at Liu. She was sitting twenty feet away from me, clutching her leg.

"Are you all right?"

She didn't answer but pulled herself up and started limping toward an alleyway. Blood was pouring from a large cut in the side of her calf. At the entry of the alley she stumbled, slumping to her feet against a wall.

I ran over, ripping some cloth from my shirt and kneeling to tie it around her.

"You need a doctor," I said, twisting the cloth into a tourniquet.

"No, no. You must go ahead."

"Forget it. I'm taking you to a hospital." I started to slip my arms under her to pick her up, but she grabbed my hand.

"No. Please. You go. I will get help later . . . after."

"After what? This is crazy, Liu! I don't have the slightest idea what's going on here!"

"You are going to catch the bad element."

"Yes, but for what?"

Liu took a deep breath and closed her eyes. Her amber skin was turning white with pain. She trembled slightly. I trembled, too, envisioning the scar this cut would leave on her beautiful leg, if she were fortunate enough to get off that easily.

She nodded toward a shed. "I will wait there. Bring the bad element back to me. We must prove he is working for Yen."

219

"For Yen?"

"Yes."

"I don't get it."

"For years he has been doing it, trying to discredit our country in the eyes of foreigners. First the French and the English. Now the Americans. He uses every method possible."

"Yen?" I repeated.

"Yes. Yen."

She pressed down with the palms of her hands and pushed herself back toward the shed. I opened the door and helped her in. Inside was a storage area for cooking utensils, the walls stacked high with old woks and bamboo vegetable steamers.

"Then all those things that happened—going over the wall, the bad elements attacking us—they were all fabrications? Yen set them up?"

"Yes. Even Fred Lisle asking to stay in Nancy Lemon's hotel room."

I smiled. No wonder Fred had been so pissed off. But then I stopped smiling. Yen was clearly a clever man, one who studied his subjects closely and worked off their own vulnerability. And at the moment, I never felt more vulnerable.

"Why is he doing it?" I asked.

"To sabotage relations between our countries . . . to prevent normalization between China and America."

"For whom?"

"Our enemies."

"The Taiwanese?"

"Perhaps . . . maybe the Russians."

"But I don't understand. Why do you need me? Why don't you just accuse him yourself?"

"First, because I think he has an American confederate. Someone who has brought money. You must find that out. But more important, because of who I was."

"Your class background?"

220

She shook her head.

"Then what?"

"It does not matter for you to know."

"Liu!"

"You would not understand."

"Goddamn it! I don't care if I don't understand. I just want to know what the hell's going on!"

"It is not good for you to know."

"And it's not good for you to sit around some dusty shed getting gangrene in your leg. Now, why the hell couldn't you do this yourself?"

"Because of her," she mumbled.

"Her?"

Liu's eyes closed again. "There is some water in the bag."

I lifted the overnight bag off her shoulder and took out a plastic thermos, uncorking it and holding it to her lips. She drank for several seconds before pulling away. Then she opened her eyes.

"I worked for her for seven years!" she said.

"Who? Goddamn it, Liu! Who?"

"Comrade Chiang Ching . . . I was her personal translator from the Cultural Revolution to the smashing of the Gang of Four. No one would listen to me now."

"No. I guess not."

I gave Liu another drink of water. So she was Chiang Ching's personal translator. No wonder she had had trouble obtaining a divorce. That was probably the least of it.

A fly alighted on her nose and she swatted it away. "Away with all pests," I thought, remembering Mao's poem. "Our force is irresistible!"

It had come to this, his revolution—a woman forced to prevaricate, to risk all, in order to defend it from itself. Contradictions, contradictions. Always contradictions. One always splits into two. Mao had warned that there would be those who would wave the Red Flag to attack the Red Flag. Now it was the reverse. He had also warned that a revolution was not a dinner party. No doubt he was right about that. From the looks of Liu, I doubted she would ever make it to the hors d'oeuvres table.

I doubted she wanted to, either. I marveled at her dedication, but it troubled me. Or maybe I just couldn't make the leap into serving the people. Maybe I was corrupt to the core. I had no way of knowing. I was confronted once again by the old metaphor of the Chinese boxes, opening one after another after another without end. Only now I was getting down to smaller and smaller boxes, watching them diminish beyond vision, like some puzzled graduate student searching for minutiae beyond the power of his electron microscope.

"You must go," she said.

I nodded.

"Touch my hand . . . please."

I reached out.

"Be careful, Moses. Yen will do anything. . . . That man who died in the commune—he was working with me."

XXVIII I walked through the doors of the Jin Jiang Hotel in the middle of a group of French tourists. The heavy perfume of the women seemed out of place, almost obscene, in China. I crushed with them into the elevator and went up, hoping no one would remark upon this odd American with a dirty, scraped face and torn shirt. It was a calculated risk, of course, but I assumed the last place the authorities would look for me in Shanghai would be right here in the bowels of socialist tourism. I also knew I would need a new identity, something to disguise my obvious middle-class Western persona.

The elevator opened on the third floor and I got out, leaving the French behind me as the elevator continued upward. Then I walked by the hall man without looking up until I turned the corner at the end of the corridor. I paused there a few seconds, waiting to see if he would follow me, then opened the first door. It was unlocked, of course. I had expected that, all the belongings being safe from intruders in proletarian China. I saw a tape recorder on the bureau and a Beaulieu movie camera. Then I opened the wardrobe. Inside were four or five men's suits, dark and of the European cut. I tried on one of the jackets and looked in the mirror. It wasn't a bad fit, but as a disguise it was worthless.

I closed the door and hurried on to the next room. It was occupied by two women who, between them, appeared to have brought the entire fall line from Christian Dior. I was clearly in the wrong area.

I waited for the hall man to disappear and headed down to the opposite end. The first door I tried was locked. What was this? A heresy? A lack of faith? But the next one was opened. I entered and shut the door behind me. At first I wasn't sure the room was being used. There was nothing on the bureau and the bed did not look as if it had been slept in. But when I opened the armoire it had everything I needed— it was lined from end to end with Arab *galibiyas*! I took the first one off the hanger and slipped it over my clothes. A perfect fit if I did say so myself. Then I found a red-and-white headdress, walked over to the mirror and began to adjust it.

I smiled. I had to admit I liked how I looked. It reminded me of my ancestors. And I guessed I enjoyed the irony of Moses Wine, Jewish-American, dressed in the costume I recognized immediately as that of the Palestine Liberation Organization.

My first test was the hall man and I passed it with flying colors, bowing to him with a polite "Salaam" as I waltzed into the elevator.

The lobby was not difficult either. I walked through it slowly, stopping, as a test, to peruse the postcards at the hotel post office. The woman behind the counter was good enough to point out several views of the Taching Oil Refinery with descriptions in Arabic. I demurred and left.

Outside I proceeded along the Nanching Road in the general direction of the Industrial Exhibition Hall. There was little chance the bad element would be repeating his performance for another group of foreigners, but it was the only lead I had in this city of ten million. According to my map I had a way to go, about two and a half miles, but I could use the opportunity to think things over. I had a lot to consider, all Liu had told me. I found it difficult to focus, however. I kept thinking of Liu herself, holed up in that shed, her leg throbbing as the heat built up under the corrugated roof. Three times I almost turned and went back to her, but for what—to satisfy my own needs, my own overwhelming desire to be with her, even though her purposes and mine were best served by finding the bad element and bringing Yen and his confederates to justice.

But what justice? And justice for what? Don't intrigue and conspire. Unite and don't split. Be open and aboveboard. Stop carrying on with your Gang of Four. Avoid splitism, revisionism, ismism. It was all swimming around in my head. The idea that Liu had spent seven years of her life with Chiang Ching was incredible to me—seven years with Mao's own wife, the woman who tried to turn China upside down by purifying revolutionary culture while watching Garbo movies. At the very least, it couldn't have been boring.

Before we split up that morning I had wanted to ask Liu about Chiang Ching, but the atmosphere was hardly conducive to casual inquiries. And yet my curiosity was great. Perhaps it was the detective in me, unable to resist one of the most puzzling of contemporary crimes. Was Chiang Ching guilty of sabotage or was she not? Was she an idealist bent on changing the very essence of human nature, or a clever propagandist who spent her life manipulating ideologies for her own temporal advantage, a new Dowager Empress determined to rule China politically and intellectually. It was a fascinating conundrum. Even now, as I moved swiftly down the Nanching Road, my consciousness was dominated by the image of a photo I had seen in *Time*, of the young actress riding into the Red base in Yenan, 1937, almost as beautiful herself as her idol, Garbo. What had those men thought, monkishly celibate in their radical redoubt, when this lady from Shanghai appeared among them? No wonder their leader disregarded his own doctrine and took her for his own. No wonder the others resisted and then later made a cult of the new wife. No wonder in his dotage he sponsored her ascendancy and then pulled back.

No wonder . . . no wonder . . . "Chiang Ching has wild ambitions."

The counterattack was vitriolic. Vicious.

Or was it merely a question of Women's Liberation? Who could know? But the Chinese have their own special character for death from exhaustion during intercourse. And I assume, although I have never seen it, that it isn't the woman who dies.

I rounded the corner and caught my first glimpse of the Exhibition Hall. It was crowded, about half a dozen buses lined up along the periphery of the vast concrete patio. A tour leader with a bullhorn was urging on a group of about sixty uniformed Japanese, who marched in a line, waving little white flags as the essentially unruly Chinese looked on with amusement. I followed them in, stopping to buy a ticket for twenty fen at the window in the lobby. For a split second I was startled by the figure reflected in the glass. I had forgotten about my disguise. By the grave of Allah, I muttered, bowing to my reflection, and continued into the center. Although it had only been four days since I had been there, it seemed several weeks. I barely remembered the exhibitions. They appeared to have been rearranged, changed or modernized.

The Japanese descended the step into the main room, which was filled with turbines and generators. I headed after them, stepping carefully for fear I would trip on my *galibiya*. A group of Chinese students approached me on the stairs, pausing to stare at me from below as if I were some refugee from the *Arabian Nights* whose camel got lost on the way to the oasis. My hand shook under the sleeve. I nodded to them without stopping and continued to the bottom of the stairs, hesitating on the last step.

Neither the bad element nor any of his cohorts was in sight. I was beginning to feel faintly ridiculous. If Yen were as intelligent as I assumed he was, he would never repeat a performance and certainly not at the same location. He wouldn't use the same people, either. He probably paid off the son-of-a-bitch and left it at that. And everything was doubtless done through intermediaries. I wouldn't be able to get much out of him. In a society like this, the slightest untied shoelace could send you tripping all the way to Outer Mongolia.

My perplexed expression must have been obvious, because a doughty woman in a gray tunic came up to me, pointing behind a steam turbine and talking a blue streak in a strange language I knew wasn't Chinese. In a split second I realized what it was when a group of Arabs, half of them in Palestinian headdresses just like mine, emerged from the back of the turbine. I looked from them to their doughty guide, wondering for one odd moment where on earth she had learned Arabic. Then I panicked. I backed up the stairs about three steps, turned, and bolted.

I heard shouts and what sounded like an alarm going off. I didn't dare look back. I dashed through the lobby, slowing abruptly when I hit the street, doing my best to smile innocently at the guards, and walking past them into the patio. No one appeared to be following me. I quickened my pace, planning to put as much concrete as possible between me and the Center, when my path was blocked by another bus. The figures inside started to wave at me, pursing their lips and emitting that shrill, high-pitched whistle of greeting I recognized from *The Battle of Algiers*. More Arabs.

I spun about. The Palestinians were standing in the door with some Chinese, pointing at me. I ran around the bus, dodging a truck filled with night soil, and plunged into an alley behind the school across the street, continuing on for a couple of blocks before ducking into a doorway, disrobing immediately and shoving the *galibiya* into an incinerator. Seconds later a Palestinian raced past me, accompanied by two officers from Public Security. They were the first ones I had noticed in China carrying guns.

I descended into the basement. It wasn't until I was under the stairs that I realized I was trembling so much I had to hold the railing for support.

I stayed there until nightfall, hiding behind a broken boiler and thinking about Liu. Late in the afternoon some kids came around, playing a game of something resembling hide-and-seek in the basement. I had to wedge myself far into the crack so they wouldn't see me. I listened to them laughing and I thought about my own kids. I wondered where they were then—getting ready for school, if I correctly calculated the time difference, gobbling down Suzanne's pancakes while complaining she had put too much lecithin or some other health food goop in the batter. It seemed like another world.

That night I emerged on the streets again and headed off toward the river. I had to rely on instinct. My map was gone, consumed in the incinerator with the *galibiya*. The citizens of Shanghai were out in force, playing cards, gossiping, as they had been on my first visit, but this time their eyes seemed filled with suspicion, their offhand remarks pregnant with menace. I wondered if the word was out, the connection made between the false Arab and the missing American, the People's Militia armed and ready to defend the state at all costs.

I felt a hand on my shoulder.

"How are you?" someone said.

I turned to see a young Chinese man in his early twenties smiling thinly at me.

"How are you?" he repeated.

A crowd was gathering around us, the curious Chinese always ready to stare unabashedly at a foreigner.

"Fine," I said. "I'm fine."

"Where are you going?" The man enunciated with the care of one who knows only about fifty words of a language but wants to make sure those count. I had to give him an answer.

"The Great World," I said. "I'm on my way to the Great World."

"The Great World?" The man shook his head and made a

clucking noise. Then he started to laugh. "The Great World is closed."

He turned and related this to the others in Chinese. Some of them laughed, too, but most of them looked disturbed, even sullen.

"I know it is closed. But I wanted to see it anyway."

"You want to see the Great World?" The man scrutinized me briefly, then said something to the others. "We take you to Great World."

He nodded for me to follow him and started off down the street. We hadn't gone fifty feet when I realized we weren't going alone. The whole crowd was following us. And they didn't leave when we turned the corner. I was doing undercover work in China with about five dozen observers trailing me down the street less than a quarter of a block away. It was like tailing a suspect with a cowbell dragging from your ankle and a joy buzzer going off every time you took a step. I wanted to turn around and scare them off, turn into a white devil or something, but I knew it was useless.

We crossed a couple of narrow streets and then a wide boulevard, our parade lengthening as we went. There must not have been a great deal to do at night in the PRC. I seemed to be the prime form of entertainment. I would have laughed, if I hadn't been scared shitless.

We passed a large covered market and came out on the other side of the Nanching Road. I recognized the building across the way, dark and boarded-up as it had been before.

"Is Great World," said my guide.

"I know."

"Great World bad place."

"Oh?"

"Old society. Very bad. Gambling. Bad women. Very bad."

"I know. . . . Well, I'll see you. Thanks for the help."

I waved to the long line of Chinese. They didn't move.

I shrugged and crossed the street anyway, dodging the

stream of bicycles and stopping at the curb for a second to look back at my audience. They were smiling and I had the peculiar sensation they wanted to protect me. In my turn, I felt a growing desire to help them, to demonstrate my solidarity with them and to foil this last-ditch attempt to paint China as the totalitarian monster of Asia before the inevitability of normalization.

I realized then I was standing by the gate of the Great World, only yards away from where we had been attacked in our first confrontation with the bad elements. Oddly, the padlock on the gate was missing. I pushed it open and walked through, into the courtyard of the building.

Suddenly everything was quiet, the traffic on the Nanching Road sounding miles away, my sixty companions seemingly vanished.

I looked around me. All the windows remained boarded with plywood sheets, the doors shut and painted over just as they had been since the Cultural Revolution. Not a sound from anywhere. Not even a creaking sign.

Then I saw a dim crack under a door on the other side of the yard. I walked forward, my footsteps echoing violently off the pavement.

I stopped, proceeding quietly through the portico to the door. There was a dull hum from the grate by the wall. Music. I took another step forward and listened. It was coming from a record player, all right, but the recording was so scratchy they must have been playing it with the flat end of a nail file. Even so, I recognized it immediately. The moaning and reverberation of the guitar took me back twenty years. It was Elvis singing "Don't Be Cruel."

I tried the door. It was locked but the hook-and-eye securing it was easy to slip and I eased it open, keeping my back to the wall outside. A rickety stairway led down to a subterranean area that must once have been a nightclub, judging from the flocked wallpaper and the chintz around the light bulbs. I started down, listening to my footsteps creak on the floorboards. In a room somewhere below, the music

230

switched to one of the old black groups like the Flamingoes or the Charts.

I reached the bottom of the stairs, stepping into a small anteroom with American movie posters on the wall. A half-open door led into a corridor. I could see down it to a large, L-shaped room, where the music was coming from. A couple was doing a stilted version of the twist, the girl in a print dress and the guy wearing pants with a stripe down the side. Off in the corner some others were laughing and gambling with dice near where the bad element I had seen at the baths leaned against a broken jukebox, tapping his toes to the music. I stood there transfixed, looking into this weird time-warp, half prerevolutionary China, half 1959 sock hop, when I felt a cold steel object pushing into my rib cage. I had felt it before, but not often enough to guess the caliber.

"Very good to have you with us, Mr. Wine," said Yen. "American detectives are always welcome at the Great World." He nodded across the way where a dog-eared poster of Bogart in *The Big Sleep* was taped to a screen.

"I wish I could say thanks for the hospitality, Yen."

"You are too sentimental, Mr. Wine."

"About hospitality?"

"About everything . . . about people . . . about China."

"Yeah. I guess you're right about that."

"You forget where you come from. America. She is the most wonderful country."

"I like her, too, Yen. Maybe in different ways than you. But I like her."

"You do not understand. It is not a question of liking. It is a question of truth. The truth is not with China. It is with America." He jabbed the pistol deeper in my ribs. "You do not understand what it is like here. Any of you. You do not know what it means—every day the same, getting up and working hour after hour, the same way, the same place, like a slave, for some myth of serving the people that only exists over the loudspeaker!"

"Where'd you get this . . . love . . . of America, Yen?"

"Years ago, when the first businessman came here and showed me pictures of your country—Baltimore, Dallas, Las Vegas. You are crazy to give up what you have for this!"

"Who said we were giving it up?"

"I know what you want, all you left-wing Americans. You are all the same—dreaming babies!"

He grabbed my shoulder and threw me back against the wall. One of the bad elements turned and took a step toward me, a switchblade glinting in his hand. In the corner, the dancers had stopped and were staring at us, the music seguing into "Be-Bop-a-Lula."

"Now you must perform a task for us."

"For you?"

"Yes. Your arrival is most fortunate, Mr. Wine. A member of your tour was to bring us money for our work."

"Who's that?"

"You know who it is. Anyway, he brought only a pittance —two thousand dollars in your money, when we were promised ten."

"Tough luck."

The bad element brought the knife closer to my neck.

"What do you want from me?"

"To get the rest."

"You've got to be kidding!"

"Not at all, Mr. Wine."

"How do you expect to make me do a thing like that?"

Yen smiled and turned away, wedging the pistol, a .45, in his belt. He walked over to the jukebox and began to caress its plastic shell. "Gene Vincent and the Blue Caps—you like them?"

"Not bad."

"I like all your music—Gene Vincent, Arthur Haley and the Comets, Buddy Holly."

"He died eighteen years ago."

"Yes. With the Big Bopper. You thought I was stupid, didn't you?" He nodded to the bad element, who pulled back

232

his arm and shot a vicious kung-fu punch into my solar plexus. I doubled over, clutching my stomach. "I am not stupid, Mr. Wine. When I ask you to perform a task, I know you will have good cause to do it."

Yen eyed me a moment, then walked over to the screen, kicking it back with his foot. Liu's body was lying there.

"You dirty bastard!" I lunged for Yen, slamming him against the jukebox. "You killed her!"

I grabbed for the gun. Instantly, the bad element and another man were on me, pulling me backward, the knife to my throat and my arms pinned to the small of my back.

"You killed her, you rotten son of a—"

"I didn't kill her, Mr. Wine," said Yen, dusting himself off. "That would have been a pointless thing to do—now. You should know that." He picked up a syringe from a nearby table. "Anyway, I believe it was a scientist from your country who invented sodium pentothal."

I looked over at Liu. She was drugged, all right. In my fury, I hadn't realized she was still breathing. I felt a tremendous rush of relief, but it was quickly overwhelmed by my growing hatred for Yen.

"You *are* a sentimentalist, Mr. Wine. Liu Jo-yun, of course, is not. She is a confirmed revolutionist . . . although," he smirked, "even Mrs. Liu makes her mistakes."

"You are a creep."

"Perhaps it is her excessive zeal. First for the extreme leftism of Mme. Chiang Ching and now . . ." He laughed.

"Smile all you want, Yen. But I didn't come here alone. I've got this building surrounded. There're hundred men waiting outside."

"Mr. Wine, do not play foolish games. I have been a guide of the China International Travel Service for fourteen years. Don't you think I know how the oppressed Chinese people follow foreigners through the streets? It is pathetic." He came closer. "Besides, you know nothing of what is really happening here, beneath the surface. In three years, China could all

233

be capitalist again—the Shanghai bund lined with tourist hotels and Coca-Cola stands. And people like you will feel totally betrayed."

He smirked from ear to ear. I wanted to cream him, but the bad element still had my arms doing Kundalini yoga.

"So, Mr. Wine, the situation must now be clear to you. In return for the monies owed to us by the agent on your tour, Mrs. Liu shall be freed in safety."

"Terrific."

"And one other thing."

"What's that?"

"The duck."

"The duck?"

"Of course, Mr. Wine, the duck. I'm sure you do not think I would be so naive as to stay in China after you have completed your mission." He gesticulated to his entourage. "This operation is finished . . . but with the Han Duck, our future is assured. A Han Dynasty artifact of that beauty and rarity should be worth four million yuan at least from the antiquities dealers in Taiwan."

"I didn't figure you'd be going through all this trouble for eight lousy grand, even at Third World prices."

"Quite right, Mr. Wine."

"But I don't know how you expect me to find this."

"Expect? Come now. With the intimacy shared by you and Mrs. Liu, how do you expect me to believe she did not tell you she stole the duck—if you had not already guessed it yourself?"

"Yeah. But she never told me where it was."

I looked down at Liu again. She hadn't moved an inch. On the table behind her, the syringe was now propped against the empty pentothal vial.

"Though I imagine *you* didn't have much trouble finding out."

"No. I didn't."

"Then what do you need *me* for?"

"Because it is in the possession of your aunt."

234

XXIX "I don't know how you could have had it. They searched our rooms *and* they searched our bags!"

"That's what I'm saying, shmendrik. She gave it to me afterward!"

"When?"

"After the dinner. At the restaurant. We thought it would be safer that way."

"We?"

"Yes. We."

I looked away. My brains had turned into scrambled eggs and there was a dull throbbing in my temples that wouldn't quit. Shanghai, Peking, I didn't know where I was. If this was Tuesday, it must be the Gulag Archipelago.

Outside it was May Day in August, over a million demonstrators thronging Tien An Men Square, celebrating the Eleventh Party Congress. Loud martial music carried through the windows of the hotel room, and large clusters of red balloons were visible, dissolving into a brilliant blue sky. Beneath them, giant papier-mâché effigies of Chiang Ching, Wang Hung-wen, Chang Chun-chiao and Yao Wen-yuan were being paraded through the crowd as objects of ridicule. The Gang of Four may have been smashed with one blow, but the battle was still being carried through to the end, the bitter end.

"You don't think much of me, Sonya, do you?"

"I didn't say that."

"You sure didn't. You didn't say anything!"

"Hey, it was for you she took the duck in the first place. So you would have to investigate."

"Thanks a lot."

"Look, you think you got on this tour for good behavior? You didn't go to one meeting of the Friendship Society and I sent you an invitation every time."

"All right. All right. I've lost patience. Where is it?"

"I got it locked away."

"Give it to me." I started rummaging through her bags.

"Wait a minute. Hold your horses!"

"They'll kill her, Sonya."

"They'll kill her anyway."

"Maybe. But it's the only chance we've got."

She stopped and looked at me. "Moses, why did you come here?"

"What?"

"Why are you here?"

"What do you mean, why am I here? I'm here because Yen flew me up on a CAAC jet, ostensibly to rejoin the tour, but actually to get him the goddamn duck!"

"That's not what I mean. I mean why did I get you on the tour in the first place?"

"What is this, Twenty Questions?" I opened her flight bag and rifled it, but the duck wasn't there. "Now, will you tell me where the duck is or am I going to have to commit auntfanticide?!"

"Not until you tell me what you know."

"I know we're all in trouble and she's in the deepest trouble of all of us!"

"You know what I'm talking about, Moses!"

I took a quick look in her camera bag and turned to her. A huge red banner was streaming by her window, halfway up the facade of the Peking Hotel. "I don't know anything, Sonya. I can only guess."

"Then guess."

"All right, try this . . . ever since you first went to China eight years ago, you've been bragging to me you were the only foreign friend to maintain a correspondence with a guide from the China Travel Service."

"Not the only."

"Okay, not the only, but one of the few. That doesn't matter. What does matter is who it was, and I imagine it was an eager young translator for Chiang Ching named Liu Jo-yun."

Sonya nodded.

"Now, you and Liu became very friendly, even intimate, from what you tell me of the letters, and somewhere along the line Liu got the message to you that things weren't entirely kosher in the Travel Service, that someone was using it to sabotage Sino-American relations—though I doubt she accused Yen directly. Not in the mail, anyway."

"How could she?"

"And then you found there were going to be illegal payments made to these counterrevolutionary Chinese. So you decided to get your little nephew on the case—only you didn't want to tell him what he would really have to know because he couldn't be trusted. . . ."

"Ideologically."

"You said it—ideologically. Pretty incredible, isn't it?"

"I don't think so."

"*You* wouldn't."

"You don't tell anybody more than they have to know."

"Sonya, this isn't the nineteen-thirties anymore. Nobody believes that shit!"

"They don't?"

"No, they don't!"

"Well, it was for your own protection."

"Oh, come on."

"Well, look what happened."

"What do you mean, look what happened?"

"You know what happened."

"What happened?"

"You fell in love, like an idiot, with someone you can never see again!"

"Oh, crap! At least I didn't fall in love with a CIA agent!"

"What??"

"Staughton Grey."

"Moses!" Sonya sat down on the bed and stared at me. "I don't know what this has to do with—"

"You don't?"

"No!"

"And I thought you wanted to know the truth!"

"Well . . ."

"You do or you don't?"

"I . . ." She watched apprehensively.

"How about this? Flashback—1934. . . ."

"Oh, my God!"

"Come on, Sonya. Flashback—1934!"

"Please."

"Listen, Sonya. I know it now. Some of the truth. Do you want it or don't you?"

She hesitated.

"Okay—1934. The Bronx Cooperative Movement grows like wildfire through every corner of the borough. Idealistic young organizers, among them Sonya Lieberman, stand at the brink of turning the Bronx into a commune!"

"Moses, what is this?"

"You know what it is. I've heard the story on your knee, my mother's knee, a thousand times! Flashback—1935. Another story I've heard. That same Sonya Lieberman is in love with another organizer. They live together, out of wedlock because they're socialists, but this is the real thing. Thunder, lightning, romance forever! Flashback—1936. . . ."

"Moses!"

"Let me finish. Flashback—1936 . . . something strange happens. A political outrage. At the very threshold of suc-

238

cess, the Bronx Co-op Movement is revealed as a commie front and smashed by the cops. The young organizers are arrested, Red-baited, ridiculed, lose their jobs—the whole shmeer. All of them, that is, except for Sonya Lieberman and her lover. What has happened? Who ratted? There must have been an agent provocateur, a fink, among them. But who? Surely not Sonya Lieberman, may God strike me from the heights of Sinai! But her lover . . . her lover. . . . But who was her lover? Alas, a family secret. I never knew. My mother never told me. It was a tragedy, hidden in the closet like an uncle who went insane or a cousin who was a bar girl, until . . ."

Sonya had collapsed, her face fallen in and her shoulders deflated like pumpkins the week after Halloween. She looked a hundred years old.

I sat down next to her and put my arm around her.

"I'm sorry."

"That's all right."

"It's just that none of it made sense. I couldn't figure out why you decided to come on this particular tour—or how you or Liu knew someone in *this* group was bringing money to Yen."

"Until you guessed who Staughton was."

I nodded.

"I never could get myself to say anything about him, all those years. And he kept doing it, spying on us. I knew it. In the Peace Movement, civil rights, everything. I could see his name in the papers. I just couldn't . . . talk."

"That's because you loved him, Sonya."

"No, no, no, it's not!" She angered suddenly.

"Yes, it is."

"Bourgeois sentimentality. I don't have any . . ." her voice dragged again ". . . bourgeois sentimentality."

"Without bourgeois sentimentality we would all be dead . . . Sonya."

She lowered her head. "I know."

"Where is he now?"

"In his room. He's been there for the past couple of days. By himself. I think he suspects something, Moses. Max Freed told him about those matches from the Peninsula Hotel. That's probably why he didn't give Yen all the money. He thought he might need it for his escape."

"He's got some buddies over at the Liaison Office. Maybe they'll help him."

"What're you going to do, Moses?"

"Just give me the duck."

"You're not going to give it to Yen, are you?"

"Just give it to me, Sonya! Stop screwing around. What happened between you and Staughton Grey is forty years old, but Liu Jo-yun is twenty-nine years old."

"Just tell me what you're going to do."

"Get caught."

"What?!"

"I don't know what you're so worried about. You're the one with all the faith in the People's Court. Now get me that duck before I change my mind!"

Sonya took a breath and stood up. She walked over to the closet and reached far into the back, pulling out a plastic shopping bag from Ohrbach's.

"I always take them with me," she said. "You never know when they'll come in handy."

I took the bag and opened it. Inside was a Chinese lacquer box of the inexpensive sort bought by tourists, with a picture of the Great Wall on the top. It was nailed shut and I had to pry it open with Sonya's nail file. A pile of excelsior jumped out at me, spilling onto the floor. Beneath that was the duck. I didn't want to look at it, but there was something about this vision of Han Dynasty magnificence, the centuries-old craftsmanship we could never reproduce, that held me transfixed. I had to force myself to shut the box again.

I tucked it under my arm and started for the door. Sonya followed me. "Be careful," she said.

"Don't forget to lock up."

I opened the door. Standing in the doorway across the corridor was Staughton Grey.

"What the hell do you want?"

"I thought you'd want to speak with me."

"A little late for that, isn't it?"

"I hope it isn't, Wine. I hope it's not too late for all of us. For you, for me, or for her."

I looked from him to Sonya. She was trembling. "Oh, get off it," I said.

"You're not going to turn me in, are you?"

"Maybe."

"I've got some money left. Perhaps you . . ." He reached for his pocket.

"You've got to be kidding!"

"You'll get into trouble, Wine! You don't know what you're getting into!"

"That's my problem, isn't it?"

"Your aunt's an old woman. It'll kill her!"

I looked at Sonya again. She was starting to cry. It occurred to me I had never seen her that way before, never seen any break in her tough, wisecracking exterior.

"You contemptible son of a bitch! Using her again. You claim you care for this woman, but I don't think you ever cared for anybody for ten minutes of your entire life!"

"That's not true!" He turned to Sonya. "Tell him. Tell him it's not true!"

Sonya sobbed. Her hands were covering her face.

"Why don't you leave my aunt alone? Haven't you done enough to her for one lifetime?"

I stepped out into the corridor, simultaneously shoving Grey backward and shutting the door behind me. I started for the elevator.

"At least let me explain myself," he said, following after me. "You don't understand. I had to do it. It was my patriotic duty. I did love Sonya. But she was just a dupe, you understand? A dupe. . . . Don't be fooled about those people,

Wine. The Stalin-Hitler pact, the purge trials—it's a betrayal. Always a betrayal!"

I let the elevator door shut in his face.

It opened on the lobby. I waited a moment before exiting, then I moved as quickly as I could, crossing the floor without so much as a backward glance at Comrade Huang's guards, who were calling after me as I headed through the front door of the hotel.

On the street I slipped between two tour buses and broke into a run for Tien An Men. The celebration was in full swing. I hadn't been in a crowd this dense since the antiwar march in Washington in sixty-seven. Within a block it became so tight I had to turn sideways, barreling along shoulder-first like a halfback to get through.

Soon I was in the middle of the demonstration, banners swirling about me, flags flying. A squadron of Chinese jets zoomed overhead, fanning out in formation as they passed over the Forbidden City. In front of me a band played on a temporary stand behind a choral group of about a thousand, singing the praises of the Party, Congress and Chairman Hua. Beyond them, an equally large group of gymnasts had joined together to form a human tower in an awesome display of solidarity. I pushed through toward it, the masses of Chinese parting to let the foreigner pass.

In a few minutes I reached the steps of the platform and started to mount it. The people at the bottom were disturbed. Some pushed forward, trying to stop me. A PLA officer jumped in my path but I bumped him aside and ran up to the top. Then I spread-eagled myself in front of the choral group, holding the duck aloft over my head, and yelled, "Long live Chiang Ching! Long live the Gang of Four! Long live Chiang Ching! Long live the Gang of Four!"

XXX I KNEW Nick Spitzler would be pleased he finally had a chance to see the People's Court in action. He was seated in the front row, suppressing a smile, his hands eagerly clutching the earphones for simultaneous translation.

Not far off was Max Freed, also pleased because he sensed a scoop, operating two cassette recorders on the chair next to him. He was seated beside Ruby Crystal, who had confided in me earlier that day that she had already contacted some producers back home about a movie version of our adventures.

In fact most of the group was happy, relieved it was I and not they who would be standing trial that afternoon in a basement room of the Peking Hotel. They were relieved too that a plane was scheduled to fly them out the next morning to Canton, with connections to Hong Kong the following afternoon. Indeed, had it not been for some genuine concern for my welfare, the atmosphere in the court would have been one of a going-away party.

Only Staughton Grey was not feeling it. He sat in the back of the room, with a sense of foreboding that I shared because, in the intervening two days since I was arrested, I had become convinced that I had made a mistake, both for me and for Liu.

Actually I had heard nothing about her. I had no idea where the bad elements had taken her, or even if she was still alive.

I turned from Staughton to Yen, searching the face of the senior guide for some clue to Liu's whereabouts. But I could read nothing as he stood next to Comrade Huang, confidently staring out at the audience as they took their seats.

In addition to our group, a number of Chinese were in attendance, some from the Travel Service and others whose work depended on tourists—waiters, chambermaids, hall men, elevator operators, bus drivers and so on. That was the Chinese way, to invite those directly concerned with a trial to attend so they could comment on the defendant's guilt or innocence, even recommend a sentence if they wished to.

I had spent the previous evening learning what I could of the People's Court. The proceedings were inquisitorial, not adversary like ours. Two kinds of trials were held—one for "Contradictions Among the People" and one for "Contradictions Between the People and the Enemy." The first were informal neighborhood affairs stressing group education, criticism and self-criticism. Petty crime was the community's problem. Sentences were light. Rehabilitation, not punishment, was emphasized.

Contradictions between the People and the Enemy were a different matter. These concerned forces resisting and sabotaging the Revolution and were dealt with severely. A thorough investigation was made, a three-person tribunal convened by the state. Sentences were vague, open-ended. The implications were ominous.

I didn't need to see the tribunal to know I was in the second category. But when they took their seats I recognized two of them. Comrade Tseng of the Travel Service and Comrade Huang of Public Security. The third was introduced as Mrs. Gwo, a dishwasher at the hotel. She was acting as judge.

Another representative of Public Security read a list of grievances against me: unauthorized exit from the Peking

Hotel on four separate occasions; unauthorized travel from Peking to Shanghai; theft of a Western Han Dynasty artifact from the Palace Museum; and other activities of a counter-revolutionary nature. The last, I assumed, was a euphemism for standing in front of a demonstration of a million people and shouting "Long Live the Gang of Four!"—punishable by seventy-five years transporting night soil from Manchuria to Tibet.

Judging by the angry reactions of the people in the room when the grievance was read out, I might have underestimated the sentence. A group of workers in the back cried out in Chinese and shook their fists at me. The woman seated directly behind me hissed in my ear, grabbing furiously on the armrest and pulling backward, forcing me to hold on to the next chair for support. Her neighbor was tugging at my sleeve, shaking it back and forth in a gesture of contempt.

"Do you have any comment to make on these accusations?" I imagined the question in my ear originated with Mrs. Gwo, who had just said a few words to the translator.

"Not at the moment," I responded.

"Would you like to have a Chinese citizen assist you in your defense?"

"I don't think so."

"Do you wish to make a self-criticism?"

"No."

It didn't take long for the translator to report back to Mrs. Gwo.

"Then you do not deny unauthorized exit from the Peking Hotel, unauthorized travel from Peking to Shanghai, theft of a Han Dynasty artifact and other counterrevolutionary activities?"

"I do not deny the unauthorized exits or the unauthorized travel. But I did not take the Han Duck, at least not originally, and if by 'counterrevolutionary activities' you are referring to my behavior at the demonstration celebrating the Eleventh Party Congress, its sole purpose was to draw the maximum attention to my case."

"To draw attention to your case?"

"Yes. To assure as speedy and public a trial as possible."

There were confused murmurs in the courtroom. I could see Sonya was watching me from the other side with a worried expression.

"And to prevent the murder of Liu Jo-yun of the China International Travel Service."

There was a low but audible collective gasp. I glanced at Yen, who betrayed no emotion. Comrade Huang looked stern, reaching into a briefcase for a file and placing it on the table. I could hear him ask me a question in Chinese.

"Who was going to murder Liu Jo-yun?" came the direct translation into my earphones.

"Perhaps she is already murdered."

"By whom?"

"Those working for Comrade Yen Shih. Comrade Yen is the one who should be on trial here. Not me."

More gasps.

"Comrade Yen is for five years a member of the Revolutionary Committee of the China International Travel Service."

"What difference does that make?"

"Comrade Yen is a long-standing friend of the Chinese Revolution. His father participated in the Long March under our glorious leader Chairman Mao."

"Wasn't it Lenin himself who said the dialectics of history are such that the theoretical victory of Marxism obliged its enemies to *disguise themselves* as Marxists?"

Huang looked angry. "Do not make fun of this court, Mr. Wine. We are very familiar in this country with foreign agents who familiarize themselves with the rhetoric of our society in order to overthrow it!"

"You think I'm a foreign agent?"

"How else to explain the apparent irrationality of your behavior?" He opened the file in front of him. "Comrade Yen has been good enough to provide us with these photographs of you spying on the citizens of the People's Republic of

246

China." He held up one of me staring through the gate on Shamien Island. The blurry figure of Natalie Levine stood in the background.

"That wasn't spying," I said. "That was a nursery school."

He held up another of me bending over a body I recognized as Ana Tzu.

"What's this supposed to mean?"

"One hour later this woman was in Canton Hospital for three days, yet the doctors there were never able to make a diagnosis."

"That's because she was faking. She wanted to be able to stay in Canton to visit with her relatives. Isn't that right? Tell them, Ana."

I turned to Ana but she quickly looked away from me, shielding her face with her hand to hide it from me.

Huang pulled out another photograph. It showed me sliding along a wall of the Wang Fu Ching. I could see the audience staring at it intently. He replaced this with another. It was dimly lit, but I was clearly discernible, staring out from behind a row of coats by a pool of soapy water.

"I'm sure you recognize the Bright and Flowery Bathhouse of Peking, Mr. Wine," said Huang. He eyed me with an expression bordering on menace.

I was starting to sweat. So Yen had been preparing for this all along. It had been he, or one of his confederates, who had made the call that sent me to the Bright and Flowery. The object had been to discredit me in advance, before I could be of any use to Liu. And it had obviously been successful. I looked at Yen, who had a complacent smile on his face as he said a few words to Huang which the translator did not bother to pass on. Huang turned to me again.

"We already know about the check you received from Mr. Arthur Lemon of Newport Beach, California, Mr. Wine. Are you now prepared to confess your crimes and make a self-criticism?"

"No, I am not."

Huang slammed his fist on the table. "Mr. Wine, you are

247

only making it more difficult for this court to exercise special consideration in the sentencing of a foreigner!"

A worker in the back jumped up and shouted something toward the tribunal. "Comrade Wu of hotel maintenance," came the translation, "wishes to express his anger for the death of his brother, a rice farmer, who died during the American bombing of Chinese territory during the Vietnamese Liberation War."

A woman stood up. "Comrade Chiu—a barefoot doctor—wishes to protest American support of the Kuomintang gangsters on Taiwan, who have exploited our people for so many years."

An older woman stood. "Comrade Li—a retired street cleaner—wishes to protest the death of her mother, Ch'en Ming-hsien, a textile worker, from smoke inhalation in an American-owned factory where over a third of the workers perished."

Another two people stood up.

"Tell these people I deplore those things, too," I shouted to the translator. "And I'm ashamed of them in the name of my people . . . but I am not guilty of these crimes!"

The audience stamped their feet angrily. Again Huang slammed his fist. "You have not changed your mind, Mr. Wine?"

"Where is Liu Jo-yun?"

"That is no concern of yours."

"I demand to know the whereabouts of Liu Jo-yun."

"She has gone to visit her husband in Yünnan Province." It was Yen who had answered the question, directly in English. He had a smirk on his face and I knew he was lying.

"Mr. Wine, if you have nothing substantial to say in your defense, the tribunal will begin to discuss a sentence."

Slowly, I stood up and looked around me, first at the Chinese in the audience, then at my American friends from the tour. They seemed confused, suspicious. Was there any validity to these accusations? After all, I was a private detective. Perhaps the government had hired me. It made sense, didn't it? How unlikely for me to be on the tour in the first place. Some of them averted their eyes. I turned to the tribunal.

"First I would like to say that I came here a friend of China and that I remain, despite everything, a friend of China."

"That is a lie," said Huang. "You are not a friend of China."

"How do you know how I feel?"

"I've seen what you have done. That is—"

"Let him speak," came another voice. It was Comrade Tseng.

I nodded to him and continued. "Most of the things I have seen about your society have impressed me very much—the children, the spirit of the people, the pride in the communes and the cities. Some things, like the struggle against the Gang of Four, are internal matters I do not fully understand, and some things, like certain restrictions on the individual, I admit disturb me. But as I have said, I am a friend of China and will remain a friend of China, no matter what this court decides."

I paused a moment, waiting while the audience studied me, trying to decide whether I was honest or just another foreign devil come to sell them snake oil.

"Many forces divide the world. And within them are forces inside forces, forces that divide us from ourselves and others. Iran contends with Iraq, Israel with Syria, Ethiopia with Somalia, China with the Soviet Union, the Soviet Union with the United States and so on. Inside these countries there are contentions which mirror the outside. Here in China you have had eleven struggles between the two lines. In the Soviet Union some favor Lenin and Stalin, others Khrushchev and Brezhnev. In the United States too we have had our debates, not the least of which stem out of the nineteen-sixties, when many of us felt our country had overstepped itself in an imperialistic war.

"Two nations, in effect, developed inside our country. One

249

favored peace, justice for minorities, and more economic equality. Another favored world domination, social status quo, and economic growth at all costs. Many outside our country, however, misunderstood our struggles, as we have, no doubt, misunderstood yours. It takes great effort for one individual to understand another; for one culture to understand another is extraordinarily difficult. You, for example, misjudged the seriousness of our Watergate scandal and the dislike of progressive Americans for Richard Nixon. Also, in your eagerness to have us defend the world from the Russians, you must consider that a country that has made war ten thousand miles from its shores must spend some time digesting the futility of such adventures. The lack of comprehension of China by us Americans is greater still. Somehow we learned to envision as a massive threat to our security a country half the world away from us, which doesn't have one single solitary soldier based on foreign shores."

Suddenly I felt the audience quieting. The members of the tribunal had closed the folders in front of them and were staring straight at me.

"So confusion compounds confusion and for us to communicate with each other is as treacherous in the People's Court as it is in what we call at home the 'court of popular opinion.' For us to understand each other will take extreme patience and may take ingenuity none of us has had to exercise before. That is why Liu Jo-yun had to steal a duck she never intended to keep, to make me understand her society. And that is why I had to adopt attitudes about the Gang of Four which I do not espouse, so that you'd be forced to understand mine."

Silence. The members of the tribunal looked at each other.

"You claim it was Liu Jo-yun who stole the duck?" said Comrade Tseng.

"Yes."

"Why would she have done that?" broke in Huang.

"To prevent Friendship Study Tour Five from leaving China and to expose Yen Shih."

250

"As what? He has done nothing!" Huang clenched his fist threateningly. There was another murmur in the court. Someone else in the back yelled out in anger.

"You have made many unsubstantiated accusations against Comrade Yen, Mr. Wine," said Tseng.

"I know."

"You realize at this point these accusations worsen your case rather than improve it."

"I understand. And I would not do so had not Mr. Staughton Grey of our tour given me such a detailed account of Comrade Yen's activities." I looked at Grey, who suddenly sat up in his seat. I continued quickly before he could protest. "Mr. Grey was in a unique position to do this, as he was originally a confederate of Mr. Yen's."

The members of the tribunal looked surprised. Tseng turned to Yen, who smiled and said something to him in Chinese. Yen looked over to Grey. "Were you a confederate of mine, Mr. Grey?"

"Yes, he was," I said. "Before he understood the nature of China and realized he should not be meddling in her internal affairs."

"I asked Mr. Grey," said Yen, sternly.

"He told me the day I returned to Peking—"

"I asked Mr. Grey!" Yen repeated.

"And I'm telling you what he said. That he wanted to make a self-criticism, that he saw so much in China that he appreciated—"

"Is this true, Mr. Grey?" said Tseng.

"Of course, you could say he's doing it to save his own skin," I continued, looking pointedly at Grey. "That he wouldn't want members of this group to let the Chinese know he was a CIA agent come here to bring money to an underground network of counterrevolutionary Chinese. Or if they did know it, at least to realize he'd had a change of heart, a *genuine* change of heart, so they would let him go to return to his own country, a free man, so he could work for Chinese-American friendship within his own organization, routing out those reactionaries who still oppose the bettering of relations between our countries. That is why Mr. Grey wanted to make that self-criticism. Isn't that right, Mr. Grey?"

I waited, holding my breath and hoping Grey would make the right decision. I could guess some of the things he was considering—whether he could rely on help from his lower-echelon cronies at the Liaison Office, whether Sonya would testify against him, whether she was respected enough in China to be believed. I saw Sonya watching him, her hand trembling.

Grey rose to his feet.

"It is true," he said. "I wish to make a self-criticism."

Yen jumped to his feet, shouting something in Chinese, but Grey ignored him. He turned to Sonya.

"There are many things in my life I could criticize myself for. In fact an entire lifetime . . . but most of these are not germane to the subject of this trial and would confuse most of the people here and seem very far away." He turned back to the tribunal. "I will say to you though that all of what Mr. Wine has said is true, that Yen Shih is a Taiwanese agent, and that I imagine Comrade Liu Jo-yun is in grave jeopardy. As proof of that, I will name for you the following persons, associates of Yen Shih in Shanghai and Taipei, members of an underground propaganda wing of the Taiwanese secret service—Wang Ching-chu, Wu Hsi-lien, Fang Tzu-yang, Hsu Mu-hua. . . ."

XXXI "Six hundred and thirty-eight dollars? Friederich, I never even heard of a transmission mount."

"You learn many new things when you buy a Porsche, Mr. Vine."

"Yeah. Last week I learned about a cold-start enrichment hose for three hundred and twenty-eight dollars, and two weeks before that about Servo-Lock synchronization for four hundred and thirty-two. You run a very expensive school, Friederich."

He shrugged. "It is exclusive, Mr. Vine."

I nodded and climbed into the cockpit of the Messerschmitt. "I'm going to sell it," I told Simon, who spread his Lego set all over the jump seat.

"Oh, Daddy." He looked upset.

"Dad," said Jacob, removing his face from a copy of *Oliver Twist*, "you don't want to have fun anymore. Ever since you've come back from China you've been down in the dumps."

I pulled out onto La Cienega Boulevard. "That's my privilege," I said.

"Aunt Sonya says people have a mysterious glow when they come back from China."

"Glow? The only glow she's got is from watching her old boyfriend sail off to South America."

"Aunt Sonya's got a boyfriend?" said Simon.

"She had one. Remember? I told you—forty years ago. It never worked out."

"And he's in South America?"

"South America. Somewhere. He went to China, but he didn't want to come back."

Simon looked confused. I turned on Sunset and caught Laurel up into the hills.

"Faster!" he said.

"Do you want me to get a ticket? I've told you I'm going to sell this sucker!"

"I know why *you're* so depressed," said Jacob.

"Why?"

"You've got a girl friend."

"Oh, yeah? What makes you think that?"

"Oh, I don't know."

"Come on. Stop being coy. Out with it."

"I just heard."

"From whom?"

"Mom."

He had a shit-eating grin on his face.

"What'd she tell you?"

"Nothing . . . until I made her."

"How'd you do that?"

"Threatened to tell you about Sidney."

"Who's Sidney?"

"I won't tell you until you tell me about your girl friend."

"I don't have a girl friend."

We stopped at the red light by the Canyon Store. Jacob looked at me. He had a sympathetic expression on his face. The kind kids have sometimes when the roles of father and son are reversed.

"It's okay, Dad," he said.

I nodded.

"Was she the woman who got into trouble? The one who wanted to expose Comrade Yen?"

"Boo, Comrade Yen," said Simon. I had told him the story three times.

"You were afraid she died, weren't you? Or went to jail?"

I nodded again.

"Was her name Loo Joe John or something like that?"

"Yes . . . how do you know that?"

"Mom wanted to give you this."

Jacob was holding a postcard in his hand.

"How come it came to your place?"

"I guess they had your old address."

"Yeah." I took it from him. On the front it had a photograph of a red flag flying over a rice paddy. The light turned green but I didn't move. I turned the card over and started to read:

Dear Mr. Moses WINE,

Comrade Hu of China International Travel Service has informed me of the disposition of your case. This is good news, yes? You may be interested to know that I am here at the Autumn Harvest May Seventh Cadre School in Sinkiang Region, near the Russian border, where I am fiercely studying the fifth volume of Chairman Mao Tse-tung's work so that I may combat my individualistic nature and continue the struggle against the Gang of Four. In some time, I am told, I will be able to join the Travel Service again as a guide. I hope that you too will be able to return to China, sometime, as a Responsible Person.

In friendship,
Liu Jo-yun